THE
GODS OF LOVE

NICOLA MOSTYN

piatkus

PIATKUS

First published in Great Britain in 2018 by Piatkus

3 5 7 9 10 8 6 4 2

Copyright © 2018 by Nicola Mostyn

The moral right of the author has been asserted.

A CIP catalogue record for this book
is available from the British Library.

ISBN 978-0-349-41570-3

Typeset in Sabon by M Rules
Printed and bound in Great Britain by
Clays Ltd, St Ives plc

Papers used by Piatkus are from well-managed forests
and other responsible sources.

Piatkus
An imprint of
Little, Brown Book Group
Carmelite House
50 Victoria Embankment
London EC4Y 0DZ

An Hachette UK Company
www.hachette.co.uk

www.littlebrown.co.uk

Nicola has worked as a bookseller, copywriter, journalist and fictional agony aunt. She lives in her hometown of Manchester with her partner. *The Gods of Love* is her first novel.

Find Nicola on Twitter @nicolamostyn and on Facebook as nicolamostynauthor, or visit www.nicolamostyn.com to discover Nicola's musings on relationships, phallus museums and the inevitable apes-versus-robots apocalypse.

For Nick

Chapter 1

The thing about being a divorce lawyer is you don't exactly get to see the nicer side of human nature. You can think positive all you want, but after you meet the hundredth wife whose husband has been having it away with his twenty-something colleague, you start to despair not just of the fickleness of the human race, but of their sheer failure of imagination.

That's why my client, Oona Simpson, has been in my office less than five minutes and I already know that her husband has committed far worse atrocities behind her back than the crimes against marriage she is tearfully listing. (That's the other thing about being a divorce lawyer – you need to bulk buy tissues.)

As I run through the information she's given me – thirty years of marriage, two wonderful kids, supporting his career by sacrificing hers, yada, yada, yada – I can see she's welling up again, so I grab a handful of Kleenex with aloe vera and thrust them in her direction.

'I'm so sorry,' says Oona. 'Really, I'm not usually like this. It's just – such a shock. A terrible shock. I never thought I'd find myself here.' She wipes her forefingers under her eyelashes to stop the mascara monsoon – far too late for that, alas – and stares at me with huge blue eyes. Oona is fifty-five. Assisted by some top-notch Botox, a few thousand in dental work and a haircut that probably cost more than my couch, she looks incredible for her age. But what good does that do her? Absolutely none. Because her overweight, halitosis-ridden husband, who happens to be a big cheese in the city's largest architecture firm, has persuaded some ambitious young thing to trade her buff body for his contacts and influence.

Same. Old. Story.

I don't say any of this, of course, I just nod with concern, proffer more tissues, and mentally award her another point in my private game of Divorce Buzzword Bingo. 'I never thought I'd find myself here,' is high on my list. As are, 'How could s/he do this to me?', 'What pre-nup?' and 'I want to take him/her to the cleaners'. I much prefer the last phrase. They get bonus points for that.

Still, Oona is not quite there yet. She's shocked by her husband's duplicity and frightened by the thought of being alone. She needs to let the reality of what he's done sink in. That's when the anger will come. And I can do wonders with anger. Hell really does hath no fury, etc., etc.

'Take your time,' I say. (Of course I would say that: I charge by the hour.) 'Whatever you choose, we want to do this respectfully and properly and make sure we opt for absolutely the right path for you and your children.'

She smiles at me, eyes filled with gratitude, and I take a good look at her. Gym-thin, dressed in gentle pastels, with peachy skin and delicate make-up – she looks brittle and weightless, like a human macaroon.

Some people might assume she's a wimp. But I know women like Oona, I see them every day. She's come to me because she's heard I'm the best. I'm the youngest woman in the city to have her own family law practice, and I've won my clients significantly more in their settlements than any of my nearest competitors. What can I say? I have a gift.

We wrap up – there's no point pushing her during this first meeting – and I tell her to speak to my PA, Penny, to arrange a time for our next appointment (by which time Oona might easily have taken her husband back, a dance couples can do for years before the line is finally drawn). Then she is out of the door, brave and smiling and ready for a spot of post-affair-shock retail therapy and a gin and Slimline, because the wives aren't spared their own share of clichés.

Once Oona has gone I turn to my laptop and check my emails. I find the usual junk that's crept into my inbox – 50 per cent off plastic surgery, one month's free trial to a sex-dating site, a message with the subject line: *Why Are You Still Single?* (which could easily be from my mother, if only she knew how to use a computer) – and drag them to the trash. In the sidebar, an ad plays out silently. I delete another batch of emails, and the ad catches my attention again. Intrigued, I hover my cursor over the box and click.

The screen is dark for one second, two, and then a shaft of golden light pierces the blackness, accompanied by choral music, like the portent of some divine visitation. A smooth female voiceover asks, 'Will you find the one?' and slowly, from that honeyed glow, an object comes into focus. It's a phone. A gold phone.

'The NeoONE,' runs the voiceover. 'Only ONE has been created. Only ONE will be chosen.' Then the screen goes dark again, leaving only a series of golden numbers:

14/02 @19:00.

I laugh at the audacity. It's NeoStar, of course, who else? The iconic NeoStar logo – an arrow shooting upwards – is as famous and powerful as the Hollywood sign, and it's everywhere these days: on the laptop I'm using to watch this ad, the phone on my desk, the tablet at home, the search engine I use as default and the satnav in the taxis I take. NeoStar is the largest, most influential tech company in the western world. And – here the butterflies start fluttering deep in my stomach, the harbinger of good things to come – I, Frida McKenzie, have a meeting at their head office tomorrow.

I sit back and watch for a third time as the voiceover teases and the gold phone is revealed, like the dream of everything you've ever wanted come true. I shake my head. It's an insanely good idea. Promoting the new generation NeoPhone with an exclusive edition of just one? The publicity will be off the scale. The ad runs to the end and I see again that date: 7 p.m. on Valentine's Day. Perfect. These guys are operating on a completely different level. They're an unstoppable force. And they want me.

Or they might, if I can show them how good I am.

I close my browser, checking the clock. Time to wrap up. I need to make sure that I'm fresh and on good form for tomorrow. I'm just in the middle of powering down when I hear something going on outside my office door.

'Excuse me! You can't go in there without an appointment!'

Penny sounds flustered. Penny – unlike me – is terribly posh. She never gets flustered, or angry, or anything even approaching an emotion, so this gets my attention. You have to be ready for anything in this game. I've seen a lot of angry spouses over the past twelve months. Been threatened by a good few, been propositioned by more – sometimes both in the same meeting. So, as I wait for whatever is coming through the door, I've got my mobile in one hand and, in the other, a pepper spray (recently legalised due to the spike in violent stalkings).

Like I say, my opinion of human nature is not all that high.

The door opens and a man walks into my office, quickly followed by Penny who, by the faintest flush to her china complexion, I can tell is utterly furious.

'Frida McKenzie,' he says. Not a question, more like a recognition – a hello from a long-lost friend, except I don't know this guy at all.

'You can't come in here without an appointment,' I return calmly. I scan the man's appearance to see if he matches anyone on my list of potential trouble-causers: he's of medium height, with dark brown hair, green eyes and a smattering of sexy stubble. I'm good with faces, so I know I've never met him before, but, hey, I'm a lawyer, so that's no guarantee he doesn't want to punch me in the face.

'I just need five minutes,' the guy says. 'It's important.' He stares at me intently. Those green eyes are disconcerting, and so is the intense way he's looking at me. I flick a glance to Penny and she tips her head ever so slightly: *Should I alert security?* I give a tiny shake of mine. I don't like unnecessary drama. It's bad for business.

'I appreciate that whatever this is might *seem* urgent,' I say, 'but I'm leaving the office now. If you want to see me, you'll have to book in via Penny.'

'Right,' he says. 'Well, I would, ordinarily, but I'm afraid it can't wait.'

'I don't give my time away unscheduled or for free Mr – ah ...?'

'Dan. I'm Dan,' he says and gives me a disarming smile. 'I know it's rude of me to barge in like this, but I've been searching for you for a long time, Frida. A very long time. And I need to tell you something.'

I raise an eyebrow. Maybe it's because he doesn't look

6

like the kind of client who usually ends up in my office, or maybe it's his flattering, intriguing words, but damn it, I'm tempted to hear him out.

He sees me wavering. 'Five minutes,' he says.

I've got a pretty good instinct for people and I'm getting nothing wiggy from this one. Plus, he does have lovely eyes. 'Okay,' I say. 'You've got five minutes.' I nod at Penny, who raises her eyebrows fractionally, then reluctantly departs for her desk, though she does sensibly leave the door ajar. I sit back behind my desk, slide the pepper spray back in the drawer, and gesture to the leather visitor's chair.

'So, what can I do for you?'

Something interesting happens here. The man looks ... what is it? Embarrassed? No, not quite embarrassed, but close to it. *Reluctant*. Which is weird. I mean, what kind of a person storms his way into an office to tell someone something and then doesn't want to say it?

'Ms McKenzie ... ' he begins. He meets my eyes, sighs, looks down, seems to be deciding something and then says, 'I'm what you might call gifted.'

Gifted, I think. Right. Is he angling for a job? I stay silent. Best let him get it all out.

'I see things,' he explains. 'Things that are ... going to happen.'

My heart sinks. I've completely misjudged this situation. He is a nutter after all. 'Okay,' I say, playing for time and hoping I can get him out of the door with minimum fuss. 'And what do you see?'

'I see you.'

I blink at him. 'See me doing what?' I ask, then immediately regret it. The answer is probably going to make me want to take a scalding shower. I edge towards the security button.

'There's an ... an individual,' Dan says. 'He's very dangerous. He's going to do something terrible. And only you can stop him.'

'Okay. Right. Sure.' I tuck one hand under the desk, keeping my voice level and pleasant. 'Well, thanks for letting me know, Mr – Dan. Thanks, Dan. I really do appreciate it.'

To my surprise, he laughs. 'You don't believe me. You think I'm mad.'

'I believe that you believe it,' I say in my calmest voice.

He scrubs at his face with his sleeve. 'Well, that's very nice of you.' He looks weary now, suddenly. I see the shadows under his eyes. The bitten-down nails. 'Anyway, it's fine,' he says. 'I didn't want to believe it myself, at first. But it doesn't matter. Prophecies don't lie. It's up to you to find the arrow, Frida. Only you can save us.'

I stare at him, baffled. I can't work this guy out. He seems sane, but his words are utterly crazy. I look at him more closely, as though I might find a clue to his lunacy in his clothes: T-shirt of a band I've never heard of, leather jacket, worn-in jeans, black desert boots. No tie-dye, no psychic crystals, not even the whiff of a joss stick. He looks normal. Arty, maybe, a musician or a painter.

'Who are you?' I ask.

He smiles at me then, a warm, fond sort of smile. He really is very attractive.

'I'm a friend,' he says. 'You just don't know it yet.'

Yikes.

I press the small button that alerts the guard in charge of patrolling this whole row of offices. As I do so, Dan stands up. Instinctively I jerk backwards and, wishing I'd kept the pepper spray to hand, grab the nearest sharp object.

He smiles again. 'Are you going to write me a sternly worded note?'

I glance down at the fountain pen in my hand. Oh dear. Witty, as well as mad. I better get him out of here before I start dating him.

'You need to leave,' I say, trying not to show that he's rattled me. 'I've called security. If you don't go of your own accord, you'll be arrested.'

'Okay,' he says easily. Then he puts his hand in his pocket, and I step back again. What has he got in there? A knife? A crystal ball? Instead, he withdraws a yellow sticky pad, peels off one square bearing a scrawled telephone number, and sticks it to my desk.

'Call me when you understand that this is real,' he says. His eyes meet mine with an intensity that sends a shiver through me. 'But in the meantime, Frida, it's important that you're very careful. If I know that you're the one, it won't be long before he knows it, too.'

'He?'

'Anteros,' Dan says, as though that name should mean something to me. Then I hear Donald, the security guard, on the approach. There's no mistaking his heavy footfall, he's about six foot seven and almost as wide.

Crazy Dan is still talking. 'Don't get into a car with anyone you don't know,' he's saying. 'Don't let anyone into your home. Don't eat or drink anything that hasn't been prepared by you. And don't, whatever you do, go anywhere near NeoStar.'

I frown. NeoStar. Is that just a coincidence? I hope so, because otherwise it means this guy has taken an interest in my appointment diary.

He leans over then, so our faces are close, and I feel a faint flickering between us, like wires touching for an instant, then parting.

'I thought you might know who you are, but you don't, do you?' And now his expression scares me more than his words. It's filled with pity, though why this madman should pity me I really don't know.

'Please be careful, Frida,' he says. 'You're very special.'

The door opens and Donald looks from me to Dan and then back again. His gaze lingers on the fountain pen I'm still holding aloft. 'Everything okay in here?' Donald asks, his face folded into the perpetual frown he wears as standard.

Crazy Dan turns around and holds his hands up in a sub-missive *I mean no harm* gesture. 'I was just leaving.'

'Make sure this gentleman leaves the building, will you, Donald?' I say.

Donald grunts, disappointed by the lack of action. My security alerts usually involve a bit more violence. Not to be deterred, he grabs Dan roughly by the arm and steers him towards the door. Before Dan is ejected, he shouts something back at me, something so totally apropos of nothing that it makes my head spin.

'You might want to brush up on your Greek mythology.'

$$\longrightarrow$$

Once the man has gone, I breathe a long sigh of relief. What the hell was all that about? Totally weird. I sit at my desk for a few minutes. Penny brings me a coffee and then leaves without saying anything, which is wonderful and exactly why I hired her. People talk too much in my opinion. I value those who know when to maintain a tactful silence.

I take a few fortifying sips and try to regain my equilibrium. I wasn't frightened of the guy, not really, I'm just annoyed at myself for letting him in. I think I've got good intuition, so it's galling to be proven so spectacularly wrong. What if he'd been violent? I shake the thought away. It's fine. No harm done. He wasn't dangerous. Just a bit mixed up.

I sigh. I don't know why I'm surprised. I've always attracted the wrong kind of guy. I might as well have a sign on my head. This, I remind myself, is why I haven't had a date in months. I stare out of my office window, into the darkening early evening, watching the lights of the cars and buses as they chug through the slush-covered streets.

I force myself to refocus my mind. I haven't got time for complications. January is always really busy for me. The divorce rate, already at an all-time high, gets an extra boost around this time. Relationships that have been glued shakily together all year collapse under the strain of festive expectations. All those cosy TV ads cause people to wonder when they're going to get the bright, shining love they were promised. Add to the mix some obnoxious in-laws, overwrought kids and boozy office party indiscretions and you've got a recipe for a 40 per cent increase in business. Bad for love. Good for me.

The coffee is good and strong and it makes me feel more like myself. I don't have many vices but without at least eight coffees a day I turn into a Neanderthal woman. I drain my cup then buzz through to reception: 'What's in the diary for tomorrow, Pen?'

'Your meeting at NeoStar at nine thirty,' Penny responds crisply. 'Then you've got a follow-up with Mrs Bartholomew at noon, with her husband and his solicitor. I'll be gone by then, if that's okay? You remember I'm away for two weeks from tomorrow afternoon? The agency girl starts on Monday.'

NeoStar. The madman's words come back to me. How did he know I was going there? It crosses my mind that Dan might be a competitor. NeoStar rarely hire an outside law firm, but with the divorce rate skyrocketing, it makes sense that they're looking for a go-to lawyer for employee marital disharmony. After all, nothing delays productivity like a painful, drawn-out divorce, and nothing boosts morale like winning a huge pay-out against a once-adored, now-despised ex. It would be a huge coup for me to land something like this, and plenty of my competitors would kill, or at least sabotage, for a chance to get in there first. Pretending to be psychic is a lunatic trick to play just to win a contract, sure, but I've heard of worse. This is the modern world: be the best, at any cost, or you may as well not exist.

'Frida?'

'Sorry, Penny,' I say. 'Just wool gathering. Yes, that's fine. Have a wonderful time. Send me a postcard.'

$$\longrightarrow$$

I take some work back to my flat, open a bottle of wine, and tune the radio to a soothing classical station. I begin to slice peppers, courgettes, garlic and tomatoes. I tip them into a roasting tray and drizzle them with oil and balsamic vinegar, then slide them into the oven. I sit on a bar stool and pour myself another glass of wine.

My phone buzzes and I glance down. A text message from Chris.

Hi Frida, not seen you in a while. Fancy a coffee?

I ponder the message. Chris is a business lawyer who I dated a couple of times a few years ago. We're still friends, but he's never made a secret of the fact that he wants more. I give a mental shrug. Maybe I'll meet him for coffee. It can't do any harm.

Taking my glass of wine over to my bright turquoise sofa, I fall back onto the plump fox-print cushions with a sigh of satisfaction. I love this flat and I love my life. Being single these last few years has made me realise that I make a very good partner for myself. I cook nice meals. I keep the place sparkling clean. I run scented baths after long hard days. I buy myself boxes of chocolates. I take myself to the cinema, to restaurants, to parties. What's not to like?

Work has always been much more rewarding for me than relationships, anyway. Work is logical. Invest in your career, and watch it blossom. But romantic endeavours? They make no sense. Every case I've taken (and every relationship I've had) has proven that partnerships can derail at any time, for no good reason, no matter how committed or devoted you are. *Especially* if you're devoted. And where does that leave you? I swirl the wine around my glass, staring into its deep ruby depths. Where Oona is, that's where. Where so many people end up: on the scrap heap, discovering too late that you've wasted your beautiful years on someone who didn't deserve them.

Why Are You Still Single? Choice is why. Self-preservation is why.

Before I can go any further with this train of thought, the buzzer goes. I get up to see Bryony grinning into the intercom screen. 'Got something for you,' she says. I shake my head. Bryony is the only person I know who just drops in on people unannounced, as though the mobile phone has not yet been invented.

When I open the door, I see that she's holding a large cardboard box.

'Hello, lovely,' I say, hugging her around the box. 'To what do I owe this honour? And what's in the box?'

She follows me into the kitchen, slides the box onto the counter top and breathes a sigh of pleasure. 'Oh, it's so lovely here. So clean and tidy. No crayons or tiny cars anywhere!'

I laugh. Bryony had her twin boys, Jake and Joe, two years ago and her life is a constant juggle of toys and play-dates and food stains in random places.

'How are the terrible two?'

'Firmly into their terrible twos,' she quips. 'But brilliant, hilarious, wonderful too.' I smile at her. We've known each other since school and to look at us now, you'd never put us together as friends. I'm all dresses and heels and won't put the bin bags out without a full face of make-up. Bryony favours yoga pants and loose tops, wears her gorgeous strawberry-blonde hair scraped back in a bun and only bothers with make-up on her birthday and Christmas.

'Glass of wine?' I ask.

She stares a little longingly at the open bottle, then shakes her head. 'Better make it tea,' she says. 'You know what I'm like these days, drunk after one!' She pats the box. 'I really only came to drop this off.'

I grab the kettle and fill it, then retrieve my wine glass from the coffee table. I stare at the box, intrigued. 'You know it's not my birthday until July?'

Bryony rolls her eyes. 'No, listen, so you know when Justin and I were helping my mum and dad move?'

I nod.

'Well, it turns out there was still loads of my old stuff in their garage, from when I went travelling that time. Things I never really wanted back but didn't want to throw away. You know how it is.'

I nod, though I don't. My mum erased all trace of me after I left for university. If I left a hairbrush there, she'd throw it out immediately.

'And I found this box,' Bryony continues. 'I thought I didn't recognise the stuff in it. Then I saw this.' She brings out a notepad, the cover decorated with small Pierrot dolls, and I feel a flicker of memory. 'Your name is inside!' she says. 'It's your stuff! You must have left it in the garage when we were kids.' Bryony smiles at me. 'How cute is that?'

I peer into the box. 'Wow,' I say. 'That's amazing.' I sift through the contents at the top. 'Ha! Do you remember these?' I bring out the collection of novelty rubbers that Bryony and I spent all our pocket money on.

'And this!' she says, plucking out a sticky jelly octopus that we used to throw at the wall and watch climb down.

'It's like a time capsule,' I say, smiling. 'Thanks! I'll go through it over the weekend.'

Bryony stares into the box wistfully. 'Did we ever imagine, when we were that small, what our lives would be like?'

The kettle clicks. I pour hot water over a teabag, squeeze it with a teaspoon until the brew is a deep tan colour and then add plenty of milk. One of the by-products of a long friendship is you know exactly how your pals take their hot drinks. As I stir in half a spoon of sugar, I ponder Bryony's question. I don't remember an awful lot about my childhood. My dad left when I was nine, and I think I've blocked out some stuff. Maybe it was too painful. Perhaps his leaving me and Mum, and her subsequent misery, was the catalyst for my career in righting the wrongs of sinned-against spouses. Who knows? You'd have to ask Freud. But I remember me and Bryony, aged ten, having a shared birthday party and the wishes that we made.

'Yes,' I say handing her the tea. 'We both knew that we wanted to be happy and pretty and stay best friends for ever.'

'Ah, we could see the future!' She grins and cheerses me with her mug.

'Ha, yeah,' I say, frowning as I remember the madman in my office.

'Hey,' says Bryony, noticing my expression. 'Everything okay?'

'Oh yeah, I'm fine,' I say. I take a sip of wine. 'Just a bit of a weird day, that's all. You know I get some crazy clients sometimes? Had one today who reckoned I was the subject of some prophecy.'

Bryony widens her eyes. 'Be careful, Freed. People can get very strange when they're desperate.'

I nod. I don't bother to explain that he wasn't actually a client. Bryony does not altogether understand my choice of career, but as a GP she knows quite a bit about dealing with people whose lives are going awry.

'What about you?' I ask. 'Everything okay with work?'

She sighs. 'It's good but it's tough. I just wish there was more I could do, you know?' She shakes her head, looking pensive for a moment. I do know. Bryony has told me that an increasing number of her patients are single and convinced there's something wrong with them. She does her best; tries to reassure them that they're totally fine, perfectly normal, she recommends them to therapy if it's appropriate, but still they keep coming back, seeking to get themselves fixed, or asking for pills to take away the loneliness.

'You care, Bry, and that's all you can do.'

She smiles at me sadly. 'I guess.'

We talk a bit more, about her work and mine, about the kids and Justin, about the text I got from Chris and whether or not I should meet him. Then Bry checks her phone and tips her tea back. 'Right, hun, I've got to dash. Come over for Sunday lunch this weekend?'

I return her hug. 'I'd love to.'

$\longrightarrow$

After putting my childhood toys back in the box, I fasten the lid and stow it in the store cupboard. I refill the kettle and, when it's boiled, pour the hot water onto dried pasta. Once my dinner is prepared, I resist the urge to take it over to the sofa. Instead, I sit at the table, with my pasta and a glass of good red wine. This is my life, I made it for myself, and it's a bloody good one.

Later I relax in the living room and then I do switch on the TV. I catch the end of a recent blockbuster in which an abusive husband is transformed by his wife's love. I flick and watch the start of a popular sitcom whose protagonist is a terminally single shopaholic. Flick – a feature-length advert for slimming pills. Flick – a documentary about a woman whose dead body lay undiscovered in her flat for three years.

Flick – a game show in which the contestants win ten grand for every person they can sleep with before being caught by their partner. Flick – the NeoONE ad, a golden phone appearing out of the darkness. Already, it's all anyone on social media can talk about.

I watch the ad until the end and then – click – I switch off the TV and make my way to bed.

That night, I dream of chasing a brown-haired man through a crowd, his head bobbing in the near distance, always just out of reach. When I finally catch up with him, I reach out to touch his arm and when he turns, I see that it's the guy from the office, Dan.

'Do you know?' he says, gripping my shoulders tightly. 'You're special. Do you know? Do you know? You're the one. Do you know?' His voice gets louder and more desperate until I wake up with a start, my heart pounding. But it's just a dream, and, as with all dreams, it soon drifts away, dissolving into fragments so that, when I wake in the morning, I don't remember it at all.

Chapter 2

My alarm goes off at seven and I spring up, filled with energy for my meeting.

I take my time getting ready, making sure that every detail is exactly right. I shower, then sit in my robe, drinking coffee and putting on my make-up. I pick out my best underwear, and then slip into a fitted black dress, pull on hosiery, and step into a pair of shiny black heels. I smooth my hair (scrupulously straightened but always looking for an opportunity to return to its natural frizz-bomb state), refresh my lip-gloss, slick on some more mascara and survey my reflection.

Not bad. I need the heels, since I am not terribly blessed in the height department, but I find that works in my favour. I'm small, I'm twenty-nine, and I look twenty-five. I've actually been called cute by people who've never properly met me. And that's fine by me. I find it pays to be under-estimated. That way, they don't see me coming.

Ten minutes later I'm in the taxi. The roads are thick with gritty grey snow, and the traffic is moving slowly, but I don't mind. It gives me a chance to centre myself. I have to make a good impression at this meeting. At the moment I'm a big fish in a small pond, but I have grander ambitions. I started my own business a little over two years ago, and everyone thought I was mad to be so ambitious so young. Secretly (and often not so secretly) many of my peers were hoping I'd go bust within the month. But I'm still here, just like I knew I would be.

I love being my own boss, but more, I truly love divorce law. I understand what makes people tick. After I've met someone once, I can quickly ascertain how they think, why they behave as they do and how they'll probably act next. That helps me find the chink in their armour and the flaws in their case that enables me to turn the situation to my clients' advantage.

And they need my cold impartial eye because so often they are completely caught up in the detail, so consumed by their emotional state, they don't see the bigger picture at all. Sometimes, when a client is listing among their irreconcilable differences the way their spouse left the top off the marmalade, or sneezed too loudly, or used too much loo roll, I'll take a moment just to look at the couple in question and try to imagine how truly happy they must once have been. But it's impossible. Their marriage has erased the people they once were. Behold love, the great destroyer.

The sky is white, heavy with incipient snow, and as I gaze up, the black block-lettered NeoStar sign looms into view, that airborne arrow a promise of achievement. There's a NeoStar tower in every major city now. As its headquarters, this particular building has helped put this city on the map. It's the tallest structure in the world, with 199 floors, three hotels and fifty luxury apartments.

As I climb out of the taxi, I stare up at the building. They were going for awe, those who designed this building, and they nailed it. Some people say that it's ostentatious, gratuitous, obscene, but I disagree. People look up to NeoStar, figuratively and literally, a company that began building computers and phones back in the 1970s, a humble operation, but one that embraced – and, often, innovated – every subsequent development in technology, in order to become the global leader they are today. They're aspiration writ large.

Hurrying to get inside before the snow begins again, I head to the enormous glass entrance. A blindingly polished door revolves until I'm facing a reception desk that looks something like the helm of the starship *Enterprise*. The woman at reception, a flawless blonde beauty, flashes me a perfect smile as I approach.

'Welcome to NeoStar,' she says. 'I'm Mandy. How can I help you today?'

'I have a meeting with a Clive Bailey in Human Resources,' I say. 'My name is Frida McKenzie.'

'I'll just call through to Mr Bailey and let him know you're here.'

I watch as she taps one button on the phone.

'Hello,' she says. 'It's Frida McKenzie for Mr Bailey. Very good. I'll tell her that.' She replaces the phone and smiles. 'If you'd like to take a seat on the sofa, Mr Bailey will come down to meet you.'

Very nice, I think. The personal touch.

The sofa, like everything else in this place, is seven times as large as it needs to be. I sink into its soft leather cushions and stare at the enormous screen that is fixed to the opposite wall, on which the ad for the NeoONE plays. It's even more beguiling in widescreen. I'm just wondering how it would feel to be the winner of that phone, what unique fame it would bring me, how I could leverage that for my business, when I hear my name.

'Hello. Frida, is it?'

I look up to see a man with a mop of black spiky hair and a considerable belly atop long skinny legs. He's heading towards me so I guess this must be Clive. His balloon-like face breaks into a smile of greeting as I struggle from the crack between two giant cushions with as much grace as I can muster.

'Yes, hi, Clive? I'm Frida McKenzie, from McKenzie Family Law. Nice to meet you.'

'Excellent!' he says, his round eyes seeming to bulge with enthusiasm. 'So glad you could join us! If you'd like to follow me, we'll take this to one of the upper meeting rooms.'

This is good news. Everyone knows that the higher up you go in NeoStar, the more important you are. Clive leads me to a security gate where a tall, stocky man in a black security uniform nods at my bag.

'Place the bag on the conveyer belt,' the guard says in a low droning voice.

I flash a quizzical glance at Clive.

'We take security very seriously here,' he says, smiling broadly, seeming to find the whole situation very jolly.

'Of course.' I place the bag on the belt. As it trundles into a small tunnel, I walk through the gate, and wait there for a moment for my bag to come through.

In the lift, I watch as Clive presses the tip of one bony finger into the buttons on the keypad: 1, 2, 0, star. Then he stands, arms folded, unspeaking. I know I appreciate silence but lift silence is awkward even for me.

'So, Clive,' I say eventually. 'I didn't receive very much information from your secretary when she set up this meeting. Can you tell me what will be on the agenda, and who else, if anyone, will be joining us?'

Clive shoots me a glance, almost as though he's forgotten I'm there. 'Yes, yes,' he says. 'All the information will be covered in the meeting.'

'Right,' I say. 'But, the purpose of the meeting is . . . ?'

'To answer that question. Exactly!' he says.

Right. Clear as mud. I give up. The lift ascends, flicking through the floors, and then comes to a gentle stop at level 120.

'This is us.' Clive says. 'Follow me!'

Clive sets off at a fair old pace down a very long corridor. I walk after him, struggling to keep up, my heels sinking in to the soft pile of the carpet. Clive seems a bit strange, but then lots of successful businesses are manned by eccentrics. You don't get creative answers to problems if you don't colour outside the lines, as it were. Although, I muse, as I watch Clive bounding off down the hallway, his gait jerky and unnatural, I wouldn't trust this one with jumbo crayons if he worked at my place.

Clive comes to a sudden halt in front of a solid oak door that looks identical to all the others we've passed.

'Here we are,' he says.

I forget all about Clive's strange manner as I walk into the meeting room and am hit with sudden, intense office envy. The first thing I notice is the view, which is, basically, the whole of the city. Next I notice the furnishings. Oh God, the furnishings! They're unbelievable. In just one sweep of the room I take in what looks like a Ming vase, two Chippendale chairs, and an eighteenth-century writing desk. The surfaces are dotted with intriguing ornaments and *objets d'art* that have me drooling. The walls are covered with artwork, each in a huge ornate gold frame.

I turn to Clive, eyes shining, completely unable to play it cool. 'This is incredible!' I say. Clive, oddly, is still hovering by the door. 'Aren't you joining me?'

He gives me that strange grin again. 'No, no!' he says. 'You just wait here. The others will be with you shortly. There's coffee, do help yourself.'

I nod and, as his Cheshire Cat head disappears, I let out a sigh of relief. He's just the lackey they sent to fetch me, thank God. While I'm waiting for the meeting to start, I head to a sideboard where a jug of hot coffee is happily steaming. I go to pour myself a cup, but somehow I lose my grip, and the jug slips out of my hand, falling onto the sideboard with a crack. I watch in horror as coffee spills all over the polished top, running off the edge in rivulets and dripping onto the no-doubt priceless carpet.

'Oh shit!' I mutter, pulling a handful of tissues from my bag to mop up as much as I can. I peer doubtfully at the sideboard. It doesn't look as though there's any damage; they've probably got a wax preserver on it or something. But the coffee pot is cracked and, even worse, empty.

Good start, Frida.

Determined not to do any more damage, I wander to the window in a bid to calm myself. It's an incredible view. The Town Hall, the cathedral, the churches and offices and apartments, they all look tiny from up here, humbled by the might of NeoStar. As I watch, the clouds finally let go of their cargo, and white flakes descend in thick drifts. It's like the whole city is encased in a snow globe. I'm suddenly filled with an intense need. I want this: this money, this prestige, this life, this view. I resolve to impress the hell out of them at this meeting, and make this future happen.

That's if anyone ever actually turns up. Where are they all?

I check my phone. Ten minutes have passed and no one has arrived. Maybe this is a power play, a test to see how I'll react? Stranger tricks have been played in the world of business. I decide that I'll double my hourly rate for however long this meeting ends up taking. I stare mournfully at the empty coffee cup. I really need some caffeine. Where on earth is everyone? Did Clive get the room wrong?

Thinking of one crazy man inevitably leads me to another and my mind flits, unbidden, back to Dan. I remember what he said. Prophecies. An arrow. Only I can help. Like something out of a story.

There's still no sign of anyone, so I drag my gaze away from the city view and inspect the contents of the room. I quickly become entranced by a pair of green crackle-glaze vases that I would give my right and, indeed, left arm, to own. Then I move to admire a pair of bronze horse statuettes, an art deco mirror and a tapestry that looks medieval. I was already in awe of NeoStar but all of this just blows me away. Just how much money do these guys have? Then I check my phone again. Twenty minutes, now, and there's still no sign of anyone. It's like they've forgotten I'm here. This irks me. I might be inhabiting the smaller pond just now, but my time is still valuable.

I think about calling Clive to ask him what's going on, then realise I don't have his number. Taking out my phone I find the number for Clive's secretary and dial, making a mental note to request more coffee. But instead of a ringing tone, all I hear is a loud, abrasive beeping. Engaged. I terminate the call, my frustration mounting. I'll have to try again in five minutes.

I go back and sit at the boardroom table, which is empty save for a pile of letter-headed notepads in the centre. NeoStar, says the logo, and again, that arrow, a symbol of the company's continued upwards trajectory. Though quite how they manage it, when they can't even get to a meeting on time, is anyone's guess. Or maybe that's the point – when you're this big, this powerful, you can do whatever the hell you want.

Too wound up to relax, I get up again and walk around the rest of the room. It's ten times the size of my office and I think, again, that if we could just get this meeting going, I could start to make some serious money. One entire wall is devoted to paintings. I stare at the first one. A snake-haired Medusa gazes back at me, mad-eyed, blood dripping from her severed head, mouth open in a final roar. I frown. That is a weird painting to have on a boardroom wall. I shrug. Probably another power play. An in-joke about cut-throat business.

Ha ha.

I move along. The next painting shows a pale, chubby, sleeping cherub, a Cupid depicted in light and shadow. It's an image that should be innocent but which, instead, is faintly menacing. Creeped out, I move hastily onto the next painting, hoping for a nice inoffensive landscape to soothe my jangled nerves. But this image is even worse. Though I've seen it before in a magazine it shocks me anew to see it here in all its grisly glory. It couldn't be the original. It's a Goya, the monstrous one depicting the god Saturn devouring his son.

I shake my head, feeling slightly sick. This is getting seriously weird. I quickly scan the rest of the paintings: a naked woman chained to a rock; a man in shackles attacked by a giant eagle; two more unclothed women being molested by a pair of guys on horseback. Disturbing, every one of them. I'm appalled. What sort of a meeting room requires art like this? Then something occurs to me: the subject of all these paintings is classical mythology.

You might want to brush up on your Greek mythology . . .

A deep sense of unease is growing in my stomach. The whole vibe strikes me as a bit too weird. Maybe the top dogs at NeoStar are part of some cult that thinks sacrificing divorce lawyers will bring them good fortune? This thought, meant as a joke to myself, brings me only disquiet. I check my phone again. It's 10:14. This is unacceptable. There can't be any contract in the offing – no one treats a company like this if they have any respect for them. Or possibly there's just been an almighty fuck-up somewhere, a systems glitch, and I've been asked in by mistake? That would certainly explain why Clive, the great abandoner, didn't have a clue what the meeting was about.

I call Clive's secretary again, and curse when I find the line still engaged. How does a company this huge, this tech savvy, not have a cutting-edge hold system in place? I think about sending an email, but then decide against it. Whatever has happened to delay this meeting, I can't waste any more time waiting for someone to get back to me. I sling my bag over my shoulder, head for the door, and grasp the giant brass doorknob.

That's when I find out the door is locked.

Chapter 3

I stare at the door dumbly.

I'm locked in.

Clive must have flipped a catch on the door by mistake. What a colossal idiot this guy is shaping up to be!

I grab my phone again, furious. I'm a busy woman. This is the last thing I need. I dial Clive's secretary again. Unbelievably, it's still engaged. Heading back to the boardroom table, I tear a sheet off a notepad, and stab the digits of the main telephone number into my phone. I should have done this to begin with; I'll get reception to transfer me directly to Clive. I type the last number and wait for a connection, but instead of a human voice, I hear that same horrible tone.

Shit. There must be a problem with the phone lines or something.

I stand there for a moment, thinking about my next move. If the phone lines are down, everyone is going to be frantic. Which leaves less of a chance that anyone will remember I'm even here. There's nothing for it, I'll have to call Penny and get her to sort this out. Good old über-efficient Pen. I dial her office phone but what I hear gives me a jolt of alarm. It's the same *beep beep beep*.

I stare down at my mobile. Okay, so it's my phone that's the problem. That does make more sense. Except I've got 97 per cent battery and a strong signal. So why isn't it working? I try a few more numbers just to test it – Pen's mobile, Bryony's landline and then my own home – but each attempt is met with that same shrieking tone that is starting to set my nerves on edge.

Okay, I think, so my phone is broken. No problem. When in doubt, there's always trusty old analogue. I set about searching the room for a landline. Every nook and crevice and drawer of that beautiful office. There's no phone.

No way to communicate with anyone. No way to ask for help.

What started as a sense of unease is growing now into something more like panic. I try the door again. Maybe if a catch *has* fallen down, I can jiggle it free? I bend down and study the lock. But no. It's old, like everything else in this sumptuous room, and so there is no catch, just an empty keyhole. No way to lock a person in but deliberately.

'What the hell?' I whisper to myself.

I bang on the door with my closed fist.

'Hello?' I shout, as loudly as I can. 'Hello, can anyone

hear me? I'm locked in! Anybody?' I strain my ear against the door, but there's nothing. The luxury of this place seems to swallow up all noise.

Everything's okay, I tell myself. Just think, Frida. Make a plan.

I take deep breaths because, despite myself, I'm starting to freak out. I'm not a big fan of being trapped in places, even places as decadent as this. Don't panic, I think to myself. Let's just take stock. Clive knows I'm here, and we have a meeting scheduled, so someone, surely, must be coming back here. But what if they don't? What if Clive fell and bumped his head and has been carted off to casualty? This building has 199 floors. How many of these rooms go unused? And it's Friday. Soon the building will empty out save for a few weekend grafters. I could be stuck up here for days, *weeks,* without food and water. I'll become one of those weird urban legends you hear about, that no one really believes are true.

Forcing myself to calm down, I sit back at that beautiful desk and stare at the empty jug. I need caffeine. If I had coffee, I'd be able to think clearly. I reach for one of the notepads. I'll write down my thoughts, an approach that never fails to soothe me. I stare at the NeoStar logo. Something is tugging at the corners of my mind, slipping away when I try to pin it down. Shaking my head, I grab my pen and start listing my options:

Wait for someone to arrive.

I check the time. It's almost an hour since Clive left me here, and it doesn't seem likely that he's coming back. A possibility hits me: Clive might be the husband of someone I've represented. As I roll that idea around my mind, it makes more and more sense. Of course! I must have stung Clive in a divorce settlement, and this is payback. I bite my lip. Sometimes a husband scorned can be even more hellish than his wife. All the more reason to get out of here, fast.

I write the word 'window'. I could wave something, shout, try to attract attention from the street below. I get up to check. Every one of the windows is locked. I sit back down at the notepad. 'Fire alarm?' I glance around. There's no panel that I can see.

Try to jimmy the lock.

It's the only option left. Sod it. I'll wreck the door and let the bastards bill me. I start to search the office for anything sharp that I can use to force into the lock, but somehow I come up empty. How can a room like this have nothing with a sharp edge? No letter opener? No pen holder? Not even a teaspoon? That uneasy feeling is back again. *Something is wrong here.*

Stop dramatising, I tell myself, and I realise that this is an old, long-forgotten memory of my mother, who used to tell me off for spinning stories when I was a child. *Stop being so fanciful, Frida.* But I'm not fanciful Frida any more. Haven't been for years. I'm practical, force-to-be-reckoned-with Frida. And that's who I need to be right now.

I delve into my bag – my keys have a sharp edge, it's at least worth a try – but, despite my determined fishing, my hands don't come into contact with the cold metallic bundle I keep expecting. I search for a minute longer, then, cursing, I upturn my bag onto the oh-so-valuable table. I sift through the contents. I look again and again, stupidly, just like I kept checking the door. Because I can't believe what I'm seeing. My keys are missing. I have a terrible thought, and check the objects on the desk again. My purse has gone too.

They took my keys and purse. The idea forms, impossible as it is insistent. *That security guard took them.* Okay, but why? And why not my phone? *Because you'd notice that first,* the inner voice of wisdom chimes in, too late. *Probably before you'd even got all the way up in the lift. And that could have been . . . messy.*

The instinct that let me down so badly yesterday is screaming at me now. This is bad. This is very bad.

Don't get into a car with anyone you don't know. Don't let anyone into your home . . . And don't, whatever you do, go anywhere near NeoStar.

Not my own inner expert, now, but Dan. He knew something was going to happen to me. Somehow he knew. Then my brain finally makes the connection. The thing that has been tugging at my mind. I look at the piece of letter-headed paper. The name. The arrow.

I used to love word games as a kid, and I've never lost the knack. NeoStar. Rearrange the letters and what do you get?

ANTEROS.

Chapter 4

I'm still in the room. Unbelievably, incredibly, I'm still in this bloody room. I don't know who or what Anteros is, but I'm working on the theory now that scorned husband Clive and Mad Dan are in this together, one spooking me out with his fanciful nonsense before the other finishes off the prank. But the fact remains that I am still locked in this room and I'm getting a very, very – make that VERY – bad feeling about all of this.

I stand in the middle of the room, every muscle and nerve braced, though I don't know what for. I run through everything else that might be relevant to this situation. Mad Dan left me his number, didn't he, and where is that now? I see it, in my mind's eye, resting on the top of the wastepaper basket in my office. No good to me there and even if I'd picked it up, it would be useless anyway, if they're somehow jamming my phone.

You sound mad, Frida, a small worried voice inside me says.

And I do. I know I do. But that doesn't change the fact that this is happening.

I turn back to the table and begin to sift through the contents of my bag – packet of tissues, make-up, umbrella, diary, loose change, earphones – because I travel heavy and I refuse to believe there's nothing in my bag that can help me. That's when I notice it. A yellow sticky note I've never seen before, bearing the words:

Behind Caravaggio's Cupid.

I stare at it. This is getting plain goddam surreal.

Behind Caravaggio's Cupid? Putting aside for a moment the implausibility that this note might have anything at all to do with my current situation, I walk the room again. I spot the painting of the sleeping cherub. Could that be a Caravaggio? I stand on my tiptoes and check the signature but the canvas is dark and I can't make it out. Acknowledging that what I'm doing is insane, but also that I'm going to do it anyway, I drag an ornate chair over to the painting, kick off my shoes and climb onto it.

I run my hands along the underside of the frame and then all around the edges. I'm about to give up – this is ridiculous, truly ridiculous – when at the top of the frame, in the centre, my hands encounter something. Carefully, I ease the painting forwards with one hand, grip the object with the other, and pull.

I stare at it. It's a mobile phone, exactly like mine but with the battery missing. There's another yellow note stuck to it.

Call me.

I'm suddenly convinced that I haven't woken up yet today, that this whole thing is just a dream. And so with dream logic, I take the battery from my own phone and insert it into this one, switch it on, and scroll to contacts.

There's just one name.

He picks up on the second ring.

'You went to NeoStar.' A statement, not a question.

I blink, then quickly recover myself. 'Yes. And now I'm locked in a room. Would you mind telling me what kind of game you're playing?'

'No game, Frida. Have you eaten or drunk anything since you've been there?'

My mind flashes to the coffee currently staining the carpet.

'Nothing. Why?'

'Doesn't matter. Just don't, okay?'

There's a silence. 'Okay,' I say.

'How long did they leave you alone?'

'It's been about an hour and a half.' Then I add in a quieter voice, 'They left me some coffee, but I spilled it.'

He sucks in a breath. 'Okay, then they probably think you're drugged,' he says, like that's a perfectly normal sentence. 'So you have a bit of time. Here's what I want you to do. Look around the room. Do you notice an air-conditioning unit in the ceiling?'

I look up and scan the ceiling for anything grid-like.

'No.'

'Check again. It'll be hidden.'

I pace the room and then I see it; a square of white on white.

'I see it.'

'Okay. Drag the desk over to the vent, but do NOT make any noise. Climb up and remove the cover, then pull the vent. Then pull down the rope that's fastened inside.'

Rope? I'm silent as I absorb this.

'Frida, you still there?'

'Yeah,' I say faintly, sure now that this is a dream.

'Put the phone down and do that now. We don't have much time.'

I look at the distance between the table and the vent. It's about three metres. I walk to the width end of the table, grip it with both hands, and start to shove. The table is solid but I'm strong. Like I say, it pays to be underestimated. Slowly, slowly, I inch the table towards the vent and, when I'm sure I'll have enough room to balance, I climb up onto the table.

I almost slip when my nylon-clad feet slide over the waxed surface, so I take off my tights, too, and grip the table with my bare feet. I have a flash of Clive walking into the meeting room, all apologies: he'd had a family emergency, he'd forgotten to tell me the door sticks, he's awfully sorry, there's been a terrible mix-up . . . and then seeing me on top of this priceless desk, bare-footed, and mad-eyed as Medusa over there. But whoever is eventually going to come through that door means me no good. My instincts are firing on all cylinders now and I know that everything about this room, this building, is dead wrong.

I pull at the white cover with a grunt of effort. It comes away easily, revealing a small square grill. I thread my fingers into the holes and yank, but there's no give. I look in each corner, searching for screws I can loosen, but there's nothing, the thing seems to be moulded in. It crosses my mind that this whole thing might be a hidden camera stunt and that I'm going to look just peachy when I'm all over YouTube. Then I yank the vent one last time, giving it everything I've got, and it comes away in my hands.

I wobble like crazy, still gripping the vent, then steady myself. Breathing deeply, I lower the piece of metal onto the table and then stare up. There's now a large black hole in the ceiling, about one metre square. I reach up into the void and my hand immediately comes into contact with something coarse and hairy – a rope ladder. I unfold it and then stare, my heart sinking. Either help is coming down or I'm going up.

I think I already know which one is most likely.

I pick up the phone. 'There's no way I'm doing that. Who do you think I am, Bruce Willis?'

'It's the only way out, Frida.'

'Listen,' I say, finding refuge in rational argument, 'clearly you were up here already today planting phones and rope ladders and the like, so why can't you just come back with a sledgehammer or something and break down the door?

Or call the police for me. Yes,' I continue, this idea gaining appeal in my mind, 'call the police; tell them I'm stuck up here! Then I can get to the bottom of what's going on. I'm sure this is all just a silly mistake.'

'No police,' Dan says. 'NeoStar own them.'

'Don't be ridiculous!' I say, anger barely hiding my fear.

'Frida,' Dan says, 'listen to me. I wish I could get in there to help you, but I'll never get past security. That phone, those ladders, a friend who worked there did that for me.'

'Great!' I cry. 'Then they can come and let me out!'

There's a pause. 'That was two years ago.'

'Two years . . .' I drift off. How can Dan's friend have planted those things two years ago when he only met me yesterday? Suddenly I feel incredibly tired. 'I don't understand,' I say. 'I really don't understand what's going on.'

'It's very simple,' Dan says. 'You get out, or they come for you. What you choose is up to you.'

Chapter 5

With my shoes crammed into my bag, and my bag tightened over my shoulder, I proceed to clamber, with considerable difficulty and zero grace, into the air-conditioning shaft. It's only just big enough for a person of my size on her hands and knees, and I am hit with a sudden premonition of getting wedged in and dying up here. Another urban legend for the books. Dismissing the thought as not particularly helpful right now, I inch forwards in the direction Dan has instructed. I count one, two – great. I'm at the third vent. Once I get to the sixth, Dan assures me, there will be another ladder and I can climb down.

As I shuffle over the vent I hear muffled voices. I freeze. There's someone down there. Lying with my ear flat to the floor, I can just about make out their words.

'. . . will he be ready?'

'Not for half an hour.' It's Clive's voice, I'm sure. 'But she should be unconscious for a while. Take her up to Anteros on the trolley.'

'What's she like?'

'Oh, you know. Small. Big breasts. The sort of mortal you'd want to—'

The rest is hidden behind laughter, but I don't want to hear any more. An icy fear grips me at Clive's use of the word *mortal*. What does that mean? That I'm somehow less than them? Something dispensable? And there's that name again – Anteros. *Is* this a cult? I think, even up until this point, I still had a glimmer of hope that this whole thing was just a huge misunderstanding. But hearing this hideous exchange destroys any such hopes. The voices are getting fainter: they're heading out of the room. I move as quickly and as quietly as I can. I need to get to that sixth vent.

It feels like forever, but actually it's just five limb-cramping minutes until I get there. I push my fingers into the slats and shove, then throw down the rope ladder and climb down. I drop, my bare feet hitting carpet, and scan the room. It's a storeroom, holding dozens of filing cabinets and even more boxes. Some kind of archive. Each box and cabinet has a sticker. I need to get out of here, Dan has told me not to stop for a second. But I'm just reaching for the door handle when I see something.

I step backwards. Blink. The tag on the nearest cabinet says 'Frida McKenzie'. There are eight digits underneath it: my birth date.

What. The. Hell?

I know I have to go, but I can't make my legs work. I have to know what is in that cabinet. I backtrack two paces and open the top drawer. It looks just like any other filing cabinet, with those slim green folders and their clear plastic tabs, but it's the labels inside those tabs that freak me out. The first reads '9–14 years', then '14–19', '19–24'. I wrench open file after file, and see photographs of me as a child, a teen, an adult, pieces of paper filled with type, like transcripts. And a red stamp on each bundle of paper that reads: 'INACTIVE'. I'm scanning this, eyes wide, mind scrambled, unable to make any kind of sense of it, when I hear a shout from down the corridor.

I look up, horror dawning. I've lingered too long. They've checked on me.

They know I've gone.

I spin around, fling open the door, and run for the stairs. 'Hey!'

I look back over my shoulder and see Clive's face. He's not smiling any more, and he doesn't look like an affable dolt. His expression is pure rage. I figure I have thirty seconds on him. I see a fire alarm and I bash it with my fist, pushing myself to move faster as the siren fills my ears. I'm at the end of the corridor and in front of the door.

Frantically, I try to remember the numbers Dan gave me.

Three. Seven. Four. Seven.

Three. Seven. Four. Seven.

I type the numbers and yank the door handle. It doesn't budge. I can hear Clive behind me, he's almost on me now. I must have fluffed it. I cancel and start again, willing my shaky hand to still. Three. Seven. Four. Seven. A jolt of pure relief shoots through me as I hear the click and this time when I pull the door, blessedly it opens, revealing stairs. One hundred and twenty flights to safety.

I repeat Dan's words to myself: *Down seventy flights. Through the red double doors, down another fifty. That's where all the normal workers are. You'll be safer there. They won't do anything to cause a scene if there are people around to witness it.*

Down the stairs I go, down and down those never-ending stairs. Clive is careering down after me, just two, maybe three flights behind. I'm fast, but he's faster, and he's gaining on me. I try to increase my pace, but it's like being chased in a dream, inevitable that I'll be caught. Only this isn't a dream, I can't just wake myself up; this is real life and then, suddenly, I've done it, I'm there, at the red doors, and freedom is just metres away.

But so is Clive.

I type in the second code – three, three, three, five – and this time I get it first time, but I'm not going to make it, he's too fast, and all I'm thinking is that I can't let him take me back up there, to those horrible pictures, to whatever they have planned for me, I'll go mad if they do. And anyway, I didn't climb through an air vent just to get caught. Then my glance falls on my bag and I know what to do.

In a fluid movement I grab the door, throw myself through it, slam it shut and, whipping my tights from my bag, thread them through first one handle then the other and tie them. Maybe they should have confiscated those at the security gate, too, I think with grim satisfaction, if they wanted to keep me locked up.

As I give the knot one big yank, I take a last look through the small bevelled window. Clive's face looms up at me, twisted in anger. He doesn't even look human any more. Then I'm off again, down and down, like Alice down the rabbit hole, except that I'm doing the reverse, going from madness to normality, because now, at each floor that I pass, there are more people, ordinary people. Young men in their first suits flirting with their colleagues. People frowning, mobiles to ears, complaining about the interruption to their very important meeting. Giddy young girls with expertly curled hair and HD brows, glad of the respite from the dull Friday grind.

Soon I'm just one flight from the ground floor and I can see the reception desk through the plate-glass windows. Mandy is surrounded by five men dressed in black security uniforms, and she's showing them something on her screen. I watch as the men split up and head for the exits and, with a sinking feeling, I realise they've been told to find me. They're going to check everyone as they leave.

I spot a multicoloured scarf trailing from the tote of the girl in front of me. As she chats on her phone, I grab the end of it, whip it from her bag like a magician, and wrap it around my hair. Then I slow down, let a few groups pass, and mingle in with a bunch of forty-something women dressed in brightly coloured blouses, black skirts and sharp black stilettoes. I drift casually down the stairs with them, praying no one notices my bare feet.

This is it. The ground floor. The group heads for the exit.

'Hey, ladies!' I say, and link arms with the woman nearest to me. She frowns and looks down at me.

'What are we doing for lunch?' I ask jovially as we pass the security guard. 'Shall we go to Leroy's again?'

'I'm sorry,' the woman says, looking at me in confusion. 'Do I know you?'

'Oh my Gosh!' I say. 'You look just like my colleague Janet!' Then I separate from the herd, and step into the giant revolving door.

I don't want to look back but I can't stop myself. Over the heads of the women I see Clive arrive at the bottom of the stairs. Before I can turn away we lock eyes and he points over, communicating his orders in gestures to the guards. But there are too many people; they can't get to me without drawing attention. I have to believe Dan when he says they don't want to make a scene.

The five seconds it takes for the door to revolve are the longest of my life, every single moment I expect the machinery to jerk to a halt, and that will be it. I'll be trapped like a spider under a glass. But then I feel fresh air on my face, and I'm out and I'm running, my heart hammering, my bare feet hitting the cold wet pavement, and anyone who saw me would think that I was running for my life.

Chapter 6

I weave down side streets, diving down alleys and turning endless corners, until I'm sure that no one is following me. I'm coatless, and frozen, and my bare feet are drawing more than a few curious glances, so I stop for a moment to take my shoes from my bag and put them on. Immediately, I feel more like myself.

Then I walk on, going over in my mind what just happened. It was madness to climb through that ventilation shaft. I can't have heard what I thought I heard. Perhaps the door really did just stick? But that still leaves the question: how did Dan know I'd be trapped in there? And that brings me to the filing cabinet. I know I didn't imagine that. Unless I did.

I stop for a moment and take a deep breath. Right. So, either the largest tech company in the world has got it in for me or I'm losing the plot. Right now, I don't know which of those possibilities I'd prefer.

The planted phone rings in my bag, and I know it's going to be Dan checking to see if I got out okay. He's expecting me to meet him in some café near the train station. But as I listen to the ringtone I suddenly realise that I'm not going to do that. I don't know what crazy shit is going on here between Dan and NeoStar, and I don't want to know. I'm not getting myself in any deeper. I'm going to my office and I'll sort it out from there. It's daylight, in the middle of a busy city. I'm safe. I have to be.

Dan's phone pings with a text.

Frida, please don't be stupid. You need to come to the café NOW.

I frown at it. I don't know what riles me most, him calling me stupid, or those capital letters. Either way, I'm not going.

I take the battery out of the phone he left for me, put it back in mine and turn it on. It vibrates, signalling new mail and my eyes widen. It's from Clive's secretary. Heart racing, I thumb it open:

Mr Bailey sends his apologies for the mix-up. He'd like to connect again to discuss terms that he believes would be mutually beneficial. Please return to the office at your earliest convenience.

What the hell? Has he really just chased me out of the building and then sent me an invitation for a follow-up meeting? I shake my head. This day just gets more and more weird. I need to get back to my office. Ken, the building custodian, will let me in. I'll collect the spare keys I keep in my drawer and then head back to my flat. Then I'll call the police and tell them everything. I'm a lawyer, for God's sake. They can't do this to me.

I stow the phone back in my bag and walk. The closer I get to my office, the better I feel. The normal world is all still here, after all. The courts, which I class as my third home, after my flat and my office. The multiplex, with the kids hanging around outside trying to muster snowballs from the sludge. My favourite bookshop-cum-coffee house, with its witty chalkboard quotes that change daily. The library, with its two grand stone lions standing guard. By the time I get to the Chapterhouse café bar it's quarter to twelve and I have half-convinced myself that this morning never happened.

I slip into the loos and inspect the damage. My dress is covered in streaks of dust and grime from the air vent, and the snow has sprung my hair into curls. I smooth it down as best I can, then bat the dust from my dress. I take out my make-up bag and after adding a dash of lipstick and mascara I feel better. More normal. I count the loose change in the zipped pocket of my bag and scrape together enough for a small takeaway coffee. I can't wait to head home and pour myself a bucket of wine. This day is a write-off.

It starts to snow again as I walk to the office. Shivering, I take out my mobile and call my bank about my lost cards, but I don't understand what the customer service person is saying. Something about all my cards having already been cancelled.

'No,' I say tersely. 'I'm calling to report them stolen.'

'Ms McKenzie, your bank accounts have been frozen,' the man says. 'No funds may be transferred in or out.'

I stop walking and frown, trying to process the customer service advisor's words, and then I see that the front door to my office is wedged open. There's a removal van parked outside, and two men in baseball caps and leather jackets are angling my desk out onto the street. And not carefully either.

'I have to go,' I say and I start to run.

'Hey, hey!' I say to the burly guy in the red baseball cap who is walking backwards towards the open boot of his van. 'This is my stuff. What do you think you're doing?'

Red Baseball Cap gives me the once over. 'You Ms McKenzie?'

'Yes, this is my office,' I say, then I tap on the wooden table top which is rapidly gathering a layer of crisp snow. 'This is my desk.'

Red Cap sniffs. 'Repossession order.' He nods at Blue Baseball Cap, and they lower the desk to the pavement. Red Cap retrieves a tablet from the back pocket of his jeans and hands it to me.

I scan the screen quickly, unable to compute what I'm seeing. 'This is a mistake,' I say. 'I don't owe any money.'

Red Cap shrugs. 'Nothing to do with me, love; I just collect the stuff.'

'But . . . this is . . .' I don't finish. I can't. I'm literally lost for words regarding what this is. I take a deep breath and aim for a calm tone. 'Look, this isn't legal. Can you just stop moving that desk, and let me call someone and sort this out?'

He shakes his head. 'Sorry, love. No can do. We'll take the stuff and if it turns out it's all been a mistake, you'll get it all back, see? And the stuff from your flat too.'

'My flat! What have you done? I swear to God, I'll . . .' But Red Cap isn't listening, he's too busy loading my belongings into his van. Furious, I carry on reading the notice. It lists unpaid rent on my office and mortgage arrears on my flat, going back twelve months, and a final notice of eviction for both premises, which, according to this document, they sent to me eight weeks ago.

This is unacceptable. Taking out my mobile, I dial the contact number at the top of the screen, stabbing the digits furiously. Then I hear something that fills my veins with ice: an ear-piercing, rhythmic beeping that's horribly familiar. I hang up and, while the men are busy loading my desk into the van, I slip through the open door of the office, up the stairs and into reception. I stare at Penny's desk, empty now except for the grey, cordless landline. Picking up the receiver, I try the same number again. All I get is that same regular, piercing beep.

This can't be happening.

I stand there for a minute, trying to get things straight in my head. First they try to imprison me. Then they chase me. Then they evict me from my office and home, and freeze my bank accounts. What the hell is going on?

My skin prickles. Dan was right. I'm not safe. They're trying to force me into a corner. Leave me with nowhere to hide. It was stupid to come back here. They could be coming for me at any minute, a sleek black car pulling up outside, some anaesthetic applied to my mouth and nose. And then – what? I wake up chained to an altar while a load of crazed business types in masks stand around me chanting?

I'm still holding the phone. For a second, my finger hovers over the 9. Should I? I don't know. Even if what Dan said about the police isn't true – and it could be; I'm only too aware of how corrupt this city can be – what evidence do I have against NeoStar? A door that sticks. A filing cabinet that will be long gone before anyone gets around to investigating. A jug of drugged coffee spilled on a carpet that's probably been removed too. And two notices for eviction which, I'm willing to bet, have all the legitimacy your average police officer would require to be convinced that it's me, and not NeoStar, who is the guilty party. After all, I realise with a blank sort of dread, they probably made the systems used by the banks. What's to stop them hacking in and falsifying my records?

That's crazy talk, my mind chides. *That's ridiculous!*

But then other voices chime in. *Bit off more than she could chew,* I imagine my old law school acquaintances saying. *Too ambitious by far.* It strikes me that NeoStar know me very well. This – the evictions, the sudden lack of funds – is outrageous, yes, but it's also oddly credible if you're a person surrounded by peers all too eager to believe in your downfall. The more spectacular that downfall the better. And why not throw in a paranoid nervous break-down for good measure?

My body floods with shame as I think about all of this coming out in the press. What they'll all say about me, how much they'll enjoy it. And that decides it. I'll take care of this myself. Quietly.

No police then.

So, what now? I try to think. Where can I go? Who can help me? Bryony would take me in in a heartbeat, but I don't want to drag her and her family into this. Not until I understand exactly what 'this' is.

My mother? A laughable idea.

Where then? Who?

I take out my phone and read Clive's message: *Please return to the office at your earliest convenience.*

I think about Dan's message: *You need to come to the café NOW.*

I reach down, open a drawer and take out the petty cash tray. Fifty pounds in notes and three pounds in coins. I palm the money just as Red and Blue Cap stomp in and start disconnecting my TV monitor. I take an old parka from lost property, pull it on and slip the money in the pocket. Not exactly my style, but needs must.

My head is starting to ache. I take a sip of lukewarm coffee from the takeaway cup.

What do I do now? Who do I know that can help me?

Then I have an idea.

Chapter 7

When he opens the door, it's such a relief to see a friendly face that I want to wrap my arms around him and bury my face in his chest, except I don't want to give him the wrong idea so I just smile.

'Thanks for letting me come over,' I say. 'I didn't know where else to go.'

Chris smiles back. He looks glad to see me. 'Not a problem. I've just opened a bottle of wine. Want a glass?'

He always did have a knack of saying exactly the right thing. 'I'd love one,' I say, letting out a long, slow sigh of relief. I follow Chris into his impeccable house, shrug off the coat, and then sit on a bar stool at his pristine granite kitchen worktop. He hands me a glass, looking me up and down.

'Have you been sweeping a chimney?'

I give a faint smile. 'Not exactly.' My mind flashes back to crawling through the air-conditioning shaft and I shudder. Accepting the glass gratefully, I take a long swig. 'You look well,' I say. And he does. Blond hair, winter tan. Healthy and wholesome. 'How's work?'

Chris takes a small sip of wine. 'It's going great,' he says, nodding slowly. 'Some interesting opportunities coming up.'

'Really? Fantastic.' Chris is very, very good at what he does. He has a penchant for detail and a determination that entirely suits him to the structure of the corporate world. It also makes him the best possible person to untangle this unholy mess I find myself in.

'So,' he says, 'want to tell me what's going on? You said on the phone you had a problem you needed my help with?'

I take a sip of wine. 'Something weird has happened, Chris, and I need your take on it. It's to do with NeoStar.' I recount an abridged version of the story, detailing my bizarre meeting, the locked door, the filing cabinets, the eviction notices and my suddenly frozen bank accounts. Chris listens, nodding his head every so often. To his credit, he doesn't interrupt, even if he does widen his eyes as I recount climbing up a rope ladder and exiting via the ventilation shaft.

'It sounds mad, I know,' I say. I feel better now I've told someone. It's good to get the craziness out of my head. 'But it's all true, and I need you to help me work out what their game is. What they want with me.'

'Well,' Chris says, unfazed, 'it's certainly unorthodox. It all sounds very odd and rather frightening. You did very well. Don't worry, we'll get to the bottom of this.'

I nod, feeling pleasantly light headed as the red wine hits my system. 'Thanks so much. You're such a good friend.'

He smiles. 'Not at all, Frida. You know I'd do anything for you.'

He holds my gaze for a moment, and then snaps his fingers. 'I worked for a client who was suing NeoStar a few years ago,' he says. 'I'll get the file and we can take a look. There might be something in there that's useful.'

'That would be great,' I say, relieved by his enthusiasm. As he goes upstairs to retrieve his laptop, I look around the room. There are a few changes since I was last here. A new lamp in soft dove grey. A rug with a geometric pattern. Some expensive modern art. It really is a lovely room. I sigh. Why didn't I think I could make it work with Chris? I find I can't remember.

He comes back down, laptop under his arm, then refills both our glasses. I feel myself start to relax for the first time today. When I give another long, drawn-out sigh, Chris puts his arms around me. His hand snakes up to the nape of my neck and he begins to stroke me there, soft pulses that ease my tension.

'It's all going to be okay,' he says gently. 'You can stay here tonight. We'll look at all this with fresh eyes in the morning.' His hand moves down to stroke the top of my shoulders. I don't stop him.

'It was just all so horrible,' I say in a small voice that doesn't sound like mine. 'I mean, what do NeoStar want with me? I can't work out what their angle is.'

'Shhh,' he says. 'Don't think about NeoStar or Bailey or any of it right now.'

I'm so lulled by his warmth, his closeness, the reassuring feeling that he's going to sort this terrible mess out for me, that I'm practically falling asleep right here in his arms and I almost don't register it.

Almost.

I sit up. 'What did you say?'

Chris rubs the tops of my arms. 'I said don't think about any of it.'

I pull away from him and tip my head back.

'No, you said don't think about Bailey.'

Chris blinks at me. 'Right yeah, that's what I said. Clive Bailey, NeoStar, don't think about any of it.'

I swallow a lump that has formed in my throat. 'I didn't tell you his surname.'

In the split second before an expression of laid-back puzzlement can arrive on Chris' face, I see something else there – a look of animal cunning – then it's gone and he's the Chris I know: attentive, confident, in charge.

'Of course you mentioned it, Frida,' he laughs. 'How else would I know his name?' But his breeziness sounds entirely hollow and adrenalin floods through me in panicky waves.

'I didn't mention his surname,' I say again.

Chris's smile is becoming frayed at the edges. 'Well, then,' he says, 'perhaps his name is in one of these files, and your story jogged my memory?'

Now I know he's lying. If he were telling the truth, he wouldn't deign to explain himself. It's not his way.

'I have to go,' I say, getting up off the stool.

Chris doesn't let go of my arms. 'Frida,' he says silkily.

'Wait! You're overwrought. You're not thinking straight. You know how sometimes you drink too much and forget things.'

I look down at those hands. Hands that have touched me, held me. Liar's hands.

'Let me go,' I say. 'Or I swear to God, I will break your arms.'

He looks into my eyes, sees that I'm not messing around and drops his arms. 'Okay, fine,' he says, shaking his head. 'Have it your own way.'

I pull on the coat hurriedly and pick up my bag. With trembling hands I take out my phone, remove the battery, and insert it into Dan's mobile. I've made a terrible mistake coming here. I see that now. I swing my bag over my shoulder and turn to face Chris, shaking with anger.

'What's going on, Chris? Why are you helping them?'

Chris shakes his head. 'Frida, Frida, calm down! They just want to talk to you, that's all. Clive called me right after you did. He explained you'd had a misunderstanding, that you'd walked out of a meeting. He asked me to help you see sense.'

'See sense?' I gape at him. 'Chris, they kidnapped me! They have files on me going back to when I was nine years old! Does that sound like it makes any sense to you?'

'I don't know what you thought you saw, Frida,' Chris says firmly, 'but I can assure you that Clive is a perfectly reasonable man, and of course he would ask me, as a mutual friend and a person well respected in such circles as this, to help—'

'Oh please!' I say. I see it now, in his puffed-up chest, his defensive tone. I laugh. 'They promised you a job, didn't they? Wow. You are one cold, climbing sonofabitch.'

'*I'm* cold?' Chris's face tightens. 'What about you, Frida? Leading me on all these years and never sealing the deal.' His expression is mean and peevish, a frustrated toddler. Amazing how the people you know so well can change in front of your eyes, just like that.

'I liked you, Frida,' he goes on. 'We had chemistry, didn't we? We could have been good together. But no.' He sniffs. 'You have to play your games.'

He darts a glance at the clock and I realise, with a sudden shock, that they're on their way. He must have called them when he was upstairs. All that comforting then, all these horrible words now, he's just stalling me.

I'm such a fool.

I'm at the front door, opening it, looking behind me to check Chris isn't trying to stop me and so I don't see them before it's too late. Two enormous men in black security outfits getting out of a shiny black van.

Again, the thought comes, as though by thinking it I can make it true.

This. Can't. Be. Happening.

But it is happening.

They've come to get me.

Chapter 8

'Mmmppf pff gggg.'

I'm tied up in the back of the van. There are two security guards on each side of me and I'm facing Clive.

'So,' he says. 'You have not responded to my message, Ms McKenzie. Rather rude, isn't it?'

'Mfff pff,' I say, gesturing to the gag with my eyes. They'd put it on when I wouldn't stop screaming for help. Nobody came. I'm guessing this van is soundproof, just like the boardroom of death.

'Remove it,' Clive says and one of the men in black yanks the cloth from my mouth.

I flex my jaw and glare at Clive. 'You need to let me go right now.'

Clive smiles. 'Straight to the point. I do admire that. I'll respond in kind: what do you know about the arrow?'

The arrow. Dan mentioned an arrow too. Is it code for something?

'I don't know anything about an arrow,' I say, trying not to show how scared I am.

Clive smiles pleasantly. 'Then why did you run?'

My eyes widen at this. 'How about because you locked me in a fucking boardroom and tried to drug me?'

Unperturbed, Clive shakes his head. 'I think there is more to this story, Ms McKenzie. For instance, this.' Clive opens his gloved palm, to reveal a scrunched-up sticky note. My heart sinks. Why didn't I take the blasted note with me?

'"Behind Caravaggio's Cupid",' Clive muses. 'Who left this for you?'

I sense I am on the edge of deep waters here. I must tread carefully. 'A man came to see me, yesterday,' I say. 'He said some crazy stuff. He left the note in my bag. I'd never seen him before then.'

'A man? Who is this man?'

'I told you, I've no idea!' I cry. 'Truly, I don't know what any of this is about!'

Clive regards me with detached curiosity. I breathe out, trying to slow my hammering heart.

'Listen to me, Mr Bailey,' I say levelly. 'You have made a mistake. You and this guy clearly have me confused with someone else. A person you believe has done something with this arrow.' His eyes shine when I say the word, and I curse myself. It's clearly a hot-button topic, whatever it is. 'What I'm trying to say is, I'm no threat at all. I don't know anything. If you let me go, I promise you I won't tell anyone. I'll go home and forget any of this ever happened.'

Clive is watching me carefully, appraisingly. I think I'm getting somewhere.

'I couldn't prove anything, could I, anyway?' I go on. 'I don't have enough evidence. I know that, because I am a lawyer.' I'm babbling now, in danger of lurching into panic any second. I take a deep breath. 'So, you can let me go. Please.'

Clive's gaze has intensified. 'Do you know the whereabouts of this man?'

My skin prickles. Dan is waiting at the café right now. I could give him up. Maybe that's what all this is about. Perhaps, once they have him, they'll leave me alone. But then an image of Chris comes into my mind, his mean, arrogant face; his quick, sneaky glances at the clock, and just like that, I'm decided. Whoever these people are, whatever they want, I couldn't hand anyone over to them and live with myself.

I raise my eyes to meet Clive's shining gaze and shrug. 'No idea.'

'So, it is like that.' Clive says. He pauses. 'I feel, Ms McKenzie, that we are both participating in a charade, each playing our part, when actually some veracity would be altogether more helpful.'

I frown as I watch him glance at the guards and nod. I don't like the look of this one little bit.

'There is no charade!' I say. 'Please. Just let me go!'

Clive shakes his head with undisguised impatience. 'The time for pretence is over,' he says. 'We will show you what

62

we are. And then you will tell me the truth about who *you* are.'

'No,' I say, my voice hoarse and low, suddenly dead certain that I don't want to see whatever it is Clive wants to reveal.

'Yes,' says Clive and he stares at me and I stop protesting then. I'm mesmerised by his eyes. Already bulbous, they seem to be growing larger and darker until they are shiny, turquoise-black and malevolent. Insect eyes. Horrified, I drag my gaze away, but there's no escape because, oh God, the guards' faces are different now too, turned unnaturally flat, their blank expressions almost bovine.

No! It's some sort of trick, another mind game. I have to keep calm. I stare down at the floor of the van, at the dark grey speckled carpet, and remind myself to breathe. *Just breathe, Frida; none of this is real.*

'We have shed our disguises, Frida,' Clive says companionably. 'Isn't it time you shed yours?'

I keep my eyes fixed on the carpet. My mother was right about me all along. Fanciful Frida. Bad Frida. But no, that isn't me. I'm not her any more. Something lights up in my bag. I glance at it and have just enough time to see the message on the phone screen – Get down! – when the van door opens. I dive to the floor, and something explodes with a smoky BANG.

Then there's silence.

I lie there for a moment.

'Frida?'

I open my eyes. Still alive then. I climb up, coughing in

63

the charcoal air. Through the grey haze, I see Clive and the men in black, their faces still distorted. None of them are moving, at least, which is a bonus. As the fog clears, I see Dan reaching out an arm.

'Come on!' he says. 'It's only Ophiotaurus powder. It knocks them out, but it doesn't last long. We need to get to Tony's.'

I don't bother to ask who Tony is. I just reach out a hand, and he grasps it and yanks me up. As we start down the street, I have just enough time to see Chris's face at the window, his brow puckered, no doubt wondering what all of this will mean for his career trajectory, and then I'm running for my life for the second time today.

Chapter 9

Tony's is not a person but a place – the café at which I neglected to meet Dan all those hours ago. It's a ramshackle place in an area of town where the boutiques and bars give way to graffiti and sex-shops. Its red booth seats are cracked, leaking stuffing, and the once black and white checked floor is greyed out by footfall. Not somewhere NeoStar would think to look for the Frida McKenzie they have on their files. Still, you can't be too sure. I do a quick check of the other people in the café: an old man in a grimy mustard-coloured anorak, two students sharing an ice-cream sundae. No sign of Clive or the men in black.

Dan sees me scouting the area anxiously. 'Don't worry,' he says. 'There's a protection spell over this place. They can't find you here.'

I stare at him. Protection spells. Exploding powder.

Whatever the hell happened to Clive's face. I don't even ask. I'm too stunned by it all.

Dan surveys my expression. 'Sit down, Frida. I'll get us a coffee, and then I'll explain everything.'

He comes back with two large steaming mugs and, after a few sips, I start to feel fractionally better. The café might be grubby but at least the coffee is good and strong.

'First things first, keep the battery out of your phone. They'll be tracking it, okay?' he explains. I nod silently.

'I guess you saw their real faces, then, in the van?'

Remembering Clive's bulbous eyes, and the strange blank gaze of his security guards, I supress a shudder.

'Are you okay?'

Am I okay? I start to laugh then, and once I start it's like I have no control, like I might never, ever, stop.

'Frida,' Dan says, placing a hand on my arm and patting it awkwardly, 'I know you've had a shock, but you're safe here.'

I stare down at his hand until he moves it away. When I look up to meet Dan's eyes, he looks concerned and uncertain. 'You really don't know anything, do you?' he says.

I glance at my coffee. The mug says, *World's Greatest DAD*. This surreal detail almost sets me off again. I have to be careful. I have to get a grip. I take a deep, calming breath. 'I know lots of things,' I say firmly. 'Except who Clive is and why he seems hell bent on locking me up in increasingly small spaces. And what did he do to his eyes? Is he on drugs? Is this a cult thing? They're a cult, aren't they?'

Dan has that look on his face again. The pitying one.

'No, Frida, it's not a cult. Clive is a . . . Well, you're probably going to find this hard to believe but Clive is a god.'

I blink at him. 'Excuse me?'

'He's a god. One of the lesser deities. A pestilence god, in fact. That's why he kind of looks like a fly. The security staff are descendants of a cattle god, which means they're unnaturally strong but docile and obedient.'

'Right,' I say. 'No, wait. What?'

Dan sighs. 'It's a lot to take in.'

'And are you some sort of god, too?' I say it sarcastically, but even so I can't believe the words that are leaving my mouth.

'No,' he says. 'I'm the Oracle.'

'As in . . . the Oracle at Delphi. Visions of the future and so forth?'

'Yep.'

I stare at him. 'I've gone mad, haven't I?' I ask, with impressive calm.

'No.' He sighs again. 'Although Anteros would love you to think so.'

There's a silence. The air hangs heavy with the question Dan is waiting for me to ask. I want to resist but in the end, I can't. The lawyer in me needs all the facts.

'Who the hell is Anteros?'

'He's a god of love. Very powerful. Utterly evil.'

'Cupid is the god of love,' I return, fending off the sensation that I'm drowning by clinging on to the facts. 'Everyone knows that.'

'Yeah, Cupid – or Eros as he's known in the Greek

myths – is one of the gods of love,' Dan agrees. 'Anteros is his younger brother.'

'I've never even heard of him.'

Dan gives a sardonic smile. 'No,' he says. 'Unfortunately that isn't going to prevent him from hunting you down and interrogating you.'

'Interrogating me about what?'

'The same thing they always ask you about when they bring you in. The arrow.'

I gawp at him. 'You're not making any sense. Today is the first time I've ever been to NeoStar.'

'No,' he says levelly, 'it isn't. Five years ago, and five years before that, they brought you in for questioning.'

'You're wrong,' I say, but my skin is starting to crawl.

Dan continues as though I haven't spoken. 'When they were sure you weren't a threat, they let you go. I saw some of your past in my visions. I assumed you were playing for time,' Dan says, searching my face. Then the hope goes out of his eyes. 'But you're not faking. You really don't know.'

'I'm getting pretty sick of hearing that,' I snap, 'when clearly it's you who doesn't know anything. I'm telling you, I've never been in that building before in my life!'

'Lethe water,' Dan says shortly. 'It's from the river of forgetfulness. One sip and any memories of magical activity are wiped.'

'Okay, that's it.' I stand up, hitching my bag over my shoulder. 'I can't stay here and listen to this supernatural conspiracy theory bullshit. If you won't help me understand what's really going on, I'll have to call the police.'

'Frida, sit down,' Dan says a trifle wearily. 'If you were going to the police, you'd have done it already. But you haven't, because you understand on some level that the police are not equipped to deal with what is going on here.'

There's some kind of challenge in his gaze. I stare him down, longing to make good on my word and storm out, but in the end self-preservation proves too strong a force. I sit back down, and put my hand to my head. It feels like a rock – dense, compacted. I still don't believe any of this is happening. Soon enough, I'll wake up, ready for that important meeting, vowing never to eat parmesan after eight o'clock again.

Except there's no waking up from this.

'You are aware of how ridiculous all this sounds?' I ask.

'Well, I'm aware that it sounds ridiculous to *you*,' Dan says. 'I'm from a long line of Oracles so I grew up with this stuff.' He sets his jaw firm. 'Anyway, you saw their real faces, Frida. You can lie to me, but please don't lie to yourself. You know that Clive and his guards are not of this world.'

I don't answer.

'Don't you?' he pushes.

I meet his eyes. Every fibre of my being wants to deny what he's saying but what I saw in that van is etched on my brain. And it was not human.

'Yes,' I whisper. Even as I am saying it, I'm shaking my head, unable to accept it, logical Frida fighting with fanciful Frida. But, then, to deny what I saw, what I *felt*, in that room, in that van – that would be the real self-delusion.

'Good,' Dan says, satisfied, 'because we don't have much time. Anteros knows who you are now, so he'll put everything he's got into the search for the arrow, we have to—'

'Wait a second, wait a second.' I hold up my hand. 'What are you talking about? What is this arrow? And what do you mean he knows who I am?'

Dan looks at me for a moment, sizes me up, seems to find me wanting but carries on anyway. 'There's an ancient prophecy,' he says, 'that tells of the lost arrow of the love gods, a powerful weapon buried somewhere on earth. Anteros has been looking for it for centuries—'

'Okay,' I say. 'Fine. So what? Is it hidden under my flat or something?'

There's a silence then, and I don't like at all the way Dan is looking at me. Suddenly, a deep unease, the beginnings of a very real fear, begins to gather in the pit of my stomach. It's the same feeling of dread I had with Clive in the van. This is where I see things I can't un-see, hear things I can't un-hear.

'The prophecy also foretells that a descendant of Eros will rise,' Dan says. 'That this person will find the arrow first, and destroy it, saving the mortal race from Anteros.' Dan locks eyes with me, his gaze so intense it gives me goosebumps. 'NeoStar believe that person is you.'

$$\longrightarrow$$

I stare at him for a long time without saying a word. If I thought I was surprised before this point, I had seriously underestimated my capacity to be dumbstruck.

'But they're wrong, obviously,' I say eventually, through a mouth that feels cottony and dry.

His face is impassive. 'No. The ancient writings passed down my family, the visions I've been having of you for two years, they all say the same thing. Come on,' he urges. 'You must have known, deep down, that you were different? Special? You must have felt it?'

I lock eyes with him, and something deep within me stirs. *Yes*.

'No,' I say. 'Not at all. I can assure you that I'm one hundred per cent normal human.' My head is now throbbing painfully. 'Listen,' I say, 'I can just about accept that all this magical shit is real. I mean, okay, it's a bit of a shocker, but hey, fine, whatever. "There are more things in heaven and earth, Horatio", and all that. But I can assure you that all of this has NOTHING to do with me. Come on! I'm the descendant of a god?' I laugh. 'I suck at this. I've already been kidnapped twice today and it's not even six o'clock. Surely they must see that I'm just a normal, innocent human being? I mean, I cannot understand, even for a moment, why they'd think that I . . . '

Clive's words come back to me. His bulbous eyes gleaming, insistent, as he asked me: *Then why did you run?*

'Oh my God,' I say, pointing an accusatory finger at Dan. 'This is your fault.'

Dan blinks at me. 'Sorry?'

'This whole magical interlude only began when you warned me about NeoStar. That's probably why I dropped the coffee, some lingering subconscious memory. If you'd never come to see me I'd have stayed in that room and drunk the drugged coffee and they'd have questioned me, found out I didn't know anything about the arrow, then wiped my brain and let me go back to my nice normal boring un-mythical life, right? But,' I continue, 'because I ran, Anteros and Clive think I've got something to hide. It's all your fault!'

Dan stares at me, incredulous. 'Let me get this straight. I've just told you that you are the subject of an ancient prophecy that says you are destined to save the world, and you're pissed off because I didn't let them violate your memories?' He shakes his head. 'You really are something else, Frida. Jesus. And to think I—' He stops, an inscrutable expression on his face. 'I didn't need to warn you, you know,' he says tersely. 'I shouldn't even be here. I came because you needed help.' He holds up a hand. 'But, really, no need to thank me. Your gracious demeanour is thanks enough.'

I roll my eyes. 'Thank you? For bringing this shit storm to my door? You've totally fucked this up, oh wondrous Oracle. You've got the wrong woman.'

'No, I haven't,' he says steadily. 'You're the one, Frida. It is written. The only reason Anteros has never taken you seriously as a threat before now is because you haven't yet appeared in a seer's vision, and because—'

'What?'

'Well, they were expecting a man.'

I widen my eyes. 'Seriously? I'm not even going to glorify that with a response,' I sniff.

'The seers' powers are weaker than mine,' Dan goes on,

'but they'd have seen you eventually and then Anteros would have come for you not just suspecting but *knowing* who you are. And that would have been much, much worse for you.'

I stare down at a scattering of fallen sugar speckling the table top. Such an ordinary sight, and yet I feel as though nothing will ever be ordinary again.

'What if I run?'

He looks at me sadly. 'They'll find you.'

'What if I just tell them I have no interest in the arrow? That I don't want to fulfil this bloody prophecy?'

Dan shakes his head. 'Won't work. Anyway, anything you do to avoid your fate will just wind up making it happen. It's sort of a thing with prophecies.'

'I don't believe in fate or crackpot prophecies,' I say, anger building as Dan blocks my every option. 'I believe in free will.'

'So did Oedipus,' Dan says drily. 'And look how that worked out.'

'Oedipus Schmoedipus!'

Dan starts to laugh, shaking his head at me. 'A fine counter-argument. Eat your heart out, Cicero.'

I glare at him, prickling with fury. 'Great. Laugh it up. I don't know if you've noticed but I've just had my whole life torn away from me. Is that somehow funny to you?'

Dan at least has the good grace to look abashed. 'I'm sorry,' he says softly. 'It's just, sometimes in this world, if you don't laugh ...' He shrugs. 'But you're right, Frida. I shouldn't be flippant. I keep forgetting that we're not—'

'Not what?'

A cloud passes over his eyes.

'Nothing. It doesn't matter.'

I roll my eyes. It would help matters if this guy was able to finish a goddam sentence. I drain my coffee and slump back in my seat. What a mess. What a fucking mess. 'What am I going to do? I've got no money, no office, no home. NeoStar have taken everything.'

'Hey, don't worry,' Dan says. 'You can stay with me.' He holds his hands up palms facing me as I flick him a suspicious glance. 'It's okay, I'm not going to try to persuade you to do this, Frida. I can't force you to do anything.' He looks heavenwards. 'Hopefully they can see that I tried.'

'They?' I look up at the grubby polystyrene ceiling tiles.

'Eros and Zeus,' he says. 'On Olympus.'

'Oh,' I say. 'Right.' Worrying how normal all this is starting to sound to me.

Dan stands up, hitching his bag over his shoulder. I don't get up. I need to think about his offer. The last thing I want to do is get myself any more embroiled in this horrible world of gods and prophecies and magical arrows. But there are practicalities to consider. I need to get out of these grimy clothes, I need to eat, and I need about seventeen more cups of coffee before I can work out my next move. Also, I have zero other options.

'Okay,' I say. 'So where exactly does an oracle live?'

Chapter 10

It turns out Dan doesn't just frequent the café, he lives above it. As I follow him up the stairs, eyeing the worn carpet and wide black cracks in the walls, it crosses my mind that, just a few hours earlier, this would have featured in my top-ten serial-killer certain-death scenarios. It says a lot about the dramatic events of the day that now I'm following this stranger, if not entirely willingly, then with a certain resignation to the inevitable.

Dan unlocks his front door and I follow him down the hallway, past the open door of what seems to be the lounge – large tan sofa, matching armchair, tiny gas fire casting a warm glow over the grey tufted rug – until we come to a small, bare box room, where a single bed is made up. Folded on top of the bed is a black knitted jumper and a faded pair of jeans, clearly both belonging to Dan, and a towel.

'You were expecting me?'

He shrugs. 'The perks of being the Oracle.' He nods at the clothes. 'I thought they might do for now. There's a credit card on the bedside table. Buy anything else you need online. Don't worry about money, I have plenty. Family money,' he says quickly. 'For exactly this kind of situation.'

I cast a dubious eye at the threadbare carpet, the stained ceiling, and I raise an eyebrow. 'You have loads of money and you live here?'

'It serves its purpose.'

I snort. 'Yeah, if that purpose is to serve as the set of a torture porn film.'

Dan raises his eyebrows. 'No offence taken. Settle in and I'll make us some food.'

'Great,' I say, 'and do you have any coffee?'

He nods.

'Dan,' I say.

He stops at the door and looks back.

'Thank you,' I say, 'for letting me stay,' nobly restraining myself from adding *even though we both know this is all your fault*.

He nods again and then leaves the room, closing the door softly behind him.

I place my bag on the tiny bed, shuck off the parka and take off my shoes, then I walk over to the small smudged window, looking longingly out at the people trudging along, wrapped up in hats and scarves and huge coats, faces braced against the sleet, completely oblivious to the danger lingering just below the surface of their safe little lives. The lucky bastards.

The jumper and the jeans are way too big for me, of course, but they smell fresh, like lavender and baby soap. I roll up the legs and the sleeves and pull the belt tight and they're serviceable. Then I pick up the phone Dan gave me and stare at it sadly. I badly want to call Bryony and talk to her about everything that's happened, but I can't. It isn't safe.

Dropping the phone back in my bag with a sigh, I pad out into the hallway in bare feet. I can hear the clanking of pots in the kitchen, but instead of joining Dan in there I decide to have a look around. I push open the door closest to me – inside the room there's a double bed, a bookcase, a guitar and an easel, a sheet of paper bearing a few bold pencil strokes. Dan's bedroom. I close the door again quietly.

The next room is the lounge. Walking in, I do a double take at what I see here. Ladies and gentlemen, we are back in serial-killer territory. One entire wall is covered with newspaper clippings, photographs, charts, maps and yellow sticky notes. Two whiteboards are propped up at either end, bearing graphs and furious scribbles. Open books are piled onto a small rickety pine table, and more stand in towers all over the floor.

I approach the wall and take a closer look. One half is filled with articles about crimes of passion, stalkings, murders, the national divorce rate, the national suicide rate. All very grim reading. The other half contains dozens of stories about NeoStar: its unique success, the new businesses acquired, its year-on-year growth, its latest investments.

I walk over to a whiteboard and see a graph plotting the crimes listed against the business growth.

I've been absorbed in the articles for almost ten minutes when there's a noise behind me. I turn to see Dan in the hall, a mug in either hand. He looks me up and down. A faint smile touches his lips.

'You okay?' he says, handing me a coffee.

'I'm fine.' I gesture to the wall. 'What is all this?'

'Research.'

I stare at him. 'You seriously think there's a link between all of these crimes and NeoStar?'

'I know there is.'

'But how? Why?'

Dan sighs. 'How? By any means necessary. Why? Because that's what he does. What he's always done.' He gestures to a bunch of pages torn from books and pinned on the wall. They're all myths about the god Eros, except that his name has been crossed out and replaced by 'Anteros'.

Apollo mocks Anteros's archery skills, and so Anteros shoots an arrow at the sun god, making him lust after a river nymph, Daphne. Anteros then shoots Daphne with a lead-tipped arrow to incite in her hatred for Apollo, so that, rather than be captured by the god, she begs to be turned into a tree.

Theban hero and hunter Actaeon, shot by Anteros, falls madly in love with the huntress goddess Artemis when he chances upon her bathing naked. Furious, Artemis turns him into a stag so he can never speak of what he has seen. Actaeon is promptly ripped apart by his own hounds.

Anteros shoots the sorceress Medea, so that she would fall in love with the hero Jason, but when Jason abandons her, she punishes her lover by killing their children.

Anteros shoots an arrow at Helen, causing her to fall in love with Paris, leave her husband, Menelaus, thereby inciting the bloody ten-year Trojan War.

I turn to Dan. 'Why is Eros's name crossed out?'

'Anteros did those things,' Dan says, 'but nobody knew it was him. They still don't.'

'Okay,' I say, struggling to make sense of any of this, 'but why is he here, now? And where are the other gods?'

'Sometime after Troy, Zeus banished Anteros to earth for forty days without his arrows. Then the portal between worlds closed suddenly, trapping him here.' Dan turns his gaze to the news clippings. 'He's been punishing us ever since.'

A chill goes through me. Because there is a horrible similarity between the heinous actions of Medea and the horrific article about the man who killed his wife and his kids and then himself because she told him she wanted a divorce. Between Apollo's pursuit of Daphne and the story of the woman who was so terrorised by the ex-colleague who had stalked her for seven years that she committed suicide.

If this is true, if Anteros is actually real . . . I think about the reach of NeoStar and my blood runs cold. 'What about Eros and Zeus? Can't they stop him?'

Dan shakes his head. 'They're stuck on Olympus, just like Anteros is stuck on earth. All they can do is send the visions to the Oracle, to warn us of what's to come.'

I ponder this for a moment and quickly find a flaw in Dan's argument. 'Hang on. If Eros is stuck on Olympus, how can I be of his bloodline?'

Dan rubs at his temple. 'You know, Frida, you can ask questions all day long but at some point you're just going to have to take this on faith.'

I frown. This sounds exactly like the kind of thing my clients' spouses say to them when they're up to no good. Personally, I'd rather put my faith in facts. 'I'm going to need an answer,' I say tartly.

He sighs. 'Eros's wife and their mortal child were trapped down here too. You're their descendant, on your father's side.'

That gives me pause. 'My father?'

Dan nods. 'You never heard anything about this? Not even an old family story? Usually these things are passed down the family line.'

'My dad walked out on us when I was nine,' I say dully. 'I haven't seen him since.'

'Oh,' Dan says awkwardly. 'I'm sorry.'

I shake off his sympathy and move to the last section of the wall. There's a sketch pinned up, showing a man with dark shoulder-length hair, intelligent, soulful black-brown eyes, and cheekbones you could cut yourself on.

'Is this Anteros?'

'Yep.'

'Wow.' From behind Anteros's muscular arms, huge wings are visible, like those of a butterfly, white, then grey, then fanning out to black. The picture has a weird, buzzy

80

aliveness to it, as though the god might at any minute burst from the paper and into the room.

I catch sight of another drawing lying on top of a pile of books. The eyes are a little brighter, the hair a little wilder, but still, there's no doubt who this is supposed to be.

'Why did you draw me?'

'So that I could look for you,' Dan says.

'Well, that's just creepy.'

'Think of it more like a photofit if it makes you feel better.'

'Ha ha,' I say. 'So hilarious.'

Tiredness hits me then. I've had just about enough of this wall of doom. Wearily, I take my coffee over to the squashy leather sofa and sit down. Close my eyes. By now, my head is pounding fit to burst.

'Are you okay?'

I don't open my eyes. 'Well, let's see,' I say, massaging my temples. 'Hunted by gods. Evicted from my life. Subject of a prophecy. Absolutely starving. Yeah,' I say. 'I'm great. Never better.'

'That last one I can do something about,' says Dan. 'Is spaghetti okay?'

'Sounds good,' I say. I open my eyes. 'Dan?'

He turns at the door. 'Yeah?'

There's a question I haven't yet asked him. It's one I'm not sure I even want the answer to.

'What will Anteros do with the arrow, if he finds it?'

Dan stares at me, as though deciding something, then he walks over to the bookcase, picks up a stack of drawings and holds them out to me. For a moment I leave him there, arm outstretched, unable to force myself to take them. Then I reach out my hand.

There are a dozen sketches, maybe more, and as I lay them out on the table a dark fear blooms in my stomach. The scene that unfolds is of a writhing mass of human bodies, some in the throes of terrible violence, some contorted in pain, every pair of eyes glittering with madness.

It's horrifying, more horrifying by far than anything I saw on that boardroom wall.

'What *are* these?' I ask, my voice shaky.

'Scenes from my visions,' Dan says. 'I see the same things over and over.' He shrugs. 'It helps me to draw it.'

Little wonder. Who could stand having all that stuck inside their head? I stare at the images, repulsed but unable to drag my focus away. 'What does it mean?'

'It's a warning, I think,' he says. 'Of what he's planning. Of one possible future.'

I look at Dan sharply. 'If I refuse to help, you mean?' But his gaze isn't accusatory, just very, very tired. I see, suddenly, the burden he's been carrying and it's too much. I have to look away.

We stay like that for what feels like a long time: me sitting, Dan standing, neither of us speaking. It would make a nice tableau for one of Dan's drawings. Title: *The Impasse*.

Eventually Dan breaks the silence. 'You need to eat, Frida,' he says softly. 'Rest up here and I'll go and make a start.'

Once alone, I gather the drawings into a pile and turn

them so the pictures are facing downwards, but I can still see those violent pencil marks through the page. A wave of fear and nausea threatens to engulf me, and I push it back with everything I've got. Come on, Frida, I urge myself. Keep it together. You have to make a plan. There has to be a way out of this.

Calmly, methodically, I run through all my options. But it's no good. Each one leads me right back to Anteros. He's too powerful. Panic begins to cloud my mind. I'm utterly out of my depth. I can't do this. How can I stand against someone who is capable of . . . ? My eyes flick to the drawings and then skitter away again. No.

Pulling my legs up under me, I tug the jumper cuffs down over my hands and curl into a ball. I sit there for a while, arms wrapped around myself, and as the heat from the fire reaches me the numbness that has been protecting me so far begins to thaw, and in its place I find only despair. I can't do what Dan expects of me, what these prophecies say I am destined to do. This is not my world; I didn't ask for any of this. I wish I'd never learned that these creatures are real, that magic exists. It's too much, too frightening. I just want things to go back to the way they were.

Here, in amongst the wreckage of my wretched, churning thoughts, something sparks. Not an idea, alas, but my Divorce Buzzword Bingo alarm. Because this is something my clients say all the time. *I just want things to go back to the way they were.* And what do I tell them? That you can't run from the truth. That you have to accept the facts, no matter how awful and impossible they seem. That when you try to hide from reality, you become a victim, an easy target.

I counsel myself then, just like I would counsel a client, and slowly, slowly, the hopelessness begins to abate and a new fledgling clarity emerges. There's no running from this. The only way to put this situation right is to find what Anteros is searching for and destroy it. Once the arrow is out of play, I'll have nothing valuable that NeoStar need.

And, after all, it's only one measly arrow. How difficult can it be?

When Dan returns ten minutes later, holding two bowls of steaming, fragrant pasta, I'm back in front of the evidence wall, staring at the picture of Anteros, trying to read those liquid eyes, that faint, menacing half-smile. My first rule of the courtroom has always been: know your enemy.

I turn to Dan and see an expression on his face that's equal parts hope and fear.

'Okay,' I say, 'where do we start?'

Chapter 11

When I agreed to assume the mantle of the chosen one, I think I had imagined it might involve some action, some adventure, maybe even a sexy outfit. I mean, if this were a film, we'd be cutting straight to the montage scene:

Here's me settling bravely into this new, strange environment (which in my film would be an art deco mansion, and not a crummy flat above a café).

Here's me undertaking several tests of strength and ingenuity, which reveal that I am faster, stronger and more intelligent than the average human. (In this scene, my hair does not frizz, even in the rain.)

Here I am again, practising several kick-ass ancient martial arts that will not only protect me from the likes of the repellent Clive, but have the added bonus of contributing to fat loss and core strength.

Here's me undergoing a makeover – gold arm cuffs, a white flowing dress, some sort of tiara – that really makes my inner goddess pop.

And finally, here's me with Dan, burning the midnight oil, both of us tired, but plucky (him casting me admiring glances when he thinks I'm not looking), as we pore over the ancient map I discovered in his extensive, beautifully furnished (and sadly, imaginary) library – a map that – any moment now, will lead us directly to the arrow.

Now let's cut to the reality, shall we?

Today will be the third day I've been cooped up in the café studying musty old textbooks.

The closest I've come to excitement is when I asked for a bran muffin and got chocolate chip instead. The closest I've come to proving my extraordinary strength is not telling Dan where he can stick his ancient prophecy. The closest I've come to a makeover is the state of my hair, which, after a single application of Dan's 2-in-1 shampoo has doubled in personality and now refuses to be cowed into submission no matter how much product I slap on it.

And the closest we have come to finding the arrow is . . . well, not close at all. We are nowhere near. We haven't got a single lead.

'Can't I call someone?' I ask for the tenth time. 'I know loads of people. Lawyers, judges, mayors, academics. They have to be able to help.'

Dan looks up from his text, a no-doubt thrilling tome on the weapons of the classical gods. 'I've told you, Frida: you can't call anyone.'

'But we can't just keep hiding out, reading and hoping to come across a clue!'

Dan shrugs. 'This is how it's done.'

'Why?' I ask. 'Because it is written?' I say, in a portentous voice, mimicking Dan's growly tones. 'I'm not being funny, Dan, but it's not written, is it? Otherwise, we'd have read it already.'

Dan conveniently didn't tell me, as he was waxing lyrical about my mission to save the world, that he doesn't have the first clue where this arrow is or how to find it. This has rapidly become a bone of contention between us. What (I have asked him a few dozen times) is the point of recruiting someone to your epic cause if you don't even have the semblance of a plan?

I'm worried about what I'm going to tell people if I can't get this mess cleared up soon. I'm lucky that Pen is on holiday: all I had to do was email and cancel the temp and all my appointments for the next two weeks. But what about Bryony? My mum? My colleagues and friends and clients? How will I explain where I am?

Being the chosen one is turning out to be really inconvenient.

'Don't you get anything useful in these visions?' I ask. 'You know, clues? Landmarks?'

Dan looks up again. 'GPS coordinates? Sadly, no. That's not how they work.'

'Well, they're pretty useless visions then, aren't they?' I huff.

Dan raises an eyebrow. 'You're not exactly bringing much

to the table yourself, Frida, unless you count complaining about my choice in shampoo and hammering my cafetière.'

'Ha ha,' I say. I get up, stretching my cramped limbs. 'Fancy some lunch?'

Dan looks at me. 'It's five past eleven.'

'Elevenses, then.'

He shakes his head. 'Just a coffee for me, thanks.'

I head to the counter. Dan and I have found a way of rubbing along in these extraordinary circumstances, and it's heavily based on liberal quantities of caffeine and sarcasm. But I also know that there's truth behind his quips and it burns. He's disappointed in me.

I return to the table with two coffees and a cheese and ham toastie and resume reading, munching dolefully. I swear I can feel my thighs getting bigger by the second. It's all this inactivity. I'm eating just for the sense of accomplishment. I sigh. I miss the gym. I miss my juicer. I miss a time when my hair didn't smell of burger grease. Dan looks up, sees me spilling crumbs on the pages of the book, and gives me a look of exasperation.

I smile sweetly back at him.

The problem with Dan is he's been having visions about me for years and so feels that he knows me quite well already. At the same time, he imagined I'd be much more impressive in the flesh than I actually am. It's probably like meeting your internet date after a lengthy correspondence and discovering they're a poor copy of the fantasy you'd imagined.

Well, tough, I think to myself, taking another bite of

toasted sandwich. I never asked to be the subject of any-body's prophecy. I roll my neck to get rid of the crick that sleeping in Dan's spare room has caused. The flat makes strange noises throughout the night. There's woodchip on the walls and the bay windows leak all the warmth, so I have to pile on three blankets and bury my head under the covers to get to sleep.

It's not all terrible. The lounge is homely enough if you can ignore the wall of doom, (which I've found can be successfully achieved via the application of half a bottle of Rioja) but it's all a bit rustic for my tastes. Basically, I'm getting through this experience by pretending the whole thing is a kind of outward-bound holiday and reminding myself that it won't last for ever.

Which it won't, if we can ever find the arrow.

'We have a bit of time,' Dan says, in an appeasing tone that winds me up even more.

I look up. 'How so?'

'They're currently looking for the arrow in Greece, but they won't find it there.'

'How do you know?'

'I just know.'

'Okay,' I say, pretending to scribble on my pad. 'Possible places we might find the arrow: not Greece.' I hold up my pen and cock my head inquisitively. 'Anywhere else the arrow isn't?'

'So funny,' Dan replies, but at least he's smiling. 'Just make yourself useful and read those books, eh?'

'It's incredible this secret hasn't got out,' I say, pushing my crumby plate away. 'How is it possible in the age of social media that no one has leaked that there's something weird going on at the heart of NeoStar?'

Dan raises his eyebrows. I'm still annoying him with my questions, but since I agreed to help find the arrow he's felt obliged to pacify me somewhat.

'Aren't there plenty of buried secrets in this city, ones that you know about personally, that you have helped keep?'

I flush. 'That's different,' I say, thinking of the indiscretions I've unearthed over the years, then used as leverage to help my clients get good settlements.

'Not really. Any secret can be kept if you have enough power. But mostly it stays hidden because normal people aren't predisposed to believe in magic. They rationalise it, just like you did. And if someone does witness something they shouldn't,' Dan shrugs, 'there's always Lethe water.'

I think of Chris at the window, his tanned face turned pale. Will he be carrying on with his normal life right now with no memory of ever having betrayed me?

Then my mind turns to all those NeoStar employees. There are so many humans in service to Anteros, working on NeoStar's anti-love technology, oblivious about who they're really working for, and to what end. I haven't mentioned to Dan that I've actively encouraged my clients to use some of NeoStar's specialist software – the kind that turns your partner's laptop into a bug, or lets you read a person's texts remotely – when we've suspected their partner was lying about their affairs, either financial or sexual. I feel sick about it now, of course, but it's just more evidence of the tools Anteros has at his disposal. Whereas Team Frida and Dan? Not so much.

I try again. 'Dan, I've been on a few David and Goliath cases in my time, so I totally get this whole small-but-scrappy vibe you've got going on. But, honestly? I think we're in trouble here. We have two people and a pile of musty books. Anteros has a global corporation spanning several continents and the most advanced technical knowledge the world has ever seen. If we're going to find this arrow before him, we need help. Isn't there some, I don't know, mystical shit we can use to locate the damn thing?'

'The visions,' Dan says, without looking up. 'They are the mystical shit of which you speak.'

I gaze up at the grease-spotted ceiling. 'Can they see us?' I ask. 'Zeus and Eros and all the rest?'

'I think so,' says Dan. 'My ancestors believed so. They *will* help us, Frida. You just have to have faith, and patience. The visions don't come on demand.'

'Well, yeah. But, it'd be nice if they could send one soon-ish, don't you think?'

'Agreed. But in the meantime, let's jusss—' Dan stops talking suddenly. I watch as his eyes roll back, his feet drum the floor and he clutches his head, letting out a terrible moan.

'Dan? What's wrong?'

His face is deadly pale now, and his eyes are white and large in their sockets. My first thought is that he has been poisoned, this place must not be under protection after all and I have a shock of purely selfish terror. Oh please God no, I think, don't leave me alone in all this. Then finally my body unlocks and I leap to his side.

I touch his face; his forehead is waxy and cold. 'Dan. Dan! Are you okay? Can you hear me?' But he can't, he's totally out of it, like he's having some sort of fit. I grab his phone, dial 999 with a shaking hand and I'm about to press 'Call' when I feel his hand on my arm.

'I'm . . . okay . . . ' Dan says, his voice faint.

'Are you sure?' I say. 'Because you didn't look okay. You looked kind of fucking awful.'

He smiles weakly. A layer of sweat has broken out on his brow. 'That's the visions for you.'

'That was a vision?' I ask, appalled. 'Hang on. I'm getting you some water.'

I'm back in thirty seconds with the water and a flapjack. 'Eat something,' I say. 'You look like you need sugar.'

Dan takes one sip of the water then another, and then bites into the flapjack. 'The visions don't come on demand, huh?' I say, staring at the ceiling. 'God, I'm sorry, Dan, I didn't realise, when I was asking for one . . . are they always like that?'

He shakes his head, smiling weakly. 'No, I don't usually get a flapjack afterwards.'

'I'm serious! That looked really painful.'

'They are painful,' he says and takes another sip of water. 'But it's okay.'

Slowly the colour starts to come back to his cheeks. 'It's so brutal,' I say. 'Why are these gods such colossal pains in the arse? This is the twenty-first century! Couldn't they just

92

send you a nice painless text message? I tell you, if I ever meet Zeus or Eros, I am going to have serious words with the pair of them.' I'm ranting now, out of adrenalised relief that he isn't dead.

But Dan isn't listening. Now he's coming back to himself, his eyes are shining and he doesn't just look better, he looks positively ecstatic. I don't think it can be the flapjack, because they're really quite disgusting.

Dan grabs my hand, and grips it hard. 'I saw it, Frida. I know how to find the arrow.'

Chapter 12

Thirty minutes later we're walking into the entrance of the City Museum. This is the first time I've left Dan's flat or the café in two days. It feels weird. Everything is really loud, and bright, and I see Clive's face everywhere. I look warily up at the CCTV cameras in front of the entrance. We're both carrying bushels of some root in our pockets which, apparently, will shield us from detection from Anteros and NeoStar. Again, I just don't ask. There is already way too much I don't understand.

The current exhibition is entitled *Gods and Monsters*. 'That's quite the coincidence. This exhibition, in the city, now,' I venture.

'No such thing as coincidence,' Dan says distractedly.

We head in and walk through the first gallery room, and then the second, then the third. I follow Dan from painting to painting, biting my lip.

'Is it here?' I ask eventually.

'I don't know,' he says. 'We were here, in the vision. It's just . . . ' He stands in the middle of a room and turns 360 degrees. 'None of these rooms look right.'

'Well, there's another floor. Let's keep looking.'

As we carry on through the building, I feel a small thrill of excitement. By the end of today we'll have found the arrow and destroyed it and all of this will be over. I have a glorious vision of myself in the bath, eating chocolates, drinking champagne and washing the burger grease out of my hair.

We inspect dozens more exhibits, but none of them are what Dan is looking for. As we work our way around the paintings, I feel increasingly queasy. It's the same feeling I had back in the NeoStar boardroom. The world of the gods was a violent place, filled with abduction, rape and murder. Now that I am starting to understand that these were real people, real monsters, real gods, this display is nightmarish to me. I want to tell all these erudite academics, standing around, analysing the images in the context of art history. I want to say, 'This happened! This was real!' But, of course, they'd think I was insane.

After finding nothing promising on the first floor, we head up the stairs. I linger by a white marble statue of a tall young man with huge wings, poised to shoot an arrow from his bow. Eros. I reach out a hand and touch one of his cold stone arms. This is my family? I mean, really?

'Ms McKenzie?'

I turn to see a blonde woman in an ivory mohair coat

regarding me with interest. I blink. It takes me a minute to remember who she is.

'Oona,' I say, recovering myself and smiling. 'How are you?'

'Oh, fine, fine.' She casts an anxious glance up the stairs. 'I'm with Robert, actually. We're having lunch in the Mezzanine.' She approaches me and says in a low voice, 'I meant to get in touch with you, in fact. I would be very grateful if you didn't mention our meeting to anyone.'

'Of course, Oona. That goes without saying.' I take in her red-rimmed eyes, her pale complexion underneath flawless make-up. 'Are you working things out, then?' I ask.

'Yes,' she says. 'We talked. He says he's been in a difficult place.'

Like in between his intern's legs? For one horrified minute I think that I have spoken this out loud, but Oona is still wearing that faint, nervous smile and I realise that, thankfully, it was just in my head.

She casts a puzzled glance over me. My hair is spiralling in corkscrews as it does when I leave it to dry naturally and I'm wearing an outfit made up of clothes I hastily ordered online: a black shirt dress, black tights and grey ankle boots, with Dan's old leather jacket slung over the top. An outfit suitable for running, should the need arise.

'You look … different,' she says. 'Are you here for the exhibition?'

'Yes, I'm just here with a friend.' I look around to find Dan heading towards me, worry turning to relief as he sees I'm okay. When he spots Oona, he looks wary, then pastes on a smile.

'Hi!' he says. 'I wondered where you'd got to.'

'Dan, this is Oona, she's a friend of mine. Oona this is Dan, also a . . . friend.' I watch as these two people who are not my friends smile and make polite and awkward noises at one another.

'Anyway,' I say, eyeing Dan, 'there's one exhibit we've made a special trip to see, so we'd better go and find it.' I smile at Oona. 'Enjoy your lunch. I'm glad things are working out for you.' As I glance back, Oona is climbing the marble stairs to her meal with her husband, a mixture of trepidation and hope on her face. I have a bad feeling for her. The research I did on Robert did not suggest a man prone to reflection or repentance, though he certainly is a man prone to lunch. I shrug. Time will tell. It always does.

In the next gallery room, all the paintings are by an artist called Charles-Joseph Natoire.

'These illustrate the story of Psyche, Eros's wife,' Dan tells me. 'They depict the story of her trials at the hands of Aphrodite, when she was trying to make her way back to Eros.'

I stare at the paintings. Another of my long-lost relatives. She's so beautiful. I turn to Dan and cut to the chase. 'So, is the arrow here?'

'I think so.'

'There's a link, at least,' I muse. 'Psyche being Eros's wife. Maybe that's a clue.' As we walk around studying the paintings, I read the accompanying text and piece together the myth.

Aphrodite was jealous of Psyche's beauty, so she asked

Eros to make Psyche fall in love with a beast. (Dan points out that she would have asked Anteros, not Eros, and that, once again, the myths got it wrong.) Eros visited Psyche (possibly to protect her from his brother), but was so taken with her beauty that he pricked himself with his own arrow, and fell in love with the princess.

Fearing his mother's actions, he took Psyche to a wonderful palace where he could keep her safe from the machinations of Aphrodite, but, in order to protect her from the shock of his godliness, he only visited her in darkness. (Note to self – the gods are super weird.)

Psyche, having never seen her lover, was understandably worried that she had indeed been married to a beast, and so one night, while Eros lay asleep next to her, she lit a lamp. Overjoyed to see her handsome bedmate was the god of love himself, she was so giddy she accidentally spilled burning oil on Eros, and he flew away to nurse his injury.

Psyche, desperate to find Eros, pleaded with Aphrodite for help. The goddess agreed, but only if Psyche could complete three trials.

I read on, moving around the paintings that help to tell the story. Psyche's first task, if she is ever to see her lover again, is to separate a pile of grains, beans and lintels before nightfall – an impossible mission, but one that she achieves with the help of some sympathetic ants. The second task, to retrieve a golden fleece, she does with the help of a river god. The third task is to visit Persephone in the Underworld, and ask her to drain a little of her beauty into a box as a gift.

Dan has stopped in front of this picture. The sign

underneath reads: *Psyche Obtaining the Elixir of Beauty from Proserpine*.

'Proserpine?' I ask.

'It's the Roman name for Persephone,' Dan explains.

'Ah,' I say. As if there wasn't enough for me to get my head around without having Roman names for the gods, too. I stare at the figure of Psyche, standing before Persephone and Hades.

There's something about the way Dan is looking at the painting that alerts my attention. 'Is it here?' I ask. 'Is this the one?'

'It's weird,' he says, shaking his head. 'This painting is the same scene I saw in my vision. But . . . it's still not quite right. The picture I saw was more of a sketch.' Dan's eyes drift to a green door on the other side of the room. 'There.'

We hurry over. There's a sign on the door stating that the room beyond is currently only open to staff. I look around, and, seeing no one, grasp the handle.

It turns.

Dan starts to smile as he sees the contents of the room: works by the same artist, but smaller, pencil and chalk sketches.

'Preparatory studies,' Dan says, his eyes lighting up. 'I haven't seen these before.'

He walks around the room peering at first one drawing, then another. Eventually, he stops at a sketch in a gilt frame labelled, *Black chalk with white highlights on blue paper*. It's the Psyche meets Hades and Persephone scene again.

'Is this it?' I ask. 'Should we take it down?'

But Dan isn't listening. He's staring at the picture, as though mesmerised. 'I've only ever seen the finished paintings,' he says. 'I didn't realise, I had no idea . . .'

'Realise what?' I ask, trying to follow his gaze. 'What have you seen?'

'It's there,' he says, and points to something embedded in the base of Hades' throne.

I lean in and examine the marks. It does look a bit like an arrow. 'Oh,' I say, standing back. 'So is that a clue? Is the arrow behind the sketch? Maybe taped to the frame somewhere?' I cast a glance at the door, to check no one's coming, before starting to feel around the back of the picture. I frown. 'There doesn't seem to be anything here. Want to help me lift it down?' I ask Dan. 'Maybe it's concealed between the canvas and the frame?'

But Dan doesn't move. He's just staring at the arrow.

'That's how it survived all these years,' he says in wonder.

I look at the image and then at Dan and then back at the picture. 'What do you mean?'

He grabs my hands, and there's a tingle, a flicker, as his skin makes contact with mine, before his next words shake all such thoughts from my head.

'The arrow isn't on earth at all,' he says. 'It's in the Underworld.'

Chapter 13

I stare at Dan, struggling to take in his words. The arrow isn't here. This won't be over today, or tomorrow, or anytime soon. My disappointment is so great, it feels like a vice is crushing my chest.

'I thought you said the arrow was here,' I say, my voice tight.

Dan's eyes have a faraway look. 'No, I said that we would find the arrow here. And we have found it.'

'So, you lied.'

'No.' He shrugs. 'Maybe I was a little oblique. But I'm the Oracle, that's how it works.'

'So, it's in the Underworld? Does that mean it's lost for ever? That it was only ever a myth? What?' I stop when I see Dan's expression. 'You're going to tell me the Underworld exists, aren't you?'

'Of course it exists, just like earth and Olympus do,' Dan says.

We stare at the picture.

'It's just a doodle,' I protest. 'It could be a slip of the chalk.'

'It's the arrow,' Dan says firmly. 'It makes sense now that I see it. I don't know why I didn't think of it before. You know the myth of Hades and Persephone?'

'Sort of.' I don't. It was probably in the pile of books, but I've not really retained all that much. It's okay for Dan, these stories were passed down his family line. The closest I have to a heritage of classical myth is a copy of *Clash of The Titans* and I was mostly just staring at Sam Worthington's thighs the whole time.

'Refresh me,' I say now.

'Okay, Anteros was bored one day and looking for trouble, so he fired an arrow into Hades' heart, causing him to fall violently in love with Persephone, right? So much so that Hades kidnapped her and took her to the Underworld to be his queen.'

'Okay, so what?'

'Well, Hades must have taken the arrow with him as a sort of memento. That's how it survived all this time.'

'Jesus,' I say. 'News just in: romance is definitely dead.'

But Dan is still following his own train of thought. 'This will be difficult, but not impossible. But we're going to need some help. There are only a few people who have been to the Underworld and returned,' he says. 'Odysseus, of course. Heracles. And Orpheus went to rescue Eurydice—'

'And failed,' I say pointedly. Dan flashes me a look of surprise. 'What?' I say. 'I saw the opera.'

'They're no use to us anyway,' he muses. 'They're either dead or absent. We need someone who's been down there, but it has to be someone who has a vested interest in helping us stop Anteros.'

'Yes,' I say with heavy sarcasm. 'Form an orderly queue, candidates. I mean, who fits that description?' I shake my head, but secretly I'm pleased. There's no way we can do this, which means I'm no threat to Anteros, which means he has to leave me alone. Doesn't he?

But then Dan turns back to the sketch, his eyes bright with excitement. 'You're looking at her.'

Chapter 14

I stare at the chalk drawing of my beautiful ancient ancestor. 'What, you mean Psyche?' I ask. 'She's still alive?'

Dan doesn't seem to register the enormity of this revelation. 'If the arrow is in the Underworld, the only way Natoire could know that is if Psyche mentioned it when she sat for him.'

This is starting to make me dizzy. 'Wait a minute.' I hold up a hand. 'Psyche modelled for her own paintings?'

He shrugs. 'She was the muse for many men, so I've heard. Remember her beauty was so great it made even Aphrodite jealous. Natoire probably assumed Psyche was just taking the whole muse thing to extremes, but he must have liked the detail about the arrow, and included it in one of his early drafts, before deciding against it in the final painting. That's why I've never seen it in my research. These drawings haven't been seen for hundreds of years.'

'Right,' I say, my brain now properly starting to hurt. 'Can I just get clear what you're saying? Psyche, my great-, great-, however many times great-grandmother, is still alive somewhere?' I feel something rising in me and I realise what it is: anger at being surprised yet again, just when I'd started to wrap my head around this crazy situation. I don't like not knowing what I'm dealing with. I like being lied to even less. And I can't shake the feeling that I've been duped here somehow.

Dan frowns at me, annoyed at this distraction. 'Of course she is. Didn't you read the books? She's immortal.'

'I know that!' I say. 'But I assumed . . . ' I stop there. What had I assumed? Nothing. It hadn't even occurred to me that someone in my family line who knew about all this stuff would still be around. I refocus my argument. 'I would have thought you might have mentioned a little fact like I have a long-distant immortal relative hanging around the place!'

Dan gives me a look and I see something in his face I don't like. 'I tell you what you need to know, Frida. I don't have time to give you the Cliff Notes to mythology when the world is in peril.'

His words hit me like cold water. 'Excuse me?'

'Listen,' he says, clearly aiming for a calmer tone, 'we finally have a break. We know where the arrow is, and we know how to get it. I thought you'd be pleased that we can get this thing over with and you can get back to that lovely normal life you keep going on about.'

I glare at him. 'Of course I'm pleased we've found the arrow,' I say through gritted teeth, 'but are you surprised

I'm in no hurry to enter hell to get it?' I fold my arms. I'm so furious, I can't control my anger. I can feel it coming off me in hot waves. 'Believe me,' I say, 'I'm as keen to escape your shitty little flat as you are to be rid of me, but I've already been kidnapped twice. I'd rather not become Hades' next permanent sleepover buddy, if that's okay with you!'

'Why do you have to make everything so dramatic?'

'Dramatic? You barge into my office, tell me I'm the subject of some prophecy, and recruit me to this impossible cause, and *I'm* dramatic? Take a look in the mirror, why don't you?'

'Well, if you'd actually listened to me when I came to you, then you wouldn't have been kidnapped, would you?' Dan fumes.

'And if you'd just left me alone in the first place, none of this would be happening to me!' I shout.

We glare at each other for a moment, boiling, neither willing to back down.

The door to the private room opens and a woman with long braids and tortoiseshell glasses peers in at us. 'What are you doing in here?' she asks, looking sternly over her spectacles. 'This room is off limits to the public until next week. Please go back to the main galleries.'

'I need some air anyway,' I mutter, and head out of the room.

I'm approaching the gallery exit when I feel Dan's hand on my shoulder. I turn and am shocked by how pale and tired he looks.

'I'm sorry,' he says.

I don't say anything.

'Look, I'm an idiot,' he says. 'I was just excited that we have a lead, but you're right to be scared. Of course you are. And you don't have to go into the Underworld. I'll retrieve the arrow. It will be fine.'

I let out a long breath. The rage in me came out of nowhere, but really, is it any wonder? My emotions are all over the place. I'm frightened and the only person I have to rely on is almost a stranger; worse, a stranger who has been keeping secrets. I take in Dan's rueful expression and think about dragging this out, letting him see that he can't talk to me like that. I might be new to this world, but I'm not some stupid little girl.

But he's clearly exhausted. I'm tired, and I've only been wrapped up in this mess for a few days. He's been involved in it for years. And he did have that horrible violent-looking vision. Angel and demon wrestle on my shoulder for while, but angel eventually pips it and I relent. There's no point making things worse than they already are.

'Let's just try to find Psyche and see what happens from there,' I say stiffly and he smiles and nods, happy to have brokered peace. As we head back to his flat Dan is unusually talkative, explaining his family's long-standing relationship with Psyche, how they lost touch a few generations ago, how exciting it will be to finally meet her. I smile and nod, but, try as I might, those words of his won't leave me: *I tell you what you need to know.*

$\longrightarrow$

That evening, I sit in Dan's kitchen, drinking a cup of hot chocolate as he cooks some pasta. He's being extra nice to me, and I'm letting him. Time to restore the power balance. I watch as he twists salt into the pan, adds rigatoni to the bubbling water, studs a camembert with garlic and rosemary and slides it into the oven – all foods he knows I like. It's freaky how much he knows about me when I think about how little I know about him or this bizarre world I've been dragged into.

We eat dinner in near silence, Dan flashing me concerned glances. After collecting our plates and placing them in the sink, he says he's going to call Greece and find out what information his family still have about Psyche's whereabouts. I listen to him talking Greek for a few minutes, and marvel again at how little I really know this guy. Then I go to my room.

After what happened today, I've realised how passive I've been these last few days, how pathetic. I haven't tried to understand this world of gods because the myths are complicated and contradictory and I have the sort of brain that likes logic and order. But there's something else, something I don't want to admit to myself. A way I get sometimes. Soft, spineless, like someone I don't even recognise.

But that's not me. Not any more. I have to take control. I have to stop relying on Dan so much. I don't want any more surprises.

Sitting on the bed, I draw a blanket over my knees and open a book about Eros and Psyche. I flip a few pages – it's the third task I need to know about. According to the story, the trip to the Underworld was filled with its own trials. First Psyche had to get Charon, the ferryman of the dead, to take her across the river. Then she had to face three spectres designed to distract her from her mission. Then she had to drug the three-headed dog, Cerberus, before entering the palace of Hades and Persephone and asking Persephone for the box of beauty.

According to the myth, Persephone gave Psyche the box, but, as soon as she re-entered the light of day, Psyche made a mistake. Wanting to sneak some beauty for herself so that she would look her best for her reunion with Eros, she opened the box. But instead of beauty, the box contained infernal sleep and it sent Psyche into a terrible torpor.

She would have remained asleep for ever, except that Eros woke up and, realising what Aphrodite had done, flew down to earth and rescued Psyche, wiping the infernal sleep from her eyes. Then he took her back to Olympus, she was made immortal and Eros and Psyche were married and, eventually, had a child. A real happy ending, if you don't count the 'being separated by an unexpectedly closing portal between worlds' aspect of things.

I lean back against the pillows and pull the blanket up further around me. What must it have been like to be trapped in this world for nearly three thousand years? Psyche must have seen some amazing and terrible things. She'll have watched her mortal daughter die of old age. She must have watched, too, as her husband's brother, the enemy, took his punishment and turned it into revenge against her people.

And she's family. My family.

Just then, there's a gentle knock on my door.

I close the book and slide it under the covers. 'Come in.'

'I've found her,' Dan says. His face is lit up. 'She's only seventy miles away!'

'That's a coincidence,' I say.

'There's no such thing as coincidence.'

'I know,' I say, raising my eyebrow. 'That was sarcasm.'

'Oh, right,' he says. There's an awkward silence.

'So what now? Do you have a phone number for her?' I ask. 'An email?'

'No. I was thinking we could just go down there first thing tomorrow.'

'Tomorrow?'

'Well,' Dan says, 'the sooner we get Psyche's help to recover the arrow, the sooner we can both get back to our normal lives, right?'

I stare at him. 'Exactly right.'

He hovers in the doorway. 'There's a glass of wine out here with your name on it, if you want it?'

I meet his eyes but I'm not sure what I see in them. Apology? Fear? Something else? I'm too tired to think about it. I need to stay strong.

'I'm going to get an early night, actually,' I say. 'I want to be on my game for meeting my three-thousand-year-old great-grandmother, don't I?'

'Right,' Dan says again. 'Of course. Well, goodnight, Frida.'

'Goodnight, Dan,' I say.

I turn off the light and lie there in the dark, thinking

about the argument today, the trip we're taking tomorrow. No matter what Dan thinks, I am pleased that we've located the arrow. I need to get this done. Because I'm seriously worried about what's happening to me. At first this whole situation felt like a dream, something I'd eventually wake up from. But each day I spend here, it's my old life – my business, my flat, my office, my clients, my friends – that feels unreal. Something I made up. A life too good to be true.

Chapter 15

'Are you warm enough?' Dan asks, fiddling with the heater of his ancient car.

'Yes,' I say. 'Thanks.'

We're on our way to visit – or more accurately, ambush – Psyche. Things are thawing a little bit after yesterday's heated exchange and subsequent awkwardness. Part of me wants to have the whole thing out, but I feel too mixed up. I need to keep things simple. Dan and I will only have to be in each other's company until Psyche can help us get the arrow, and we destroy it. In the meantime, I'll just keep a professional distance and be friendly. Civil.

Dan flicks a glance into the rear-view mirror.

I twist to look. 'Is somebody following us?'

'No, don't worry. They can't track us.'

'How do you know?'

'Because of the protection spell.'

'But what about Psyche? Won't he be watching her? I would have thought Anteros would have taken great pleasure in tormenting Eros's wife.'

'Well, he would, probably, but remember she's been down here as long as he has, so she knows some tricks. My aunt told me that Psyche has been using the same protection spells we Oracles use. That way, as long as she keeps her head down, Anteros can't find her.'

I think about this. That's how I'd be living if I had decided to run from this. Always looking over my shoulder. Waiting for the inevitable. I give an involuntary shiver, and Dan flicks a glance at me and starts fiddling with the heater again.

I stare out of the window, where grey clouds mottle the sky. I suppose we should be pleased it hasn't snowed. Dan swings the car down a slip road, where dull motorway turns to frozen fields, frigid hay bales and lone horses poised at intervals, like pieces on a chess board.

I feel a twist of homesickness. I posted a card to Bryony this morning before we left, telling her I was staying with a friend and would see her soon. I wish I could call her. Even just to talk about normal stuff. But I can't. Dan's right, people aren't built to believe in magic, and even if it was safe to call her, to speak to her and hide all of this from her would make me feel lonelier than ever. I sneak a look at Dan. Maybe that's why, yesterday's incident aside, I do actually feel comfortable with him. He's the only one who understands.

'When did you find out you were the Oracle?' I ask.

He gives me a surprised look, then focuses back on the road. I notice his jaw clench. Interesting. So, not a happy memory, then.

'I got my first vision at my grandmother's funeral back in Greece,' he says eventually. 'No one had expected it to be me.' He laughs gently. 'The Oracle is usually a woman.'

'What happened when you found out?'

He pauses. 'I didn't believe it. I had a good life, before all this. I had a house, a wife—'

This takes me aback. 'You had a wife?'

He nods. 'My family tried to persuade me to move back to Delphi. They'd been upholding the tradition of giving prophecies to everyone who visited them, and they insisted that I do the same.'

'So why didn't you?'

He shrugs. 'Because I intended to ignore the visions and carry on with my life.'

I absorb this information. Dan has been so gung-ho about this whole prophecy thing, it never occurred to me he'd ever have felt otherwise. 'What happened?'

Dan sighs. 'It became very clear that wasn't a possibility. If I ignore the visions, they just become more frequent. And more painful.'

'Did you tell your wife the truth?' I ask, curious.

'Of course.'

'And it was too much for her?'

He stares straight ahead, his face blank. 'Something like that.'

'So what happened next?' I persist.

'I started to tell my family what I had been seeing and they got very excited and pointed me in the direction of the ancient prophecy. So I read everything I could about Anteros, did some digging into NeoStar. And I realised that it was actually happening.' He smiles ruefully. 'For centuries my family had been nothing more than two-bit fortune tellers, offering people snippets of the future that the gods were pushing through between the worlds to keep the Oracle line alive.'

'Why?'

He shoots me a look. 'So we'd be ready for you when you came.'

I absorb this information. 'So, it's a bit like pass the parcel? Which Oracle would be stuck with the prophecy when the music stopped?'

Dan laughs. 'You could put it like that.'

'Lucky you,' I say. 'So is that where you saw me? In those visions?'

'At first it was just Anteros and the arrow,' he says. 'Then, later, you. Once I'd read everything, I understood what was happening, what it meant. And I realised I had to find you.'

'How long ago was that?'

'Two years ago.'

I widen my eyes. 'You'd been trying to find me for two years?'

'Yeah. All I had to go on was what you looked like. In one of my visions I saw you walking into NeoStar headquarters, so I figured that you must be somewhere in the area, or that you would be, eventually. So I gave up my job, moved above the café, and started looking. Hoping that I'd get to you before Anteros did.'

As all of this sinks in, I start to feel a little bit guilty. In my anger at the disruption of my nice, perfect life, I'd over-looked the fact that Dan, too, was once just a regular guy with a life he loved.

'So how *did* you find me?'

'I saw a picture of you online in an article about a big case you'd just won for one of your clients.'

'Oh,' I say. The information wounds me, like a splinter bomb from my old life. There used to be a lot of those articles. There's a silence as I listen to the humming of the engine, then I take a deep breath and ask what I have been wanting to ask since that first day in the café.

'So what have you seen, about me and the arrow?'

A split second of hesitation. 'It's not clear,' Dan says, and his eyes flick away. 'What I know is that you find the arrow, and it's crucial to stopping Anteros.'

I want to press him, to tell him that if there's more to know, then I need to know it, but Dan swings the car into a sharp left and down a long gravel drive, then pulls up in front of a wall of brambles and turns off the engine.

'This is it,' he says. 'We're here.'

Chapter 16

A freezing wind assaults us as we climb out of the car. I pull on my coat and stare, perplexed, at the row of brambles that stands in front of us, like something out of *Sleeping Beauty*.

This is no fairy tale, Frida. I pull on my gloves and, approaching the thicket, I part the branches. The house visible through the small gap is huge, a greyish white, and seemingly derelict. We find an opening in the brambles and push our way through.

'Are you sure this is the place?' I ask as I gaze up at the building.

Dan looks up. 'Pretty sure,' he says, sounding anything but.

'It looks abandoned.'

He frowns. 'Yeah.'

We walk up to the door. Dan grasps the knocker (which is

in the shape of a lion's head and looks pretty ancient itself) and gives it a good bash. When there's no answer, he pounds it again. Still nothing. I walk a few paces back.

'Try again.' As he does, I see a tiny movement from the upstairs window.

'There's someone up there.'

I approach the door and push the letterbox. From the resistance and the subsequent flaking of rust, I'm the first person to do that in quite some time.

'Psyche,' I shout. 'We know you're in there. I'm Frida, a distant relative of yours. And this is Dan, he's the Oracle. We have to speak to you about something very important.'

Nothing.

'The fate of the mortal world is at stake,' I say, sounding ridiculous even to myself.

More silence.

I straighten up and pull a face. 'She's not keen.'

Dan manages a smile. 'Seemingly not.'

Luckily, I like a challenge and persuasive argument is my bread and butter. I bend to the letterbox again. 'Psyche,' I say levelly, 'we wouldn't have intruded on you if it wasn't extremely urgent. We need to find the lost arrow, and we think you can help. We need to stop Anteros,' I say. 'You want that, don't you?' I pause. The air is taut with silence. I picture her, at the top of the stairs, listening. I give it one last attempt.

'Isn't that what Eros would have wanted you to do? Save the mortal race from his brother?'

We wait. Still nothing. I shrug. 'I don't see how we can

force her to—' And then I hear it – the clicking of locks, the jangling of a chain.

I watch, holding my breath, as the door opens a crack.

'Psyche?' Dan says into the black slit between the door and the frame.

'Psyche,' I say. 'I'm Frida, this is Dan, we—'

The door opens a fraction wider and I see a pair of dark grey eyes in a pale, heart-shaped face. I blink. One thing is for sure: she doesn't look like anybody's gran.

'Psyche, hi,' Dan says. 'I'm the new Oracle. And Frida is the one from the prophecy. She's the one everyone has been waiting for.'

I feel stupid as this sentence lands, and even more so when Psyche's eyes rest on me, her expression filled with scorn.

'A woman!' she says, her voice low and husky.

All thoughts of a cosy family reunion rapidly flee as my ever-ready anger kicks in again: 'Yes, I'm a woman! So what?'

Psyche opens the door fully now, and, well, there's no other word for it – we gawp at her. Because no painting can do this woman justice. Psyche is spectacularly, phenomenally beautiful. Her skin is smooth and creamy, with the faintest natural rose in her cheeks. Those grey eyes are verging on navy blue, the colour of a sky just before a storm breaks. Long shiny white-blonde hair. Rosebud mouth, currently pursed in a frown.

She's wearing a fitted white sweater and indigo jeans. Her feet are bare on the cold concrete floor. The one concession to make-up is that her toenails are painted a dark burgundy. She looks the way an off-duty supermodel might look, although only after some intensive Photoshopping. I put my hand to my hair, trying to smooth down the curls, and wish I'd worn a dress.

I turn away from Psyche's unimpressed expression and look nervously at Dan. I feel sure that Psyche's going to slam the door in our faces, but instead she turns and walks into the house. Dan and I exchange another look, and Dan shrugs. Then we follow.

$$\longrightarrow$$

The inside of the grand old house is in even worse shape than the exterior. There are cobwebs hanging from every available corner and, lonely in the cavernous lounge, a few sticks of battered furniture stand, including a small, discoloured, tapestry-covered couch and a cream leather armchair. The only cheery note is the orange glow of the crackling fire and the dog on the rug in front of it, nose tucked into tail, deep in sleep.

Psyche flicks a hand dismissively at the couch. When Dan sits down, a cloud of dust rises, causing me to sneeze. I lower myself gingerly next to him. Psyche sits in the armchair, folding one bare foot over her knee gracefully. Every move she makes is beautiful. Imagine looking like this and hiding in here, all alone, no one to appreciate you. What a waste. I'd get myself a plinth.

'So you're the one, are you?' she says, one exquisite eyebrow raised.

'So I'm told,' I say, helpless not to match her insouciant tone.

Dan fires me an annoyed glance. 'She is,' he says firmly. 'Anteros tried to detain her, but she escaped.'

Psyche picks up her glass and takes a slow sip of what looks like whiskey. I notice she hasn't offered us anything to drink. Not quite the family reunion I was hoping for.

'How long have you been preparing for this?' she asks.

I flush. 'I've only known what I am for a few days.'

Psyche widens her eyes, then turns her gaze to Dan. 'And you're the new Oracle, are you?'

Dan nods.

'Are you also entirely green?'

'I've known what I am for three years,' Dan says. 'And about the Oracle line all my life. But that's irrelevant.' He frowns and his tone changes. 'We haven't come here to see whether we pass muster with you, Psyche. We've come because we believe you might know the whereabouts of the last arrow of the love gods, and you have a responsibility to help us destroy it before Anteros gets hold of it. You saw it, didn't you, in the Underworld?'

'I saw a lot of things.' She shrugs.

'But you did see the arrow?' I ask eagerly. 'We think you must have mentioned it to a painter. We saw some sketches.'

She turns that stormy gaze on me. 'Child, do you have any idea how many conversations I've had in my life so far?' She shakes her head. 'Too many. I can't be expected to remember what I told to whom.'

It's both annoying and disconcerting to be called a child

by someone who looks ten years younger than me. 'Please, we just need to know, did you see the arrow or not?'

She locks eyes with me, hers cold as marble, mine full of pleading, like a cocker spaniel. Then she sighs. 'Yes, okay,' she says. 'It's down there.'

I glance at Dan. His expression is one of cautious excitement.

'Where?' he asks.

Psyche raises an eyebrow. 'Oh, so now it's my turn to pass a test, is it, Oracle?' She raises the glass to her lips and takes a sip. 'I told Natoire it was embedded in Hades' throne,' she says, shrugging. 'But that's not where it is, really.' Her mouth gives a bitter twist. 'It's in the bed he and Persephone share. Always was a romantic devil, that one.'

Dan and I exchange a glance.

'Psyche,' I say, 'we need you to help us get that arrow.'

She widens her eyes. 'I'm immortal, darling,' she says. 'No immortal can enter the Underworld. It takes a flesh-and-blood human to fool Charon. What place would an immortal have in the Underworld?' She sniffs. 'We can't die.'

'Plenty of immortals have been down to the Underworld,' Dan says. 'What about Hermes?'

She flicks her hand dismissively. 'Oh well, Hermes is a law unto himself. He used to go anywhere with those winged shoes of his. Although that was before Hades became fearful that some other god would steal his bride away and decreed the No-Immortals law. No, Charon won't take me in his boat any more,' she says. 'He'll smell my immortality from a mile away.' She looks at Dan, incredulous. 'You didn't know that? What kind of Oracle are you, anyway? You should be at Delphi, that's your proper place. Is there no respect for tradition any more?'

Dan looks uncomfortable at Psyche's probing. 'I had to find Frida. To warn her about the prophecy. She didn't know who she was.'

'Yes, well, how old is that prophecy? It's been promising us a hero to fight Anteros for thousands of years!' She looks at me again and shakes her head, rolling her eyes at Dan. 'All this time waiting. You could at least have brought me a man, someone with muscles. An Achilles or a Perseus! I admire your faith in this venture, in trying to stop Anteros, but really, this is your hero? She's quaking in her boots. She's just a child.'

'I'm twenty-nine!' I say, in a squeak that rather undermines the point I'm trying to make.

'A whole twenty-nine!' Psyche says drily. 'You must have seen so much in your long, long life.'

Dan looks utterly crushed. He stands. 'I'm sorry, Frida. We've had a wasted journey. We'll have to think of something else. Let's go.'

A small part of me is taking this as a sign – Psyche can't enter the Underworld, and we won't survive without a guide. But I don't want to leave, having got this far. She's the only lead we've got. If we don't get hold of the arrow, it's only a matter of time before Anteros does. Dan's terrible sketches come back to me, and I stay seated. 'You remember it, though?' I ask Psyche. 'You could talk us through it, or draw us a map that will lead us to the arrow?'

Psyche turns that oceanic gaze on me. 'I'll never forget my experience in the Underworld,' she says. She surveys me now with new interest, then shakes her head. 'But you're not ready. You're scared. You don't understand what you've got yourself into.'

I meet her gaze steadily. 'I am ready.' As I say this, I wonder why I'm arguing with her, when I should be agreeing with her. I'm *not* ready, I *am* scared, and I *don't* know what I'm in for down in the Underworld. But something about the way nobody thinks I'm up to the task – and because I'm a woman, no less – makes me determined to prove them wrong. I have to persuade Psyche to see things my way.

Looking around, my eye is caught by the dog in the fireplace. It hasn't moved a single whisker since we arrived, and in a sudden flash of insight, I understand. Why this house is so derelict and bare. Why the dog is static by the fire. Why she won't help.

'I may be young,' I say carefully, 'but I've met enough heartbroken mortals to know when someone is frozen with grief.' I nod at the fireplace. 'How many dogs died in your arms before you decided enough was enough?'

I'm not really talking about her stuffed animal. I'm talking about Psyche losing Eros and her life on Olympus, and then her daughter. Her grandchildren. Her great-grandchildren. All the loved ones she must have had to watch grow old and die, before she understood that, for as long as she lived, to love would always mean to lose.

'Listen, I get it,' I say. 'You don't want to help us because you are afraid to hope for something and then lose it. You're

124

afraid to connect with people again. But we can do this. I know it. I just need you to trust us.'

I hold my breath. Psyche's face goes blank, like a shut door. Dan looks at me and nods. It's time to leave. We've done everything we can, and it hasn't worked. But then Psyche smiles and, for the first time, I see why she was worshipped. Her smile is like the sun on your face after a long winter.

'Well, maybe you've got something of your grandfather in you, after all,' she says.

She gets up, stretches her long limbs, showing an inch of pale, perfectly toned midriff. She nods at me. 'Let's take a walk.'

Chapter 17

We leave Dan happily immersed in Psyche's library of ancient first editions and head out into the fields. Psyche lights a cigarette and we walk, following a stream in her overgrown acres of land, our feet crunching on the frozen grass.

'It's beautiful here,' I say. 'So quiet.'

'Yes,' she says. 'Peace is so hard to find these days.' She takes a long drag on her cigarette, lets the smoke drift out of the corner of her mouth. 'It used to be that I could lay low, stay out of the cities, keep away from media and technology and other people, but Anteros has eyes everywhere now. His fingerprints are on everything.' She sighs. 'He's colonised the human race and they're too stupid to even know it.'

'That's a bit harsh,' I say. 'After all, how could we know?'

'The world is harsh, Frida, Anteros has seen to that. But that doesn't stop you worshipping him.'

I stare at her. 'We don't worship him. We don't even know he exists!'

'Of course you worship him,' she says. 'What else would you call the reverence with which you all treat that arrow icon?'

That gives me pause. I think about the advert. The NeoONE, emerging in a shaft of golden light. The attention the phone has already created around the world, the urgency that people feel to be the one to find it, to own it, to be chosen. And how we have been groomed to think that way about love, too. Something to be bought. Attained. Upgraded. *He* did that.

'But what about before NeoStar?' I ask. 'What was he doing then?'

'Oh, then it was the TV company, the publishing house, the government office, the church.' She shrugs. 'Whatever position held most influence over the mortals, that's where he'd show up next. I've watched him play his trick a thousand times, Frida, and every time, the mortals lap it up.'

'My God,' I say, stunned at the scale of Anteros's reach.

Psyche nods. 'In the beginning, he had very little power,' she says. 'A leaked secret here, a whisper of suspicion there. Back then he was limited by the conventions of what society would allow. But the more freedoms you gained, the more Anteros's influence grew. He lived amongst you. He learned all about you. And he used your so-called liberty to forge your chains.'

'But that's hardly our fault,' I say. 'We didn't know it was him!'

She rolls her eyes. 'You never do. That's what started all this in the first place.'

'What do you mean?'

She doesn't answer for a minute, and we pass in silence through a gate, the river lapping beside us, a gentle, innocent sound. I can see why Psyche likes it here. It's wild and unfettered. It feels free in a way that the constrained, always-on city never does. Psyche nods back to the house. 'What has your friend told you, about why Anteros does what he does?'

I think about it. Detailed explanations are not really Dan's strong point. 'He just said that Anteros likes the game.'

Psyche frowns. 'But that's not the whole story. Anteros wasn't always as he is now. He and Eros were partners once, equals. Eros was the god of love, Anteros the god of love returned and the punisher of those who scorned it.'

I blink at her. This is news. 'So what the hell happened?'

'The mortals happened,' she says. 'Right from the start, they adored Eros. Sang songs about him, built statues, offered sacrifices in his honour. But never once did they speak of Anteros.' Psyche takes a last drag and then throws her cigarette to the ground where it sparks in the cold reeds. 'Eventually Anteros got tired of being overlooked and decided to make his presence felt. He used his arrows to punish the mortals and the other gods – the ones tipped with gold to provoke obsessive desire, the ones tipped with lead to cause hatred and indifference.'

She gives a bitter laugh. 'But guess what? Even after all

that pain, the mortals still didn't recognise Anteros. They just attributed his terrible acts to his brother, and began to call Eros fickle or mischievous or blind.'

I nod. That all fits with the stories I saw on Dan's wall. And it also explains why, up until a week ago, I'd never even heard of Anteros.

Psyche pulls the packet of cigarettes from her jeans pocket, taps one out and lights it. She inhales hard, her eyes faraway. 'In the end Anteros stopped trying to make the mortals see him. He gave himself a new identity, as the god of anti-love' – she turns to meets my gaze, her eyes dark – 'and he set about making them suffer.'

As we walk on, I try to process everything she's told me. There is so much Psyche knows, so much she can teach me. For the first time, I'm starting to feel that I might actually be able to do this, if I have her by my side. She's family, I think, and that notion sends a warm glow through me.

'What was Eros like?' I ask.

Psyche smiles, but it's tinged with sadness. 'He was joyful,' she says. 'Filled with light. Eros saw the best in everyone, including his younger brother. He was convinced Anteros was just mixed up, that they were the same, underneath.' She laughs. 'He should have known better. Yes, they shared the same mother, but Eros's father was Hermes, god of communication. Anteros was fathered by Mars, making him the product of—'

'Love and war,' I finish grimly. It all makes a horrible kind of sense now.

'Exactly. By the time Eros realised what his brother was

really capable of, Troy was already underway. Ten years of violence, relentless, merciless, until the city was razed to the ground.' She drops her gaze and stares at the frozen blades of grass. 'I had never seen so much blood.'

'And because of that, they banished him to earth? And then the portal closed?'

'Yes,' she says. 'And here we are,' she spreads her arms wide, 'in a world of puppets who believe they are free.'

I think about this. 'It's just . . . horrible,' I say.

'It is.' Psyche flicks the tower of ash off her cigarette, her expression thoughtful. 'Of course, the mortals know, deep down, that there's something wrong with the way they're trying to love,' she says, 'but they don't know what else to do. Anteros has given them a black hole instead of a heart and it can never be filled. Honestly, I don't think even Anteros could have imagined that his reign on earth would be so successful.' She shakes her head. 'But never underestimate the human capacity to bear pain, Frida, to tolerate it, and then, eventually, even to welcome it,' she goes on. 'It's a sickness, really.'

We don't speak for a long time, then. Just walk along the cold hard path, breathing in air so fresh it makes my lungs hurt. The stream widens out until it becomes a small lake. A bird calls from the high branches of a bare oak. This is *our* world, I think, it was never supposed to be his.

'What if Anteros had never been trapped down here?' I ask eventually. 'Would we be different? Better?'

Psyche shrugs. 'Eros always believed in the mortals, that they had some innate goodness that made them powerful

somehow.' She sniffs. 'Not sure I ever saw it. But it's irrelevant anyway, Frida. You can't go back. All you can do is
stop things from getting much worse.'

At her words, Dan's terrible drawings flash back to me,
all those tortured, manic faces. Worse than Troy, far, far
worse. 'Do you know?' I ask. 'What's coming, what he's
planning?'

'I don't want to know.' Psyche throws the end of her
cigarette down and crushes it with the toe of her boot. 'So,'
she says, turning to face me, 'how long have you known
Dan?'

I frown at the sudden change of subject. 'A few days.'

'You trust him?'

I think about his words in the gallery. *I tell you what you
need to know.* Then I shake the thought from my mind. He
rescued me from Anteros twice. He's been working on this
mission for years. He deserves my loyalty, no matter what
my control-freak tendencies have to say about being kept
in the dark.

'I do,' I say. 'He's one of the good guys.'

She nods and then gestures to a bench that overlooks the
lake. 'Sit,' she says. She lights another cigarette and smokes
it silently. I watch a robin hopping around on the lake's icy
edge, pecking for berries. A fish bobs its head above the
water, then ducks back down with a gentle *plip*.

'I've spent my whole life hiding from Anteros,' Psyche
says eventually. 'If there's a chance to stop him then I'll help
you, but if it fails, then it puts me in great danger.'

'I understand.'

She cocks her head. 'Do you? There will be trials in the Underworld, mind tricks, terrors, that you could never imagine. Are you willing to face that?'

'If it stops Anteros, then I have to do it,' I say. 'What choice do I have?'

'You always have a choice, Frida.'

'Okay,' I say. 'Well then, I choose to do it.'

Psyche looks at me for a long moment. Then she nods. 'Then I will help you.'

'Great,' I say. 'If you can draw us a map then—'

'A map won't help you,' she says, shaking her head. 'You'll soon lose your way. But ...' Psyche thinks for a moment. 'Two-way radios should do the trick.'

'Really?'

'Of course. Radios work off frequencies. Frequencies are energy. Energy is universal.'

'Right.' I nod sagely, trying to suggest I know what she's talking about.

'We'll be in contact the whole time. I can talk you through it step by step,' she says.

'Psyche, that's amazing. Thank you.'

She dismisses my thanks with a shake of her head. 'It needs to be soon,' she says. 'Before they know that you've found me. I have protection spells on the house and the grounds, but with the tech that NeoStar have at their disposal, you can never assume you're safe.'

'Soon works for me,' I say. 'Do you know how we get down there?'

'The Underworld is just another dimension, like

Olympus. I have a key to the entrance. But you'll need to get hold of the radios and a few other items before you can make the journey. What day is it now?' she asks.

'Tuesday.'

'Okay,' she says. 'Be back here just after dawn on Thursday morning. That should give you enough time to collect everything you need and . . . uh . . . tie up any loose ends.'

I blink at her. Then I understand. 'Oh. Right. What, in case we die?'

She touches my shoulder gently. 'I will do everything in my power to make sure you find that arrow and get out of the Underworld safely, Frida. I promise you that.'

I feel a rush of relief at her words. 'Thank you,' I say. 'I know that you were probably hoping for someone a bit more swords and sandals, but I promise you, I'm tougher than I look.'

She smiles. 'It runs in the family.'

$\longrightarrow$

As Dan pulls away from Psyche's house, we're in silence. My head is a jumble of thoughts that I'm struggling to process.

Dan shoots me a few worried glances.

'What?' I ask eventually.

'Are you sure about this? You don't have to come down there with me, you know. I wasn't expecting you to volunteer.'

'I'm sure,' I say. And somehow, I am. After my conversation with Psyche, something has clicked. This is what I

133

am meant to do; this crazy mission really is my destiny. As hard as it is to accept that, it's even harder to keep pushing it away.

Dan breathes out a sigh of what may be worry or relief. 'Tomorrow, then, we collect everything we need. And head back on Thursday morning.'

'Yep.'

'Are you sure you're okay?' he asks again.

'I don't know,' I say. 'I think so. I'm scared, but I also feel sort of . . . '

'What?'

'This is going to sound stupid, but, I feel kind of . . . happy. Terrified, yes, but also, oddly content. Does that sound mad?'

Dan smiles. 'Not at all. I felt the same way when I finally started paying attention to the visions. You have a destiny, Frida. All roads lead to it. And there's no better feeling in the world than fulfilling what you were born to do.'

I raise an eyebrow. 'Even if it means being eaten by a giant three-headed dog?'

Dan laughs. 'Apparently so.'

He's right. I feel it running through me, a buzz of adrenalin coupled with a sense of *right-ness*, somehow. 'So that's what this is,' I murmur, 'the feeling of being exactly where you're meant to be.' Dan flicks me an amused glance and I flush. 'I don't mean rattling around in this old heap,' I say. 'I'm more of a Mercedes kind of girl, myself.'

'I knew what you meant,' Dan says softly, and I know that he does, and it gives me a warm feeling inside.

'I want to go and see someone before we come back here. Will it be safe?'

Dan looks at me. 'Yeah. We can make sure it's safe.'

He doesn't ask who I want to see. I gaze out of the window, and the trees are a blur of green that turns gradually to grey as the city comes back into view. I take a deep breath. If I'm going to risk everything by going down in to the Underworld, then it's time I faced one daunting encounter that's a little closer to home.

Chapter 18

There's a famous quote: 'Home is the place where, when you have to go there, they have to take you in.' That's never been true for me. Home was my university dorm. Home was my house share. Home is my gorgeous flat, my office, the courts, the streets of the city I love. Home is something I had to create for myself and then carry with me.

I stare at the neat white semi-detached. Home hasn't been this house for so long. And yet, here I am.

With a pounding heart, I ring the bell. I called ahead to tell her that I was coming, but even so, my mother does her surprised face when she appears at the door, because she never wants things to be easy for me, when they've been so hard for her.

'Frida!' she says, in that tone I've learned to hate – one part wariness, two parts disapproval.

'Hi, Mum,' I say, 'good to see you.' I follow her into the lounge.

She has tea and biscuits waiting. All very polite. I sit down on the embroidered high-backed chair and watch as she pours us both a cup of weak Earl Grey.

'Thanks,' I say, taking the cup and saucer.

She eyes me anxiously and I look back at her with equal trepidation, searching to see how she is. She looks much the same as when I last saw her: short curly hair turning to grey, bright blue eyes that are never still, nervy birdlike gestures. Just being around her sets my heart hammering, I pick up her tension like a tuning fork, always have.

'What is it?' she asks now.

I blink at her. 'What is what?'

'Why are you here?'

'Oh, no reason. Just ... I'm going on holiday and I wanted to drop in before I went.'

'What about work, Frida?' she asks querulously.

I sigh. 'Everything is under control, Mum.'

'And what about Billy? Is he going with you?'

I close my eyes. *Seriously?* I swear she does this on purpose. 'We split up. You know that.'

'Oh dear,' she says. She takes little hurried sips of her tea. 'I don't know what's wrong with you, Frida, I really don't.'

I shake my head. I don't either but I can hazard a guess.

'So how have you been?' I ask.

'Oh, you know.' She waves a hand in the air with a jagged motion. 'I get by. My back has not been right since last year, it gives me terrible pain. Terrible pain . . . ' She sighs bravely. 'But I soldier on. And of course, they still don't know what's wrong with my eye, but it does keep watering, and I've read that can be the first sign of a brain tumour.'

I grimace. If she gets started, she can go all day just on ailments alone, and if she runs out of her own, she'll start on someone else's. A black feeling inside tells me this might not have been the best idea I've ever had. What did I imagine would happen? That we'd bridge the brittle distance that has grown between us ever since my adolescence and start to relate to each other in real, human terms? I'm deluding myself. My mother has sealed herself off from me, from everyone. There's a wall of glass around her, and that's exactly how she likes it.

I sip my tea and pick up a biscuit. This was a mistake. I need to begin my Underworld task strong and determined, but my mother is like a wraith, her very presence drains my energy. I want to be back with Dan, collecting the radios, the cakes, the coins. Not here, having what little confidence I have left ground into sand.

I glance around the room. It must be two years since I was last here, but nothing has changed. The horse brasses. The milkmaid statues. The tapestry, declaring 'Home Sweet Home', another pretty lie. There are no pictures of Dad, of course. I'm not even allowed to speak about him. And in amongst images of her sister's children, all high achievers, all golden girls and boys, there's only one of me, which I have always known she only keeps on the wall so that she doesn't look weird when people ask if she has kids.

138

I'm around eight years old in the picture, in a pretty pink dress, my hair in pigtails. My mum is still talking – something about the neighbour's hedge bringing her out in a rash – but I zone her voice out as my attention is drawn to the photograph. There's something there I've never noticed before. I get up and look more closely at the picture. I'm wearing a necklace. A gold necklace, with a charm dangling from it.

My chest contracts. Because it looks like a heart with an arrow shot through it. I swallow hard. 'What's this?' I ask, interrupting my mum mid flow.

'What, dear?'

'This.' I point to the photo. 'What am I wearing around my neck in this picture?'

Mum doesn't even look. 'Oh, I don't know. Just some costume jewellery, probably.' I glance at her and she averts her eyes. I've never had trouble discerning when people are lying to me, and this time is no exception.

'It looks like a heart with an arrow through it,' I say, my voice shaking. 'Is that what it is?' I try to stay calm. The necklace could be coincidence.

There's no such thing as coincidence.

'Frida, I really don't know what you are talking about!'

I stare furiously at the picture. I don't remember the day the picture was taken. I don't remember the dress. And I don't remember the chain.

'Did Dad give it to me?'

'Frida, really! Why are you raking all of this up now?'

I stare at her. She has pink spots high on her cheeks and

139

her eyes flicker everywhere but never meet mine. I take a deep breath.

'I need to know about Dad, Mum.'

'There's nothing to know.' My mother gets up and starts to clear away the biscuits. I've mentioned him. Broken the ultimate taboo. But I don't think I want to live by my mother's rules any more. There's too much at stake. The world is bigger than I thought. She might think that bringing up my errant father is the end of the world, but I know different.

'He's my only other blood relation,' I say. 'Don't I have a right to know who he was, what he was like? All these years you've refused to talk about him, don't you understand how hard that has been for me?'

She ignores me. As she reaches for a teacup I grab her arm and the cup goes clattering to the floor. She stares at me, eyes wide and frightened. This feels wretched, but I know I have to push her.

'What do you know about that necklace, Mum?'

She shakes her head. 'Nothing.'

'What do you know about Dad?'

'Your father was a foolish man,' she says, frowning. 'He had some silly ideas.'

My heart thumps. 'What kind of ideas?'

My mother's mouth pinches. 'Does it matter?' she bursts out. 'It's ancient history now, Frida, you have a successful life, why isn't that enough for you?'

'Mum,' I say, trying to keep my voice level, sensible, the only version of me she has ever been able to tolerate. 'There are things I've been told, about Dad, where he came from.

Strange things which sound like they are made up, but they're not, they're true. So if you know something it's okay to tell me. I promise I won't freak out.'

She meets my eyes then, and there's a world of bad in them. 'It was for your own good,' she says dully.

I stare at her, a terrible realisation dawning. Here I am trying to protect her from the truth, from this terrible world I have found myself in, and she already knows.

She has always known.

'Oh God, Mum,' I say. 'What did you do?'

Chapter 19

'When I met your father,' Mum says, 'he used to tell these stories. That's what I thought they were, anyway. At first I didn't mind, I thought he was just an artistic person, a bit of a joker, but eventually I began to think it was more than just that. His family were odd, too. He knew I didn't like it when he spoke as though he had lived in some make-believe world, and so eventually he stopped.'

My mother looks at me, her eyes bleak. 'I thought it had gone away. But it hadn't. He was just hiding it. Then we had you.'

'And?'

She looks down. 'It began again, but worse. Your father became so determined to involve you in his fantasies, it didn't matter to him what I thought, and how upset I was, how ill it was making me. I told him I would have him locked up if he carried on poisoning your mind like that,' she says, her voice rising with emotion.

'Jesus, Mum!' I think of my dad, struggling with the knowledge of his ancestry, with a wife who didn't believe him and a daughter who had inherited the family burden.

'He was ill, Frida,' my mother says dully, folding her hands primly on her lap. 'He said scary things, always talking about this great enemy, as though he was living in a fairy tale.'

'Anteros,' I say.

'Don't you say that name!' she scolds. 'Your dad was a disturbed man. The things he believed were insane.'

'He gave me that necklace?'

She nods.

'And you took it from me.'

'No, no.' She shakes her head. 'It disappeared. I think you lost it.'

'And Dad? Did I just lose him too? Maybe he's down the back of the sofa or in the attic, huh?' I'm close to tears. I came here to make peace with my mother, and here I am, that little pigtailed girl again, just as vulnerable, just as lost.

My mum picks up her china cup and holds it in front of her, as though she can ward off all this unpleasantness with it. 'I told your father that he had to make a choice. That he would put it all behind him, or that I would speak to someone about his mental state and make sure that he never saw you again.'

My heart is loud in my chest. 'What did he choose?'

143

For once, my mother's troubled blue eyes meet mine. 'He walked out on us. That was the last time I saw him.'

I sit back. I can't believe all of this went on in my childhood and I don't remember any of it.

'When he didn't come back, I thought all the awfulness would be over. But it wasn't. He'd passed it on to you, you see. The disease. You kept asking me to tell you more of the stories. About the gods, about your legacy. I thought you'd forget it – it was just a bunch of silly stories, after all – but if anything, the older you got the more insistent you became.'

She turns her eyes to me. 'You were just a child, Frida. He shouldn't have infected your mind with such things. So I did what I had to do.'

I look up at her sharply. 'Which was what?'

'A woman at your school, a health visitor, told me there was somewhere we could take you, they'd help you rationalise that these were just stories. I was desperate,' she says. 'I didn't want you to end up like your dad.'

'Where did you take me?'

She waves a hand. 'Oh Frida, it was all so long ago.'

'Where?'

'A place in the city. It was harmless. They just talked to you alone for a few minutes. They told me not to mention anything to you about the stories, that if I didn't remind you, you'd forget them. And they were right; you never mentioned any of it again.'

NeoStar. It must have been. Those files they have on me started when I was nine. My own mother handed me over to them.

I'm shaking. 'How could you do that, Mum? How could you lie to me about who I am? Who Dad was?' And how could he leave me, I think to myself, knowing what *I* was?

'I just wanted you to be normal!' my mother cries. 'I don't know why you have to drag all of this up, Frida. Why can't you leave it in the past, where it belongs?'

I see something in her eyes then, something much worse than what she has just revealed.

'You knew,' I say wonderingly. 'You knew he was telling the truth, and you did this anyway.'

But the conversation is over for my mum. She tidies away the rest of the cups and plates and she won't answer me, no matter how much I plead with her. I stare at her as she scurries to the kitchen, back hunched against the world, mind closed to anything but the reality she chooses. I understand now why she has found it so hard to bear being around me all these years, how fragile her safe, orderly world has always felt. How hard she fought to deny the truth. After all, I think bitterly, she is only human.

'Goodbye, Mum,' I say.

She doesn't look up as I leave.

Dan is waiting for me when I walk out. When I climb in the passenger seat he turns and smiles.

'How did it go?'

I try to speak but I find I can't get the words out.

'Are you okay?'

'I don't . . .' I take a deep breath. 'Yes. I'm okay.'

'Are you sure?' he says, peering at me with concern. 'God, Frida, the Underworld holds no terrors if visiting your mother makes you look like that.'

I manage a weak smile. 'She knew.'

'Knew what?'

'What my dad was. She gave him an ultimatum and he left us. And then she took me to NeoStar and got my brain wiped so that I forgot all about it.' I turn to him. 'Did you ever hear anything about a gold chain with a heart pendant? Is that anything to do with the prophecy?'

He shakes his head. 'I don't know. I haven't heard anything. I could ask my family?'

I collapse back with a sigh. 'Yeah, maybe. I mean, it's lost, anyway, so it's kind of a moot point.'

Dan stares at me silently, a worried look on his face.

'Anyway, did you get the stuff?' I ask, keen to change the subject.

He nods. 'Everything except the coins.'

'Great,' I say shortly. 'So let's get them and then go home.'

Home. That twists my heart – that I feel more at home with this guy I hardly know than I ever did with my mother. And now I know why.

As Dan drives into town, everything I have learned churns through my mind. It's just too much for my brain to handle right now, this switch from thinking my dad didn't care about us to discovering that he knew all along about his legacy. To be told, too, that I have memories of being part of this magical world that have been wiped. I push the thoughts away. I don't have time to deal with any of that now. I need to focus.

$$\longrightarrow$$

We buy the four drachma in an antique shop, but as we head for the door, I pause. Something feels wrong.

'Maybe we should get some spares?' I ask as I look at the coins in my hand, each one bearing the head of Zeus.

Dan raises an eyebrow. 'Why?'

'I don't know. In case we drop one or something.'

Dan shrugs and heads back to the counter. As he does so, I turn to the window and see something that makes my stomach plummet.

'Dan?' I call in a low voice, trying not to attract any attention. 'Dan!'

'Blimey, woman, make up your mind would—' Dan comes back and then stops mid-sentence as he sees what I'm seeing. 'Shit,' he mutters, 'they must have an alert on the antique shops.'

'Do you think they know what we're planning?' I stare at the van. The door begins to slide open and two black-suited security guards climb out. I have a flashback of Clive's insect eyes and my heart starts to pound. I feel sick.

'I don't know.'

'What do we do?'

We look to the front door, but it's no use. They'll be on us before we've got five yards. He looks back at the shopkeeper, who is now in a corner of the shop, showing a customer a silver snuff box.

'Follow me.'

Reaching over, Dan opens and shuts the door, so that a jingle fools the proprietor into thinking that we have left. Then we sneak behind the counter and into the back. We find ourselves in a large storeroom with a solid wooden door that should lead us out to the back streets. Dan heads for it and grabs the handle.

'Locked,' he says.

I stare at him. There's no time to break it down. No time to escape through the front entrance.

'Do you have any of that powder stuff you used on the guys in the van?'

'It's back at the flat.'

'Then what do we do?'

'I don't know,' he says. 'Let me think.' I don't understand why Dan is not doing something. His face is pale; it triggers something, a memory, but I'm too panicked to process it. Clive will be in the shop in minutes. I start to look around us. There are antiques of every kind: carpets and paintings, trinkets and ornaments and clocks.

'Come on, Frida,' I mutter to myself. '*Think*.'

I spot an enormous mahogany trunk. I dart over to it and lift the heavy lid.

'Get in here!' I whisper loudly to Dan.

'Are you kidding?'

'Would you rather have a nice little chat with Clive?'

Dan looks at the trunk, then looks at me. All the colour

has gone from his face. It's the first time I've seen him not in control. I don't like it.

He sighs. 'Okay.' He climbs in. As he does, I look around and see a woven carpet. I drag that over, then climb into the trunk beside Dan. It's a bit of a squeeze but if we lie curled up, spooned, it works. 'Help me with this!' Together, we lift the carpet and pull it in after us, then I reach up and gently lower the lid.

Underneath the musty carpet, in the dark, we lie there breathing heavily, curled around each other. I am excruciatingly aware of each place our bodies are touching, which is a lot of places. We hear the bell jingle and I stiffen. Straining my ears, I can just about hear Clive talking.

There's an exchange of words, no raised voices, all very solicitous, and then the storeroom door creaks. He's here. I hold my breath, acutely aware of Dan's body next to mine, of my heartbeat, which surely Clive will be able to hear from out there. We listen, as still as statues, as Clive walks around the storeroom pretending to admire the stock. I can hear my own pulse in my ears as the footsteps grow closer and then he's above us. Dan's hand finds mine in the dark and he rubs his thumb over the soft bit between my thumb and forefinger. *It's going to be okay.*

Just go, Clive, I think. Just leave.

And it does sound as though Clive's voice is becoming fainter, he's walking away. I relax incrementally.

And then, inexplicably, Dan begins to move, small repetitive movements, like he's jiggling his leg, tapping his foot. I turn to him in the dark, incredulous. Is he trying to get us

149

caught? Then, with dread, I realise what is happening, what was familiar to me about the sight of his pale face.

Oh no. Not now.

Clive's voice is now getting closer instead of further away, and panic floods my body. I have to stop Dan making a noise, or we're sunk. I turn in the dark until I'm lying half on top of him, muffling the movements. I clamp a hand over his mouth. It's a grotesque act, intimate and terrible, to feel his warm body moving under mine, knowing his eyes are rolled back in pain. I hold him as still as I can, and pray for his vision to end.

It feels like an eternity, but is really only seconds until Dan's body is still. But it's too late. There's a thump as Clive lays his hand on the trunk – not a trunk after all but a casket, somewhere to die – and I can hear the squeak of the hinges as he begins to lift it. I brace myself, gripping Dan's hand, and then—

A phone rings.

The lid stops moving. 'Yes?' Clive barks. 'Are you sure? Okay. On my way.' Then the lid slams with a crack and I can hear Clive's footsteps getting fainter as he walks away.

I let out a long breath. I turn to Dan in the dark and I feel him shake his head. *Not yet.*

We lie there, pressed against each other for five minutes. Then Dan shifts.

'We should be okay now,' he whispers.

He reaches up, pushes open the trunk and we struggle out from underneath the carpet, blinking at each other.

'That was very close,' he says.

My cheeks are red as I climb out of the casket. Yeah, I think, it really was.

$\longrightarrow$

On the way home Dan stops the car outside the flat and hands me the keys.

'Will you order us a pizza? I've just got to do something.'

I look at him uncertainly. 'Yeah, sure,' I say. 'Need any help?' I'm still freaked out by what just happened. I want us to be joking with each other, sarcastic. Normal. But I don't know what to say to get us back there.

'No, it's fine,' he says. 'I won't be long.' No mention of where he is going.

'Okay then,' I say.

I grab the keys and the day's spoils and take them into the flat. I find a pizza leaflet pinned to Dan's kitchen corkboard. I think about his vision. He hasn't told me what he saw. He hasn't told me where he is going. I sigh. This is too many secrets for two people who are risking their lives together.

I boil some water for coffee. Call the pizza place. Then I look in the fridge and my eyes light up and, fuck it, I eschew the coffee for a large glass of white wine. I switch on the TV.

When Dan walks in he raises an eyebrow at the glass in my hand and then smiles.

'Think I'll join you.'

'Pizza is on its way.'

'Thanks,' he says. Still no mention of where he has been.

I watch him as he pads to the kitchen, gets a beer, clicks the cap off.

'Did you get what you needed?' I ask, attempting a casual tone but ending up sounding slightly strangled. I flush. I feel like the suspicious girlfriend, always looking for the betrayal. Unfortunately both the girlfriend and the lawyer in me knows there's usually always a betrayal to find, if you look hard enough.

He glances over. His smile is relaxed enough.

'It was some stuff for when we destroy the arrow. Special powder that we pour over it to remove its magic. It has to be up here, though. It won't work down in the Underworld.'

I stare at him. Is this the truth? Is it? Then the doorbell rings. 'Pizza!' he says. 'Great. I'm starving.'

I don't bring it up again.

$$\longrightarrow$$

After we eat the pizza I go to my room and unpack the clothes Dan picked up today. Black T-shirt, black hoodie, black combat pants, black trainers, black rucksack. All the better to hide in. I can't believe we are really doing it. It still feels like make-believe. On impulse I pull on the clothes. Stare at myself in the mirror. I look like I'm playing dress-up. I look ridiculous. I find a bobble in my make-up bag and pull my hair into a high pony tail, then wipe off some of the make-up. That's a little more like it.

I decide to show Dan my Lara Crofted-self, thinking it might be just the levity we need. When I get back to the lounge, he's on the sofa, reading. He looks up, and his eyes widen.

'What do you think?' I ask. 'Am I Underworld-worthy?'

He smiles. 'Most definitely,' he says. I do a few twirls as he watches.

'It suits you,' he says.

I laugh. 'If you've got a thing for black ops then, yeah, I'm every man's fantasy.'

There's an awkward silence.

'Another drink?'

'Absolutely,' I say with relief.

I flop onto the sofa as Dan heads into the kitchen. When he comes back he hands me the glass and then, instead of joining me on the sofa, he sits in the armchair. I remember how close we were just hours earlier and a blush climbs my cheeks.

'Want to talk about it?'

'What?' I say, startled. 'No! Talk about what?'

'Your mum. The dad stuff.'

I stare at him for a moment. 'I'm not really ready to think about that right now.'

He nods. 'Okay, I get that.'

I tip the glass towards him. 'Anyway, cheers,' I say. 'Here's to evading Anteros so we can descend into the depths of hell.'

'*Yamas*,' Dan returns. 'That's cheers in Greek,' he explains.

I drink. The wine tastes like sunshine. Like happiness. Like life. Dan puts some music on, and we drink more. I'm thirsty and my glass is soon empty and then full again.

'I was thinking I might call Psyche tonight,' I say. 'Make

sure she's okay and still on board.' Maybe it's what just happened with my mum, but I'm feeling my bond with Psyche even more right now. I want us to be close. Like proper family. I need her.

Dan gives me a strange look. 'Let's leave it until tomorrow. It would be nice to forget about all of that for tonight, don't you think?'

I shrug. Perhaps he's right.

'That was very quick thinking today, Frida,' Dan says, studying me from his armchair. 'I'm sorry about what happened.'

'That's okay,' I say. 'We're still here, aren't we?'

His face darkens. 'I guess. But . . . I dunno. I'm sorry for dragging you into this. I know you're scared.' He takes a sip of beer. 'I am, too.'

'Really?' I meet his eyes.

'Really.'

'I didn't think any of this scared you. You seem so . . .' I search for the right word. 'Capable.'

'This is my destiny. I accepted that a while ago. But you're only just getting used to it. You're being incredibly brave. I just wish . . .'

'Wish what?'

He meets my eyes. 'Just that we'd had longer to get to know each other,' he says lightly. 'Of course, I feel like I know you well. But I forget that you don't really know me at all.'

I take a sip of wine and feel the alcohol begin to steal a march on my blood. I should slow down. I know I won't.

'I do know you, Dan,' I say. And it's true. As the alcohol mellows my paranoia I have to trust my instincts and they tell me that whatever Dan is doing, he's doing it for the good of the mission. 'You didn't choose this life, either,' I say softly. 'I'm sorry about how I treated you when we first met.'

'All those many days ago,' he laughs. And I laugh, too, because it feels like months, years, but it really is only days.

'I was such a pain, back then,' I say, laughing. 'Back when I was but a poor, naïve mortal.'

'No, you weren't!' he says, then smiles wickedly. 'Okay, maybe just a bit.'

'A lot,' I say.

Dan laughs. 'Frida, trust me, I remember what it was like when I first realised I was part of this whole other reality. That no matter how hard I tried I'd never be able to go back to normal life, knowing what I'd seen.'

'Well, I don't know about that,' I say. 'After we've destroyed the arrow I plan to carry on like none of this has ever happened.'

'Count me in,' Dan says. 'We could both get boring jobs and moan about mortgages and public transport like regular people.'

We grin at each other, our camaraderie warming the atmosphere, our conversation zig-zagging from flippant to intense and back again. I'm vaguely aware that my brain is getting slower and more relaxed, and that I like the feeling.

'Everything will be okay, Frida,' Dan says. 'As long as we have each other's backs, that's what counts.'

Our eyes meet and there's that electricity again, undeniable. A warning goes off somewhere deep inside me. Buried, but definitely there.

'So,' I say in a brisk, all-business tone, 'this powder to destroy the arrow. You'll bring it to Psyche's so we can do it as soon as we get the arrow out?'

Dan nods. 'Do you believe in love, Frida?'

I choke on my wine and begin coughing madly. 'Wow,' I say when I can finally speak. 'You're not much for the smooth segue, are you?'

I fill up my glass, mostly to buy myself some time. Because I don't know how to answer a question like that. I think about Bryony and Justin. They're in love and happy, but happy couples like them are so rare these days. I think about my dad leaving my mum, and how miserable she has been ever since, even though it now transpires she drove him away. I think about my clients who hoped for so much, and have been so betrayed.

I look up to meet Dan's eyes. He's watching me curiously.

'Psyche told me something that stuck with me,' I say. 'She said that the mortals know on some level that the way they're trying to love is all wrong, but they can't help it. She said their hearts are like a black hole that can't be filled.'

'And you?' asks Dan. 'What do you think?'

'I think she's right,' I say. And I do. Because I've seen it. By the time people require my services, the black hole is bigger than ever. And when I've won them all the money and property they wanted, or when I've protected their assets from their grasping ex, when they have the kids, the house, the boat, the everything, I've seen it on their faces – the wretchedness that comes when they realise that it still isn't enough.

'This is what Anteros has done to us,' I say, staring into my glass, swirling the pale yellow liquid. 'He's made it so hard to be content to be alone, and he's made it so hard to be happy in a relationship. It's like we're tied up in those knots that get tighter the more you struggle.' My mind goes to Billy. All those times when I should have walked away and didn't. Was that Anteros's fault, or mine? I glance up and the way Dan is looking at me makes me wonder how much he knows – about me, about Billy – and that burns.

'And yet,' I go on, 'despite everything, we never give up, do we? We keep on trying, no matter how many times it disappoints us. And although I know that serves Anteros's agenda, too, that it keeps us addicted to the game, I wonder,' I say slowly, 'if it isn't also because we know, somehow, that there's something better, something more true, than the kind of love he is selling us.' I stop speaking. Dan is staring at me intently. Wow, that was quite a speech. I must be drunker than I thought. 'Anyway, what about you?' I ask, hastily switching the focus.

'What about me?'

'You said you were married?'

He nods.

'So, did you love your wife? Were you happy?'

He takes a slow sip of beer. 'I loved her very much, yes.'

'Tell me about her.'

He meets my eyes, his expression serious. 'I met her at a

157

music festival. She was a friend of a friend. She was – is – great. Kind and generous and sweet.'

'But she couldn't handle your ... ah ... gift?'

'It wasn't that exactly.'

'So what was it, exactly?'

He drops his eyes. Shrugs. 'I started seeing someone else,' he says.

'Oh!' I say. I hadn't seen Dan as the adulterous kind and for a moment, I'm shocked. I wonder if the disappointment shows on my face. But then he gives me a look that sends a shiver through me.

'No, Frida. I mean, I started seeing you.'

Chapter 20

I stare at Dan, open mouthed.

'I hope you're not going to spring some time-travel shit on me right now,' I say. 'Because I just *cannot* handle it.'

He laughs. 'No. I mean, I started seeing you in my visions.'

'Oh.' I let out a breath. 'Right.'

Dan is watching me closely as he speaks. 'Janie tried to help at first. She even got the job at NeoStar and helped me plant the phone. I think she reasoned that, if we worked together, I might somehow get it out of my system.'

'But?' I ask, my breath held.

Dan shrugs. 'If it had just been the visions, we would probably have been okay. But it was the mission. All I could see was your face. I couldn't think about anything else. I was dreaming about you, obsessing about you. And she had to live with that.' He stares down at the bottle in his hands and starts tugging at the label, tearing off strips. 'It was very hard on her.'

'Well, that is . . . unfortunate,' I say, although the word I nearly used was 'romantic'. I feel very hot all of a sudden, unable to stop a deep blush climbing up my cheeks.

'I'm sorry, Frida,' Dan says, looking uncomfortable. He tips his drink towards me. '*In vino veritas*. I shouldn't have told you that. I don't want you to think . . .' He lets the sentence drift.

I tip my glass against his and our fingers brush. The contact unlocks something in me. I want to touch him, run my hand over his arms, trace his tattoos, feel his lips against mine. He seems to feel it too, he meets my eyes with that intense, sexy stare, and he leans forwards, closing the distance between us, and I can feel sparks pinging all over my body and I just know he's going to kiss me. Then he sighs and rubs at his face and sits back again. 'It's getting late. Shall we call it a night?'

It's like a bucket of cold water. I fold my arms and lean back. Take a long breath.

'Yes,' I say. 'We should.' Docile, well behaved, we fill glasses with cold water, pick up our phones. The air hangs heavy with what's been said, and what has not been done. As I follow Dan down his tiny hall, I feel the connection between us, stronger than ever, like wires just waiting to touch. But he's right. It's a terrible idea. So, fine. I just won't touch him again.

I'm walking behind Dan, staring at the floor to dampen down all ardent feelings, so when he stops at his bedroom door, I bump right into him.

'Oh God, sorry,' I say as I clutch at him to steady my drunken self. His body feels so good under his thin T-shirt.

160

Damn this man and his abs. I quickly remove my hands and tuck them behind my back.

'Well, this is me,' he says.

'So it is,' I say. My voice is husky. I feel the need to clear the air of all these pheromones, at least, if not the awkwardness. 'Look, thanks for opening up down there. It helps me to know I'm not alone in this.'

'You're not alone, Frida.'

'So,' I say, 'you never said what happened in the end, with your wife? Was it amicable? Did she leave you?' I pretend to myself that I want to know because I feel badly for this woman. And I do. Sort of. But that's not the whole reason.

Dan's eyes are on my lips, my cheekbones, my hair. I feel like he's touching me even though our bodies remain scrupulously apart.

'She asked me to choose, between her and you.'

I'm dimly realising that we are drawing closer together. My eyes are wide. Those wires just want to connect.

'Oh.'

Now his voice is hoarse as he says, 'I chose you.'

Oh. I go to say again, but as my mouth opens to form the word, his lips are on mine, or mine are on his, and the connection is made and yes, it's easy, it's right, it's exciting and familiar and sweet and painful and I give in to it, and we stumble into his room, and I don't want this to end and in the back of my mind, I know that this is a terrible idea, that this is all just the booze and the fear, because we're going into the Underworld and we might not make it out alive.

But I feel alive right now and that's what counts.

Chapter 21

When I wake up in Dan's bed in the middle of the night, I have a burgeoning headache, a gigantic thirst and a terrible feeling that I've just done something very stupid. I look down and am relieved to see that I'm almost completely dressed. Dan is snoring away, dead to the world. I stare at his slumbering head and feel a rush of affection for this man. We'll laugh about this. Probably. Or maybe we'll do it again. I feel a flush of pleasure at the thought. I lean down, brush a kiss over his cheek, pick up my phone from where it has fallen onto the floor, and then head to the kitchen in search of paracetamol.

I drink two glasses of water, neck two headache capsules, and then, aware that I'm not going to get back to sleep anytime soon, give in and make myself a coffee. While I'm waiting for the coffee to percolate, I open up the Eros and Psyche book and flick through it. Charon.

Three-headed dog. Hades. Persephone. I sigh. No matter how many times I read it I can't make it real.

I close the book. It's going to get real soon enough.

My phone lights up in the semi-gloom. I pick it up, smiling in anticipation, expecting that Dan has woken up and found me gone. But it's a message from Psyche.

I'm outside. Don't wake Dan.

I frown. What the hell is she playing at? Before I can decide whether or not to tell Dan, my phone flashes again.

Garden.

I pull on my trainers and jacket and silently pad down the stairs. I open the back door carefully and squint into the gloom. I can't see anything for a few seconds but then, there she is, leaning against the shed, smoking a cigarette, almost hidden from view.

I zip up my jacket and walk over.

'Is everything okay?' I ask. 'What are you doing here, Psyche? I thought the plan was that we come to you?'

When she looks at me, it's a searching look, like she's trying to read something in me. 'That was before I knew my house was bugged.'

I blink at her. 'What?'

She sucks on the cigarette and jerks her head to the top of the house where Dan lies sleeping. 'I wonder who could have done that.'

163

It takes me a moment to understand what she's getting at.

'That's ridiculous,' I say flatly.

'He's asleep?' Psyche stubs out her fag and then takes out a packet and lights another one. Something about the way she says it gets my attention. 'Yeah, he's asleep. Why?'

She shrugs. 'Drugged his beer while you were out. Slow release. He'll be fine.'

I stare at her, in shock. 'Psyche, what are you talking about?'

She looks at me then, her beautiful face terrible and filled with sadness.

'I'm sorry to have to tell you this, darling, but your Oracle is working for Anteros.'

Chapter 22

'Impossible.'

It's bloody freezing and I'm still in the garden, trying to explain to Psyche how she's got it all hilariously, ridiculously wrong. She pulls on her cigarette impatiently.

'It's the truth, Frida.'

'He's the Oracle,' I say again. 'He came to *me*.'

Psyche, at first bordering on sympathetic, is now getting bored.

'Listen, honey, I know all of that. I came here to warn you, because whatever else you are, you're family. I didn't need to do that. So let me say what I've come to say, all right? And then you can do what you want to do, no skin off my nose.'

'Okay.' I say, 'tell me.' Not because I believe a word of what she's saying, but because once I know the facts she thinks she has, I can work out what's really going on.

'When you guys came to see me,' Psyche says, 'something

165

felt a bit off about Dan. I've visited lots of Oracles over the years,' she says. 'You can't fail to, when you've lived as long as I have. But I've never had an Oracle come to me. It goes against the grain.'

I want to protest. Dan has told me his family disapproved of his methods. But I stop myself. Psyche is old fashioned, too, despite how she looks. She could barely grasp the idea of a female hero. So I stop myself and I do what I do in my job – let everyone say their piece, and then lay out the facts. Let the truth reveal itself.

Psyche stubs out her cigarette and lights another. 'So after you left, I did a bit of digging on both of you. My contact found this.' She shows me her phone. There's a picture of an identity card, the sort you swipe into NeoStar with. And it's Dan, years younger, but undeniably him.

'So what?' I say, ignoring the sick feeling in my stomach. 'It doesn't prove anything.'

'All trace of Dan was expunged from their records,' she says. 'I only got this because my friend knows how to dig.'

'So?'

'So, according to my source, he's been working for NeoStar for the last ten years. He's *still* working for them.'

'Not possible.'

'Listen to yourself. You've known the man, what, a week?' She tosses her head scornfully. 'There's also this.' She swipes to the next image, a still from a video. It's of Dan, as he is now. He looks pretty chummy with the other person in the picture and the sick feeling in my stomach intensifies when I realise who the other person is.

Dan definitely didn't tell me he'd met Clive.

In the cold night air, my senses on high alert, I'm suddenly sober.

Psyche presses play. I don't want to watch it but I can't drag my eyes away.

Clive says, 'Are you ready?'

Dan smiles. 'Of course.'

'And the note?'

'Planted. And the phone, too. She'll either go your way or go my way, but either route, she'll end up getting us the arrow.' There's a look on Dan's face I don't recognise. It's so unfamiliar to me that it takes me a while to work out what it is: craftiness. Then Dan says something that makes my blood run cold. 'All roads lead to your destiny, am I right?'

'Could these be faked?' I ask.

Psyche shakes her head. 'I've been hiding from Anteros for a long time. I trust about two people on the planet, and my source is one of them.'

'It doesn't make any sense. Why would Dan rescue me, if he was working for Anteros? Why not just let them have me?'

She shrugs. 'Anteros is a master of manipulation. He knows everything there is to know about you. He's hedging his bets, I guess. If Dan had come to you, but then there had been no threat from Anteros, would you have believed him?'

I think about this. 'No.' Because I didn't believe him, did I?

'Right,' Psyche says. 'So Anteros kidnaps you, sets up an alternate "rescuer" and you align yourself with what you think is the good guy. You know, don't you, that Anteros is banned from killing a human up here, but down there, he can do anything he wants to you? You're on celestial territory. Different rules apply.'

I feel sick.

Psyche stares up at the windows of the flat. 'They believe you are the person in the prophecy, Frida. And they intend for you to get the arrow for them. But the only way they could do that was to get you to trust one of them. So Dan "rescues" you – a bit miraculous that he manages to plant a mobile phone in a building that is legendarily impossible to infiltrate.'

'His wife did that,' I say weakly. 'She had a job at NeoStar.'

Psyche's eyes widen. 'What wife? I've seen his records. He's never been married.'

'That can't be—' I protest but Psyche's on a roll.

'So then he has you hole up in here with him, unable to contact anyone from your old life, everything you had taken away from you. Of course you're going to trust him, who else do you have? It's classic Stockholm syndrome.'

'No,' I say. 'Seriously, Psyche. Obviously it looks bad, but there has to be some other explanation.'

A security light goes on in a nearby house, briefly illuminating our faces, and Psyche must see something then, because she stops and shakes her head sadly. 'Oh, Frida.'

'What?'

'You have feelings for him, don't you? Oh, honey, I would have thought you of all people would have known better. That's the oldest con in the book!'

168

I burn with shame and fury. This can't be happening. It can't be true! But then I think about Chris. We were friends – occasionally more – for two years. I thought he adored me. And then he sold me out. I take a deep breath. Slowly, deliberately, I strip away the emotion from the situation and leave myself with only facts. Is it possible that Dan could have fooled me? A steely, harsh core inside me tells me that yes, it is very, very possible.

This is what Anteros has built his empire on, after all. Finding people's weaknesses and exploiting them. And my weakness? A gorgeous man so devoted to me he gave up years of his life – gave up his *wife* – before he even met me. A man who is a hero, sensitive, funny, and with great arms. A man who is willing to die with me to save the world. He's the perfect bait for a drama queen like me.

I'm crushed but my heart protests. It won't listen to logic. 'Hang on,' I say. 'They nearly found us, today at the antique shop. Why would that happen if they're all in on it together?'

Psyche shrugs. 'Maybe they know I know,' she says. 'Maybe they were going for Plan B. Force you down there against your will.'

I think about how Dan flaked when it came to hiding from Clive. The convenient 'vision' that almost alerted Clive to us, the one he didn't tell me about. Was that because it never existed? Then I remember Dan persuading me not to call Psyche and my heart sinks even further.

'I can't believe he would do that to me,' I say, and at this, finally, my Divorce Buzzword Bingo alert goes off once more. How many times have I heard that phrase in my office? Dozens. Hundreds. All those people believed what they had was real, too. Because they wanted to believe. And wanting is powerful. If you want something enough, you will warp your own reality to have it.

Still, something inside me won't let go of the intimacy we just shared. I take another deep breath and try to calm my spinning thoughts. I replay the events of the last twenty-four hours through a cold eye, and I see what my lawyer self would see: Dan complimenting me, then taking a seat away from me on the armchair, a classic example of advance-then-retreat. Dan getting me drunk, and divulging intimacies, then drawing the line, reeling me in so that I make the move. Dan in control, me ignorant. He with the power, me passive and weak.

Just my type. How easy it has been to play me.

I look up at the flat, the windows dark, Dan fast asleep, drugged.

'I thought he was one of the good guys,' I say in a cold, hard voice I don't recognise.

'Sometimes it's hard to tell the good guys from the bad guys,' Psyche says. She pauses, narrows her eyes. 'There's only one more thing I need to know.' Then she grabs my arms and pins me against the brick wall, her arm hard against my windpipe. 'Did they get to you, too?'

'God, Psyche, no!' I cry. 'Psyche! I'm not with Anteros. I swear!'

'I have to be sure,' she says, not loosening her hold. 'In this game, you really can't trust anyone.'

I try to move incrementally so that her weight is not totally crushing my windpipe. 'Why would I want to help Anteros attack the human race?' I say, my voice little more than a croak.

She shrugs. 'The same reason lover boy is. Power. Money. Revenge. Love.' She stares at me, her eyes dark and stormy. 'There's always something, Frida. Something the heart wants. Something people will do anything to have. Anteros is an expert at finding that thing.'

But her grip loosens slightly at my denials. 'Psyche,' I say in my most soothing voice, 'I already have money and power – well, a bit anyway. And I don't need revenge on the human race. I've got a great little business helping human beings take revenge on each other. And as for love . . . ' My mind flashes to Dan – the Dan who doesn't even exist – and, fuelled by a fiery fury directed mainly at myself, it's like I actually feel the last bit of hope shrivel up inside me. 'Let's just say I have now given up in that department.'

She looks deep into my eyes, and I feel again that she's trying to read my very soul. But at last her grip relaxes and she takes a step back.

'Okay,' she says. 'I'm sorry, it's just this has shaken me up. Anteros was spying on me in my own home. I'll have to move on again.' She shakes her head. 'You don't know how hard that is, to always keep running.'

I rub at my neck. 'I'm so sorry, Psyche.' I'm crushed by how naïve I have been. 'So what do I do now?'

Psyche shrugs. 'Call it off. Go into hiding. I have a protection spell I can give you. It only has a month left on it but it might give you enough time to find a hide-out, change your appearance.'

Call it off. A few hours ago, that was all I wanted. Now I think about what life will be like. Always looking over my shoulder. Never safe. Knowing that Anteros won't stop until he has found me. And like Psyche said herself, NeoStar is everywhere. Where would I go?

'Of course' she says, as though reading my thoughts, 'you'd be playing into his hands, since with you gone he'll have no one to stop him. And a life on the run from Anteros and NeoStar, that's a hard one for sure.'

I nod. 'But what other choice do I have?'

She grunts an agreement, then lights another cigarette and we stand in silence for a few minutes. I think about Dan, lying up there, in blissful, drug-induced sleep. Is he being played too? But in my sinking heart, I know that what Psyche is saying is true. I've seen this too many times with my own eyes. The con marriage. Innocents beguiled by the passion of their pursuer, horrified to find the man or women they'd fallen for was just a construct, designed to weaken them and extract something valuable. Money. Loyalty. Trust.

A magical arrow.

The more I think about how Anteros and Dan have played puppet-master, the more furious I get.

'Psyche, do you know how to get hold of the powder to destroy the arrow?' I ask. There's no point looking for the

172

batch Dan 'collected' today. It's obvious now that it doesn't exist.

Psyche eyes me with reluctance. 'I guess.'

'Then I'm not calling it off.'

Seeing the expression on my face, she laughs. 'What? You're going to do it alone?'

'Not alone, if you'll still guide me. I'm the descendant of a god, aren't I? At least that's what everyone keeps telling me. I have the equipment. It's me, after all, who is destined to find the arrow, not Dan. And I can do it, too, if I have your help.' I set my face firm. 'Psyche, we have to show these men that they can't keep playing with our lives. That we are in control now.'

Psyche stares at me, indecision on her face. 'I want to talk you out of this,' she says. 'But I also agree with you about one thing. Anteros won't stop, not unless you stop him.'

'Then we do it.'

She bites her lip. 'We'd have to leave immediately. I've got a protection spell on us, so they can't see us meeting. But when Dan wakes up, it won't be long before they work out what's going on.'

'How long does what you gave him last for?'

She checks the time. 'It's two a.m. That dose will see him through to ten.'

'Eight hours. Will that be long enough?'

She nods. 'It should be plenty.'

I stand there, my arms wrapped around myself, staring up at the moon. I'm going into the Underworld alone. I'm probably going to die. They almost had me again. What a dolt I am. What a stupid, malleable mortal.

But at least I understand, now, how this game is played. It's manipulation, subterfuge, psychology. Well, I can play that game. I can play it with the best.

$$\longrightarrow$$

Still, it's with a heavy heart that I sneak back into the flat. I listen at Dan's door, but of course he's snoring, oblivious. I head to my room, change into clean underwear, pull back on my black-ops gear and zip up the black hoodie. Black socks, black trainers, black rucksack. I stare at myself in the mirror. A few hours ago I had the blush of the newly infatuated. But now I see a hardness in my expression. A final cynicism. I yank the bobble out of my hair and retie it harshly back from my face. I jut out my jaw. So, I was tricked. So what? I don't need Dan. I can handle this.

I load my rucksack with the equipment, then take the phone Dan gave me and leave it on the bed. No doubt there's a trace on this one too. By the time he finds it, it will be too late. Then I pad downstairs and slip silently out of the front door.

I meet Psyche at the side door to the café. It's off the main street and so won't draw too much attention.

As we stand in front of it, I start to shake.

'Focus,' Psyche says, catching sight of my stricken face. 'I'm with you. You can do this.'

'Okay,' I say. I take a deep breath.

'Right then,' she says. 'Do you have the gear?'

I take the equipment from my rucksack piece by piece. Plastic bag of honey-soaked barley cake and coins in the pockets of my combats. Torch around my neck. Radio clipped to my belt, earpiece in. I hand Psyche's radio to her and we test it.

She nods. 'You're almost ready.' She hands me a small tin and, in answer to my quizzical look, says, 'You'll understand when you get there.' Then she reaches into the back pocket of her jeans and brings out two black pebbles. As I watch, their colour changes from black to blue, purple, white, grey and back to black again.

'You throw one of these in front of any doorway, and it becomes a gateway into and out of the Underworld. Got it?'

'Yeah.' I take them, and stow one carefully in a tiny pocket on my thigh. The other feels cool in my hand.

'Ready?'

Oh God. I'm really not. My stomach lurches. 'Psyche, I don't know ...'

She lays a hand on my arm. 'I'll be in contact all the way, Frida. You just tell me everything you see, and I will guide you.'

'Okay,' I say.

Our eyes meet and I feel a sudden calm. I *can* do this. If Psyche did it, as terrified and young as she was at the time, then I can too. I can't prolong it any more. I turn and face the blue door, its paint peeling to reveal the split, swollen wood beneath.

'I'm ready,' I say and I throw down the stone.

I watch the door. For a moment nothing happens and I feel a sense of absolute relief – we tried, it didn't work, maybe running is the best solution after all – and then I see it. The air in front of me is changing, atoms jostling. I watch as the scene shimmers, a kaleidoscope picture, resetting itself into a new reality. I blink at the place the door once was. Now it doesn't look like a door. Now it looks like the gloomy entrance to a cave.

'Good luck,' Psyche says.

I switch on my torch. My eyes are fixed on its thin beam of light in the darkness. Then I step forwards and I enter the Underworld.

Chapter 23

I'm in a long, pitch-black tunnel. I walk for a few minutes, scanning the ground ahead of me. The torchlight is weak in the absolute gloom.

'Psyche?' I say. My voice trembles and echoes; it doesn't even sound like mine. 'Can you hear me? Psyche?' There's a crackle in my ear, then static. My heart is hammering so loud I can hear it in the silence. What if the radios don't work after all? What if I'm trapped down here alone? I have the other pebble, but for that I need a doorway, and all I can see right now is solid black stone. 'Psyche? Please, Psyche, please.' A simple, heartfelt supplication.

Another crackle. 'Frida?'

Relief courses through my body. 'Yes!' I say, laughing with delight. 'It's me. I'm here.'

'Okay,' Psyche says and I can hear she's relieved too. 'What do you see?'

'Just blackness and stone,' I say. 'I'm in a tunnel.'

'Okay, keep walking. Say nothing. I'll talk to you. Mind your footing. Keep walking, shining your torch in front of you until you see water.'

I do as she says. After a few minutes, the gloom seems to darken even more. The light flashes over something that moves. I stop and run the torch over the ground. Water.

'There's a river here,' I say.

'Do you hear anything?'

I stop still and listen.

'No, nothing,' I say.

'Listen harder.'

I listen. And then I hear it, the faint *swish, swash* of oars.

'I can hear a boat.'

Psyche sucks in a breath. 'Put a coin in your mouth,' she says.

I do it, wrinkling my nose at the metallic, greasy taste.

'Turn off your torch. You'll be okay, the boat is lit.'

'Okay,' I whisper, my voice muffled by the coin.

'Frida, this is very important. Charon will bring the boat up to the shore. You must approach him, but don't say a word. Don't try to see his face. Just get on the boat, and no matter what happens, no matter what you see, you must not cry out. You're dead. Charon won't know otherwise unless you speak.'

'Okay,' I whisper again.

'Talk to me when you get off the boat, but until then, not a word. I'm here.'

178

I couldn't answer anyway, my throat is frozen. The boat approaches, with creaks and groans. A huge structure, it looks as old as the gods themselves. My heart hammers in my chest as the spectral figure of Charon comes into view, the boat lights casting him in shadow.

He's hooded, in a torn and soiled robe, his face just a void. Charon wields a huge double-sided oar, pounding it steadily through the water, and the boat creaks onwards. I stand on the edge of the river, trying to look like a lost soul, as Charon moors the boat with one thrust of his oar. I have a strong urge to run. It's just self-preservation, biology, the most natural thing in the world, but I fight it with all my will. I stare straight ahead. I try to step forwards, but my feet won't move. Charon sweeps that horrible empty gaze towards me, and it's all I can do not to recoil. I let my eyes lose focus and then I force myself to step onto the monstrous vessel.

Don't look. Don't look. I recite this mantra as Charon's grubby hand reaches towards me. I will myself not to flinch. His disgusting fingers, creased with centuries-old death and decay, wriggle towards me like insects, and then they're in my mouth, prising it open, seeking, and at last, after what feels like an eternity, finding the coin and pulling it free.

I want to brush my teeth for a whole day. I want to take a scalding shower. I want to be anywhere but here, I want this whole thing to be a long, drawn-out nightmare. I want, I want ... But all I can do is stare straight ahead and try not to scream.

Endure, I tell myself. Be brave. Be strong. Be a hero.

Charon stares at me then, as though he can sense my thoughts, but I make my eyes as blank as his empty hood, and, after a terrifying few seconds, my breath held, my body rigid with fear, he turns and thrusts his oar deep into the water, and begins the journey back along the river.

I let out my breath slowly, silently. I'm sitting in an inch of stinking, filthy water on the bottom of the boat, which is leaking from a dozen tiny holes. It smells of death, which, as it turns out, is a mixture of wet dog, burnt hair and shit. Good to know.

'Frida,' Psyche whispers. 'You're doing wonderfully. I can just about hear that bloody boat. I know, it's awful. He's awful. But it will be over soon. Just keep doing what you are doing.'

I sit there. I wait and I try to think happy thoughts. Unbidden, my mind takes me back to a place called Happy Valley that my father used to take me to as a child. Just me and him – my mother suffered with allergies, she didn't like to be outdoors. We'd walk through the overgrown woodland naming plants and trees and birds and insects, then call at the café at the end and drink a milkshake. I was happy then. I remember the feeling. How long has it been since I've been really happy?

I'm pulled from Happy Valley with a bump as the boat rocks to an uneasy halt. I count the seconds, and, when one minute has passed, and I'm sure we've reached our final destination, I stand. Trying to look as wraith-like as possible, I step from the boat and then stand on the shore, utterly still, until I hear that terrible, mournful creaking get further and further away. I know that, if I survive this, I'll hear that creaking in my dreams.

The sound of the boat gets more and more faint. I count the seconds. When seven minutes have passed since I heard anything at all, I ease myself into a sitting position, lean forward and spit until I can spit no more. Then I wipe my tongue on my sleeve.

There's a crackle on the radio. 'Awful, isn't it? Have a mint.'

I remember the silver tin. 'Oh, brilliant!' I say with relief, cramming three in my mouth.

'What can you see?'

I swing the torch around. 'Black. Rocks. Just black rocks, generally.'

'Okay. Start walking, keeping the river on your left. And Frida? You have to be prepared for anything. Tricks, voices, ways of getting you to stop. But you must not stop, not under any circumstances. Do you understand me?'

'Got it.'

I start walking. The darkness is like nothing I've ever experienced. It's like a solid object bearing down on me. The spindle of torchlight does nothing to reduce its oppression, or the sense that the blackness wants to swallow me up, make me disappear. At one point, my foot slips and I jerk heavily forward, almost falling on my face.

'What happened?'

I lean down, hands on knees, breathing through my panic. 'I'm okay. Just slipped.'

'Be careful.'

I get back up and focus on putting one foot in front of the other. I watch the river as I walk. Its oily waters look like treacle. Then I stop.

'I hear something.'

Psyche's voice is calm. 'This is the first test,' she says. 'Just stay silent, no matter what he says.'

'He?' I ask, a trifle querulously.

Out of the gloom, a shambling figure advances.

Chapter 24

The man is horrifically thin and drags one lame foot behind him as he walks. He's leading an even more emaciated donkey, loaded with its own weight in sticks, its eyes bulging. The man's own eyes are unfocused, confused, staring madly about the place, until they land on me.

'Hello,' he says in a quavering voice. 'Hello, miss?'

'Head down,' Psyche instructs.

But the man is in the middle of the thin path alongside the river and there's no way to avoid him. The donkey's eyes are bloodshot, and caked with flies. I look at the man, and see he is covered with pus-ridden sores. As he gets closer, I pick up the foul stench emanating from the duo.

'Miss,' the man says. 'Miss, I'm lost. Do you know the way to the market?'

I try to stay still but my head shakes, half instinct, half

repulsion. I hadn't realised my body had its own rules until I came down here.

The man seizes my arm, and my skin feels as though it is crawling away from his diseased touch.

'It's so dark in here,' the man moans. Up close I see that his flesh is moving under the surface and my stomach flips and flips again until I'm certain I'm going to bring up everything that's in there.

'I'm so cold,' says the man. 'I'm so tired. I hurt my leg. Do you know how to get to the market?'

My eyes flick to the man's leg, where I glimpse a wound that goes through the cartilage, the bone glistening greasily in the torchlight.

'Won't you help me?' he asks. 'Please help me. I hurt my leg.'

I feel an overwhelming sense of despair. I try to tug my sleeve from the man's grasp. He doesn't know that he's already dead. I have to tell him, or how long will he be wandering these hellish corridors?

'Say nothing,' Psyche warns me, snapping me back. I have to stay silent, I remember. It's a trick. A trap. The man pulls on my sleeve again. My eyes fill with tears, but I refuse to look at him. I just stare down at the wet ground.

'It's so cold,' the man says again, but then the sensation of pulling lessens as he lets go of my sleeve. 'It's so dark and so cold and I'm so far from home.' The movement below the surface of his skin breaks through, and I see that the bulges are maggots, hundreds of them, eating him from the inside out.

I bite on my fist, anything to stop myself from crying out, and the man begins to shuffle onwards again, tugging on the leash, his donkey pulled along with him. I can still hear him, as he goes, muttering to himself, that it is so cold, that he is so far from home. I hug my arms around myself, shaking and shivering.

'Has he gone?' Psyche asks.

'Yes,' I say, my voice small.

'You need to get going. You've got a lot of ground to cover.'

'Just a minute.'

'Start walking.'

'Psyche, that man, he was dying!' I cry. 'He was dead but he was also dying, how can I just—'

'Stop thinking about it. Blank it out of your mind,' she said. 'You never saw it, it never happened. Keep walking.'

There's nothing else to do. I keep walking, the river lapping by my side. I'm grateful for it now, disgusting and putrid though it is. Water is still living stuff, isn't it? I'm made of water. It's a connection to the earth.

Suddenly, I hear a splash, like the sound of a large fish surfacing. I stare at the murky waters. Another splash, and then silence.

'Psyche?'

'What is it, Frida?'

'Something in the water.'

'It's the second test. Just keep walking.'

For a while it seems as though nothing is going to happen, but then, in front of my horrified eyes, the water roils, the ripples part and a figure rears up. Its face is cracked, bleached from the water but her eyes are alive.

I'm staring down at the bloated, ruined face of Bryony.

'Frida, help me. Save me.'

The dead Bryony-not-Bryony thrusts a hand the colour of a fish belly out of the water towards me. Her hair, loose from its band, drifts around her head like seaweed. She's wearing red nail polish, a small detached part of my mind notices. It must be Christmas.

'Please, Frida,' Bryony gasps, water sloshing into her open mouth. 'Help me; get me out of here, Frida. I'm drowning.'

It's monstrous. Her eyes are alive, shining and hopeful in that terrible face, and a trembling overcomes me. It's because of me. Anteros has killed Bryony, and now she's here, in the Underworld, drowning in these terrible waters.

'Frida,' Bryony says. 'Please! Help! Help!' The arm reaches out of the water impossibly far, stretching out like the bony limb of a tree, and, as though in a trance, I reach out my hand to grasp hers. Her fingers are inches from mine and I have to save her. Our fingertips are almost touching and—

'That's not your friend,' Psyche says.

Her voice, in my ear, is cool, unpanicked. It clicks something inside my brain, like a broken circuit suddenly fixed. I blink and look again at Bryony, see properly, and snatch my hand back with a cry of revulsion. The woman in the river has black, dead eyes and a fish-mouth that gapes, waiting to swallow me, razor teeth grinding and grinding; the red nail polish is actually bloody finger stumps and she's not Bryony at all, she's the river, and the river wants to devour me.

I watch as the river wraith wails, screams its frustration and is swallowed back into the Styx.

I breathe heavily, in, out, in, out.

'Frida? Are you okay?'

'I'm here,' I gasp with difficulty. Not the same thing, but it will have to do.

'Good.' There is a lot of warmth in the one word. 'Now, Frida—'

'I know. Keep walking.'

The river is disappearing under the rock. How big is this cave? Impossibly big. I'm not in the real world any more. This is a different place, and there are different rules. I want the time to last, but in no time at all there are shadows up ahead. And singing.

'Do you hear that?' I ask.

'Yeah. It's the third test. Frida, listen, keep your guard up.'

'It's okay. They're not real. I get it.'

I walk. I won't be fooled this time. Fuck the Underworld. I know the trick now. Ahead, a group of women are weaving. They are seated across the path, so I have no choice but to push through the centre of them. I keep my head down. I won't look, no matter what, I won't look.

'Hello, dear, we've been waiting for you.'

I say nothing. They smell of talcum powder, old lady smells, and something else. Something metallic, like the coin in my mouth ...

'Do you not want to stop and see your little one?'

I freeze at the words. As I turn, I'm diffused by dread. I'm in the middle of the circle. But I'm not alone. There's something else in here with me. A cradle.

'Come and see her,' says one of the women, and she smiles to reveal black holes for teeth. 'She's a bonny one.'

'Frida,' Psyche says urgently, 'keep walking.'

'Did you think you'd lost her?' another woman says, apple cheeked and homely, in a cardigan and tweed skirt. 'Och, no, you never lost her. She's been here, waiting for you, all this time.'

'She has?' I whisper.

'Frida,' Psyche says, panic in her voice, 'it's not real. They're using things from your subconscious.'

Something moves in the cot, lets out a soft sigh. A tiny hand opens and closes.

I take a step towards it.

'Frida, keep walking!'

Slowly, deliberately, I remove the earpiece.

Chapter 25

I approach the cot. I turn the blankets down, and she's there: small and pink and chubby.

'Don't you want to hold her, love?' one of the weavers says. 'She's been waiting for her mammy. Pick her up! Give her a cuddle. She's yours, you never lost her. She's been here all along.'

I stare down at the baby. I know she's not mine, I never had a child, not really. Just a small collection of cells that was there one week, and gone the next. Nonetheless, she's the child I imagined Billy and I would have together, and she's exactly as I imagined her: a girl, with my dark hair and Billy's blue eyes and his charming smile. When I lost him, I lost the possibility of her, too.

The baby stares up at me with guileless blue eyes, one small hand clenching and unclenching.

'That's it, my pet. Just you have a cuddle,' one of the women says. 'It will all be alright.'

And she's right. It's all okay. As long as I stay here, everything will be okay.

I reach down into the cot and put my hands on her tiny body. I'll pick her up. She just wants to be held, that's all she wants. To be held and to be loved.

Love.

The word echoes in my head. There's something, isn't there? Something else I need to do. What was it?

I shake my head. Whatever it was, it doesn't seem important any more, not now I'm here, with this little bundle. My baby. I'm where I belong. What else is there?

But there's that word again.

Love.

Love.

Her tiny innocent hand. Just a little hold, a cuddle, why not?

Because it was so important, wasn't it? A baby, as tiny as that one powerful word.

Love.

A voice booms in my head, not Psyche's, not my own, not the thin needling voice of my mother. Someone else. Someone powerful.

LOVE—

And I snap back to myself, staring wildly around me, like someone just woken from a nightmare, but in reverse, because what I can see is hideous, disgusting. The women, so warm and friendly before, are now wizened crones with faces of impossible evil. Their looms are handfuls of guts strung from sticks. I hardly dare look, I shouldn't look, but my gaze is pulled to the cot.

A dead cat.

I stifle a cry of revulsion. *It's a game. This whole thing. It's a sick, twisted game.* But they can still do me harm, they want to keep me here, and the crones are up, surrounding me. I push them away, flailing, mad, and break free. And then, fuck walking: I run.

Chapter 26

I run and run. I'm running and crying at the same time, my face wet with sweat and snot and tears, my chest heaving, painful. Only when I collapse to the floor do I remember Psyche. I take deep breaths, fifty of them, before I put the earpiece back in.

'I'm here,' I say. My voice sounds dull to my own ears.

There's a pause, long enough to think she's gone, that she's given up on me. And then: 'Are you okay?'

'Yes.' I'm not, far from it, but I will be okay.

'Take a minute.'

'I said I'm fine. Just tell me what's next.'

More walking. Of course.

$\longrightarrow$

The minutes turn to hours. I try to draw Psyche into conversation, but she refuses, telling me I need to get focused for what's to come.

'Are you sure this is right?' I ask at various intervals. 'Maybe I've taken a wrong turn.'

'There is no wrong turn in the Underworld,' Psyche says.

I'm about to say something sarcastic about mythical clichés when I stop and draw in a breath.

'What?' Psyche asks.

I hear it before I see it. Growling, low like thunder.

'Get the cakes,' Psyche says grimly.

With trembling hands, I fumble in my pockets and take them out.

'You're going to have to advance now,' she says.

I take a step forwards. A gigantic shadow is looming ahead of me. 'I think it's asleep,' I say. 'I can hear it – them – snoring.'

I take two more steps and cast the torchlight over the path ahead and see black matted fur on one, two ... three snorting snouts and—

'Oh, sweet Jesus,' I whisper.

'What? What's happening?'

I scan the torch gingerly over the three beastly faces of Cerberus. 'Nothing. They're asleep,' I say. 'It's just, I didn't realise they'd be so ...' I look at the dog's claws, each one is as big as a tombstone.

'Big? Yep, I know. All the more reason to sneak past unseen,' she says. 'And Frida? Be very quiet.'

Right. Hadn't thought of that.

I take another deep breath and walk slowly towards the great dog. Two of the heads are resting on the ground, snoring and snorting. One of the heads is in the air, eyes drooping, snoozing and dribbling from its enormous snout. I see a flash of teeth, two rows of jagged razors. What could one set of teeth like that do to a person, let alone three? I shake the thought from my mind. If I can get under that head, and through, I might get past without them even knowing I'm there.

I take tiny, silent steps. The floor is pitted with indents filled with slimy water and as I step over a puddle, my foot slips. My hand jerks out, grasping, and I'm centimetres away from grabbing the dog's stinking fur – I picture myself perfectly then as a Frida-flavoured doggy treat – before I manage to jerk backwards and steady myself. I bend double, gasping. Too close. Too close. I can't do this. It's madness.

'Take your time, Frida,' Psyche says. 'You're almost there.'

I shake my head, even though she can't see it. The head is now above me, so close, I can feel its doggy breath on my neck. I take one step, then another and then, miraculously, I'm through. How many years must it have been since a human has passed these boundaries? Hundreds? Thousands? And I've done it! Feeling a rush of adrenalin and relief as I keep taking careful steps, left, right, left, right, and then I'm clear, and I'm breathing again, and it's going to be okay and then—

I hear it, or rather, I don't hear it.

Cerberus has stopped snoring.

It's like something out of a bad horror film. I should run, of course I should, but once again my body betrays me, and instead of running I turn, dread dawning in my stomach and rising to choke me as I meet three pairs of yellow eyes. Mad eyes. Hungry eyes.

Oh shit.

Cerberus gives an excited bark in triplicate – *ruff, ruff, RUFF!* – and then I finally do turn, and I do run, but it's too little, too late. They're on me, hot breath on my back, all three heads snapping in order – *snap, snap, SNAP!*

'You can't run,' Psyche says, and just how is it that she can sound so calm? 'If you run, they'll eviscerate you.'

'Great,' I pant, still pegging it. 'Wonderful. Any suggestions?'

'Hide. Hide or I'm sorry, Frida, but you're dead.'

Still running, I scour the sides of the tunnel for hiding places. They're pockmarked and uneven, but they're a solid wall that refuses me shelter.

The dogs are fully awake now, and so close and I am so dead. The noise of their growling is phenomenal; it seems to shake the cave. When I feel the drip of doggy saliva on my cheeks I slam my head to the right just as I feel the *SNAP* in the space my skull just occupied. My hair is drenched with killer dog dribble and as I look up in horror I see – oh dear God, don't make me look into those eyes again – this dog is rabid and murderous. This is a *Cujo* triple bill and I'm dead meat.

Then I see it, blink, yes, it's there, a hole in the wall of the cave. With no conscious thought, I dive into the hole. My head makes contact with something sharp and then, mercifully, it all goes black.

$\longrightarrow$

When I open my eyes again there is an enormous face peering at me, licking its lips with indecent enthusiasm.

'Frida?' I hear a small, tinny voice. The earpiece has been knocked out of my ear. I pick it up – it's wet and a bit slimy. I give it a wipe on my combats and shove it back in my ear.

'Psyche?'

It crackles. 'Wh . . . the c . . . k.'

I frown and unclip the radio from my belt. Its green light flickers unsteadily. 'Psyche, you're breaking up, I think the radio got wet. Or I'm concussed. Or both. Can you repeat?'

'CAKES!' Psyche yells.

'Right, right, cakes, of course.' Maybe I *am* concussed. I'd forgotten all about the cakes. I pat my pockets. No cakes. Trying not to panic, I turn out all my pockets, wriggling awkwardly in my hidey-hole. Nothing. Shit. Then I remember, I was holding them. I grab the torch – I caught a break, it's still working – and swing it around this tiny indentation I have wedged myself into. The dog head growls.

'Nice doggy,' I say. 'I've got something for you.'

For a terrible moment I think that perhaps I let go of the cakes in my panic, but then the torchlight finds something, a glint of plastic and I reach out and grab it.

'Got them,' I say triumphantly. The dog growls a low thunderous rumble in response.

'Need . . . of them. No good,' I hear through the crappy reception.

'What?'

'. . . three, all . . . need to . . . Oth . . . zzz . . .'

I get it. I need to feed all three heads, otherwise. Otherwise what? I don't need her to spell that out. Otherwise, the remaining ones will eat me and use my bones as toothpicks.

I shuffle onto my knees, and a dog face snaps, eager for a bite of Frida-tartare. As I watch, the head is pushed out of the way by another identical head with the same rheumy yellow eyes. This one seems more watchful, though, its eyes more intelligent. I don't know how, but I peg this one as the leader. Packs of dogs all have leaders, or so I've read, and these dogs, though they share a body, might still operate as a pack.

I take one of the drugged honey cakes into the palm of my hand and throw it to the entrance of my hidey-hole. The leader sniffs it, shakes its great head, and draws back from the gap, into which another dog head appears, bends to the cake and, without so much as a speculative lick, gobbles it up whole.

'Good boy,' I say soothingly. One down.

I take the second cake and throw it into the cave. The leader watches me, anger in its mad eyes, but again refuses to touch the cake. The second head is a little more suspicious, it sniffs the cake once, twice, and seems to consider it, and then, with a snap, wolfs the snack down.

Two down. This is going better than I expected. The drugged cakes should keep them unconscious for eight hours. *Like Dan*, I think but then dismiss the thought of that lying sonofabitch with a shake of my head. I take the final cake and shuffle closer to the entrance, just out of reach. Cerberus part three reacts immediately. I feel the vibration of that great tail, wagging with pleasure at the idea of fresh meat, but when I reach forwards and place the cake at the entrance, pushing it within his reach with my torch, the dog sniffs it, again, and turns away.

No dice.

I can't see the other two heads, but I hear them as their breathing slows, becomes nasal and they begin to emit soft snores. It works!

But I have to drug them all.

'It just makes no fucking sense, actually,' I say out loud. 'It's only got one central nervous system, after all.'

The dog growls.

I shrug. Given what I've seen so far, the normal rules of biology clearly do not apply down here, so it's pointless to argue. I consider the situation. Head honcho Cerberus does not want cake. He wants fresh meat. Mine. I stare at him and he stares back, still emitting that low rumble from his throat. There's a terrible intelligence in his yellow eyes. There's hunger too. And, glinting there in the back, pure madness. This monster will not be happy until he's tasted me.

That gives me an idea.

I drag the uneaten cake back towards me using the rope loop of my torch and then turn my back on the dog. Then

I push the cake up the sleeve of my hooded sweatshirt. He won't eat anything from my hand, but if he thinks it *is* my hand . . .

It's a ridiculous plan, not least because, if my reactions are even a second too slow, I am going to lose an arm and bleed to death down here in what is, quite literally, a hell hole. But, I don't have any other option. I have to make him eat the cake, or I'm dead anyway. I'll die of starvation, or I'll make a run for it and it'll eat me. This is it.

I *have* to be quick enough. That's all.

I inch closer to the giant snarling face, my heart thumping in protest. Cerberus is giving off a crazed and stinking heat, a viral kind of bloodlust.

I reach out a hand.

'Nice doggy,' I say, and make a patting motion, my fist balled up around the honey cake. I figure I'm as terrified as it is possible for a person to be without actually having a heart attack. I stare into the face of the dog and hear that woman's voice again – *LOVE* – and something kicks in and I grow calm.

It happens almost as if in slow motion. I reach out my hand to Cerberus, the dog's head jerks up, its teeth joyously bared, and at the exact right moment, I throw the cake into his jaws and snap my arm back. The hound's razor-teeth graze my knuckles, my hand actually scrapes its hot, flabby jowls as, with a shudder, I bolt backwards, scuttling in a crouch, my heart pounding.

Cerberus gives a startled, muffled *woof*.

I look at my hand. I'm bleeding. I might well be in for

a giant dose of rabies if I get out of here alive. But I don't care. I did it!

Now I'm the one who is waiting and watching. Cerberus eyes me resentfully; he knows something is wrong. He was promised human flesh and he got honey and cake and an early bedtime.

'Yeah, you bastard,' I say. 'The hunter is hunted.' I feel slightly giddy. I'm vaguely aware that I'm definitely concussed. Concussed, and with rabies. Frida, you're such a catch these days. I laugh, a sharp, not-entirely-sane laugh, and Cerberus's eyes widen as he gives a furious, 'RUFF!' But his pupils are turning unfocused, and sure enough, as I watch, coiled with tension, his eyes start to loll backwards, showing his whites.

He resists. He knows I've done this to him and, if he has the fortune to see me again, I do not fancy my chances of a friendly lick, but eventually the drug is his match and, with a slowly dropping nod, the third dog is down.

I listen to the trio of snores – *snort, snort, SNORT!* – for a whole ten minutes before I move. Once I'm sure they are unconscious, I take out the earpiece, wipe it, and replace it. I check the radio. A red light blinks and then is steady. 'Psyche,' I say. 'Psyche!' But she's gone. The radio is kaput.

I'm on my own.

There's nothing for it. I'll have to push on. I creep out of my hidey-hole, eyes pinned on those three monstrous heads in repose, and then I turn to find out what Cerberus has been guarding so ferociously.

$\longrightarrow$

What I see is breathtaking: a glittering diamond gate, inset with a ring of fire, like some sort of celestial bangle lighting up in the dark. I turn off my torch and approach, drawn by its cold beauty. There must be hundreds of thousands of precious stones here. I expect to find it locked, but who needs a lock when you have a three-headed dog? I open the gate a crack, and see what lies behind this jewelled entryway. Ahead of me, there's a plot of land filled with bright red flowers. Poppies. That would be Persephone's Garden. Behind it, a black palace looms out of the darkness.

'Psyche?' I try one last time. Nothing but dead air.

Am I going to do this? I ask myself. Alone? Truly alone?

Then I think about Anteros, about what he's done to me, what he's planning to do to all of us. I think of Dan, just another clever liar out for what he can get. I think about how I just faced down a three-headed dog.

Yes. I'm going to do this. And what's more, I'm going to succeed.

Chapter 27

I crunch down a path of cinders, and the red-headed, black-hearted flowers nod at me creepily in a non-existent breeze.

Psyche warned me about the flowers. I won't look at them. I'll just walk straight ahead, and stay on the black cinder path until I get where I am going. The path is lined with small shiny black pebbles and, bending down for a closer look, I realise with amazement that they're the same pebbles Psyche gave to me to get into the Underworld. Hundreds of them, just lying on the ground. I turn one around in my hand and watch its colours change.

Stop.

I cock my head.

Stop, and smell the flowers. Nobody has time any more to relax. To just enjoy beauty. Why wait until you are dead to really live?

It's the flowers whispering to me, a bittersweet, beguiling voice.

What did Psyche say about the flowers again?

I stop and turn as one of the poppies attracts my attention. It seems even more beautiful than the rest. Its petals are the deepest blood red, the interior is as soft as black velvet, and the smell that reaches my nostrils is both terribly sweet and achingly spicy, a seductive perfume. If I could just smell that flower I know everything would be okay.

That's right. Just stop and smell the flowers ...

I snap to and find myself on my knees on the cinder path, my fingers clutching a poppy stem, drawing the crimson petals towards my nose. I jerk back violently, loosening my grip, and then scramble to my feet. I remember now. The flowers are magical. If I stop to enjoy their scent, I will forget what I've come for and will wander the Underworld forever.

Is there nothing in this wretched place that doesn't want to kill me?

Breathing hard, I root my feet firmly in the gravel, shove my hands in my pockets and continue walking. After what seems like hours, but in reality can only have been minutes, I come to the end of the field of poppies. I look up, and the palace rears up ahead of me. Black, huge, windowless, like a featureless face, it feels wrong, wholly unnatural, and it sets a chord of unease running through me.

Still, there's no sign of Hades' chariot, which gives me a rush of relief. Psyche assured me that Hades is usually gone all night, reappearing only at dawn. If my watch is correct after all that dog-slather, that gives me just over three hours. I approach the huge black front door and, pushing it, find it unlocked. As I survey the inside of the palace, I see that I fit right in. Everything in here is black, and I mean everything. Black furniture. Black marble staircase. Black oak doors. A black chandelier hangs down over the gloomy entrance hall casting shadowy light over a black marble polished floor. It's like the pad of a 1980s nightclub owner.

Still, there's no time to waste on critiquing the décor. There are several doors leading off from this darkly magnificent hallway, but remembering Psyche's instructions I ignore them all. The arrow will be found in Hades' bed, she said, and that's in the main room upstairs.

I approach a magnificent spiral staircase, with black steps shining like piano keys, and fervently hope that Persephone hasn't rearranged her furniture in the last three thousand years. As I make my way up the stairs, I catch glimpses of the rooms below. A library filled with black books. A black chaise longue, in a room with black drapes. A claw-footed bath straddling a black-tiled floor. I go up and up, stepping carefully and quietly, until I reach the landing.

There's only one door up here.

'Well,' I whisper to myself, 'here goes nothing.'

I grasp the handle.

I blink into the darkness as I walk into the room. Then my eyes become accustomed to the gloom and I see it. A huge black wrought-iron bedframe, magnificent and monstrous in equal measure. And there it is! The golden arrow, suspended between two twists of black metal in that horrible headboard.

I step forward and a gasp escapes me. I've been hearing about (and, let's face it, resenting) the arrow so much, I was not prepared for it to be so beautiful, nor for the way seeing it would make me feel. It's mesmerising, it draws me towards it. As I approach, the colour of the arrow begins to change. It's not gold, exactly. It's more than gold. It's incredible, no colour I have ever seen. I have to climb onto the hideous bed to reach it. I can almost feel its pull, I stretch out my hand, and I'm almost touching it when—

'I wasn't expecting company.'

I whirl around, feet slipping on satin sheets, and then I see her. Lying on a chaise longue on the far side of the room. Persephone. She has red hair that cascades around her shoulders right down to her waist, curly and wild, pre-Raphaelite style, with white flowers at her crown. Her skin is pale as milk. She wears a white dress and her feet are bare. She glows in this black room like a flower pushing out of the dark earth.

'Persephone,' I stutter. 'Hi! Psyche sent me. I'm Frida.'

She rolls her eyes. 'I know who you are.' She flicks a hand at a chair upholstered in black velvet. 'Join me for a moment, why don't you?'

I look at the chair, and then back to the arrow. I need it. I have to have it.

'Join me,' Persephone commands, and then, in a softer tone: 'Please. I so seldom have the pleasure of anybody's company.' She holds out a slender, pale hand to me. Black

205

jewels gleam on her fingers and her wrists. She sees me noticing them.

'Wedding gifts,' she says with a hint of scorn.

Can of worms; I don't really want to go there. 'It's an honour to meet you,' I say instead.

'So, sit.'

I walk over and do as I am asked. Up close, she is even more striking. Her hair is the burnt orange of a sunset, her eyes are the deep green of summer grass. I recognise the perfume she wears: *Narcisse*.

'So, you made it this far,' she says.

I nod. 'You know why I came?'

'I hear things,' she says idly. 'Rumours, myths.' She looks at me and her eyes seem to contain a challenge. 'Prophecies.'

'Then you know I need the arrow, Persephone,' I say, cutting to the chase. 'It's a matter of life and death.'

The queen's gaze travels to the bed, where the arrow gleams.

'It seems to recognise you,' she says musingly. 'It changed colour. It's never done that before.'

'Is Hades here?' I ask quietly, looking around.

She sighs. 'No,' she says with a wave of the hand. 'Why would he want to hang out here, keeping me company, when he has so many other important things to do?' She shrugs and smiles brightly. 'So, my dear Frida, we've plenty of time. Have a chocolate.'

Persephone pushes a tiny decorated box towards me. 'Individual truffles,' she says. 'Try one. They're heavenly.' She watches me closely.

I'm just reaching for a chocolate when I remember how, in Psyche's story, she was warned to refuse all food in the Underworld. Anyone who eats down here will never leave.

I draw my hand back hastily. 'I won't,' I say, 'but thank you.'

There's a tense silence as Persephone stares at me. I meet her eyes – there's that challenge in them again.

'As you wish,' she says.

'Are you going to help me?' I say. 'If you know about the prophecy, then you know what's at stake.'

Persephone reaches out one pale arm and flips the lid of a large box of chocolates. 'Well,' she says, 'that rather depends.' She takes a dark heart-shaped chocolate, toys with it delicately, then meets my eyes.

'If I am to give you the arrow, then I shall want something in return.'

Chapter 28

Fifty minutes later, I'm still there.

'Persephone,' I groan, 'please, I have to go back. I don't have much time.'

'Just one more!'

Persephone has agreed to give me the arrow, but in exchange, she has kept me in her palace for the last hour to grill me about men. These are her terms: the arrow for gossip. What are men like these days? How do they behave? Who are the good ones? Who are the bad ones? Do I have one, and if so, what's he like?

'Tell me more about Billy,' she says, licking the filling out of a coffee cream. 'He sounds *very* exciting.'

'I don't want to think about him,' I say.

'Tell me,' Persephone demands.

I sigh. 'Okay, fine. He was great. He was perfect. He was

everything I ever wanted in a guy right up until the point where he almost drove me insane.'

She widens her eyes. 'What happened?'

What happened? I've only asked myself that question about a thousand times. But I need the arrow, so I guess this time I'll have to take a shot at answering. I take a deep breath. 'I don't know,' I say. 'I think . . . what Billy felt for me, it was intense. Powerful. But, I don't know if it was love. He could be so affectionate, so devoted; he made me feel better, happier, more important than anyone I'd ever met. But then he would get angry so quickly, and freeze me out. He could be so cruel, too.' I stare down at the fibres of the plush black carpet. 'Sometimes I felt that he hated me as much as he loved me. That it was all part of the same thing somehow.'

'And then he imprisoned you?' the goddess says, nodding sagely.

I widen my eyes. I'm about to tell her that women don't stand for being imprisoned on earth any more, but then I remember the nights I spent in tears after yet another argument, constantly checking my phone to see if he had responded to my pleading texts. The phone calls trying to get through to him, trying to put things right between us. The breaking up and making up and breaking up again. Years of it. Exhausted, anxious, barely able to sleep, barely able to eat.

And then the light that somehow got through, in between the crying jags and the make-up sex. The realisation that Billy didn't want things to be right. That this fucked-up nightmare, this dramatic, painful, constant twist of the knife was not us on our way to something better. This was us, period. This was the destination. It gave him kicks, it made him feel *good*. And the understanding, that, if I stayed with him, it must be because in some sick way I enjoyed it too.

And still, I couldn't leave him.

'Yes,' I say. 'He imprisoned me. But I escaped.'

She frowns. 'Then why do you not look happy?'

I stare at the goddess. And then, because it will be buried down here, with her, for ever, I say the most honest thing I have said to anyone in a long time, the thing I won't even admit to myself.

'Because I still miss him.'

Persephone picks up another chocolate. How this woman is not thirty stone is beyond me.

'And since then? There has been no one special in your heart?'

My mind flits to Dan and I immediately junk the image. 'No one,' I say firmly. 'Now, Persephone, I really have to go.'

The look she gives me, like a disappointed child, gives me pause. 'You don't have to stay here, you know. You could come with me.'

'Well, no!' Persephone says, her pale cheeks flushing at the thought. 'I mean, who would look after my garden? Of course, I'll leave one day. Just not right now.'

My heart hurts for her, but I let it go. It has to be her choice, just like it was mine. And will she be happier when she has made it? I can't even promise her that. I stare up at the bedframe. 'So, do I have your permission to take the arrow?'

Persephone sighs daintily. 'It's yours,' she says. 'I never did like that hateful thing anyway.'

My heart lifts as I climb onto the bed for a second time, and reach up for the arrow. As it hangs there, shimmering, shifting colours, it looks so other-worldly, so CGI, that I almost believe my hand will pass right through it. But I reach out and – no. It's solid. As I close my hand around the arrow something floods through my body. Something like cells sparking in recognition. It's real. And it's mine.

I glance over to Persephone. 'Thank you. I'm so grateful— '

But she isn't listening. Instead, she's watching the door, and then she turns those emerald eyes on me.

'He's here. Hades is here.'

Chapter 29

I'm frozen with panic as I listen to the pounding of hooves, dread rising in me. I curse myself for indulging Persephone's boy-craziness. I glance over at her. She's staring at me with bright eyes. Is she actually enjoying this? Of course she is. She's bored. And she's one of them, one of the gods, playing puppeteer. We mortals are just their entertainment, after all.

I really don't want to be caught by Hades, but even more than that, I'm not letting go of this arrow. In a few quick movements, I stow the arrow in my rucksack and strap it to my back. Then, without a backward glance at Persephone, I dart out onto the landing. Gripping the banister, I peer down, trying to see if there's any way that I can get out of the front door before Hades sees me, but it's too late. The door is opening. I crouch and peer through a gap as he enters.

My mouth dries up as I look at him. Hades. God of the Underworld.

He's tall, at least seven feet, with long grey hair flowing beneath a black helmet. He pushes the visor up, revealing narrow eyes, a thin angular face and a pointy chin. Maybe it's the effects of the arrow upon me, but it's as though I can feel what he's feeling and it chills me, because it's not so much an emotion as the absence of feeling. This is a man who is devoid of mercy. Without pity.

With dawning horror, I understand why he displays the arrow. Anteros's divinely orchestrated lust for Persephone is the only thing he has ever really felt.

'Well,' Hades says, stepping into clearer view, and tugging off his gauntlets, 'you came for my arrow, little girl?' Then he turns, deliberately, closes the door and locks it with a key that he places in his cloak. He walks towards the staircase, but I can tell by the way he moves that, though he senses me, he doesn't yet know my exact location. And also, that this doesn't bother him.

He likes the hunt, the arrow whispers straight into my heart. *The dead are such poor sport.*

'Don't be in such a hurry, my pet,' he croons. I see him more clearly now. His lips are thin and red in his pale face and his eyes are an ice blue, hypnotic. He has some power over me; it's coming off him in waves. He's coming up the stairs and when he gets here it will be over. I will do whatever he asks. I will be stuck here, for ever, like Persephone.

Maybe I'll even learn to like it.

A crackle from my pocket jolts me back to sitting and I

blink, confused, then I locate the source of the sound. My earpiece. Psyche!

'. . . ida?'

The radio must have finally dried out! With a mammoth effort, I pull my gaze away from Hades and put the earpiece back in my ear.

'Psyche,' I whisper, 'are you there?'

'Th . . . k the gods,' she says. 'I thought you were a goner for sure. Can you hear me okay?'

'I can now,' I murmur.

'Okay. Tell me where you are, and I'll work out how you can get out of there.'

'Upstairs. Landing. Quickly,' I say between gritted teeth.

'My dear,' Hades has advanced to the foot of the stairs, 'Aren't you tired? Aren't you hungry? Wouldn't you just like to let everything go, give it all up?'

His voice is a beguiling, insidious serpent, coiling and writhing around my thoughts, seeking entry.

'They don't know what it's like, do they?' he whispers, his voice the caress of a shroud. 'Nobody up there understands you. But here, you can be anything you want to be . . .'

His hand is on the banister. I can feel the vibration of the atoms between us.

'Okay, Frida,' Psyche says, 'get up. Get ready.'

I rise.

'Ahhh,' Hades says. Seeing me, his eyes glint with cold delight. 'There you are.'

As he takes each step slowly, lovingly, towards me, I'm gripped by his gaze like a butterfly under a pin. I try to focus, force my feet to step backwards, but my body is indifferent and refuses to cooperate.

'Frida?' Psyche says. 'Frida, are you there?'

I open my mouth to answer, but no sound comes out. There's just Hades getting closer, his pale face, his red lips, his silver hair, his armour glinting, his cloak billowing. He's waiting for me. He is the darkness. He is the darkness that wants to swallow me whole and I don't mind it, I want it, I—

'FRIDA!' Psyche yells and a tiny portion of my mind snaps to attention. 'Behind you, to your left, there's a door. Behind the painting, there's a tunnel. That's your way out. You have to go.' She pauses and, when she doesn't hear anything from me, she says, 'Frida, you are the descendant of a god. He has no power over you. You can fight this.'

Her words trickle into my mind like sand. Hades, oblivious of Psyche's urgent instructions, advances, one pale hand outstretched towards me, as though we are going to take a walk around the park together. How very pleasant.

You are the descendant of a god.

You can fight this.

'Give in to me,' he says and he's close now. Just a few metres away. 'Give up.'

Give up.

I feel a warmth on my back, spreading through my arms and into my fingertips and then through my whole body. There's a sudden connection, an almost audible click within me, and something begins, some old internal workings start up, a switch flicks and I feel . . . I feel . . .

I feel *amazing*.

I stand and face Hades, chin up. My mind is pin-sharp. Loftily, I cast my eye over his tragic Goth outfit, his dodgy hair, the whole undead shtick. And I smile.

'Sorry, Hades,' I say, 'I'm so over the bad boys.'

Then I make my escape.

Chapter 30

The tunnel behind the painting is small, so small that I have to run with my head bent, but still, I run. I keep going. I lose the signal to Psyche, but the arrow speaks to me, in a language I didn't know I knew, a language of cells and atoms and deep, deep magic. The tunnel has been taking a steady upward climb, getting steeper and steeper until, panting, I have to slow to a walk. Then the path runs out. I flash the torch ahead of me. There's just black rock, glistening with moisture.

A dead end, in every single way possible.

'No,' I say. All this way, and I'm trapped. It can't be.

I hear a crackle, a muffled something, on the radio.

'Psyche?' I say. Nothing.

I swing the torch.

'Think, Frida,' I command myself. I train the torch

directly ahead of me, then turn, in slow incremental degrees, looking for a door, or a crack of light to tell me that there is a way out of this. I've almost come full circle, when I stop. Here, at regular intervals, rising upwards, the rock seems darker somehow, I reach out, brush it with my fingers and find indents. Steps, carved into the rock. I train my torch upwards. There's no saying where I'll be climbing to – it's possible I might end up back in Hades' bedroom, a thought that makes my stomach lurch with fear – but I don't have a choice.

I secure the rucksack – it would be heartbreaking to lose the arrow after coming all this way – and grasping the first wedge of rock, I haul myself up. My foot flails before it finds the steps, then I'm reaching, hand over hand, going upwards and upwards. I'm stronger than I was, somehow. Because of the arrow.

I climb for a long time, getting into a rhythm. I climb and I climb until my limbs feel like string, but I don't stop climbing. I take another step and then my head brushes something solid. I hang on with one hand, and, reaching for the torch, I angle it upwards. Above my head, there's a large black cylinder of rock embedded into the cave. Holding the torch in my mouth, and wedging myself against the rock wall, I reach up and push. The hole-covering moves an inch. Grunting, I push harder and it slides all the way across.

Behind it, more blackness.

It's a door, though, isn't it? And if it's a door then . . .

'Okay,' I say. 'Here goes nothing.' Keeping my balance,

I take the pebble from my pocket and, with a deep breath and not a little fear, I cast it into the hole.

There's a blinding flash of light that causes me to squeeze my eyes shut. Then I hear ...

'Frida! Frida, is that you?'

I open my eyes again and see the sky, pink and orange. Dawn is just about to break. I have never seen anything so beautiful.

Psyche's face appears.

'Psyche!' I cry. 'Oh, thank God. Help me out!'

She holds out her hands and hauls me up, until I'm lying, panting, on the cold, hard ground.

'Where are we?' I gasp.

'Manhole. Just a few yards from the café.'

I blink up into the weak sunlight. I don't think I realised how much I believed I was going to die down there until right now.

'Did you get the arrow?' she asks.

I nod and point to my backpack.

Psyche crouches next to me. 'Here, have some water. You'll be in shock.'

I take the flask from her and drink a long draught. The water is cold and delicious. 'I can't believe I did it!' I say, laughing. 'I actually did it!'

'Let's see it, then,' she says, and strips the rucksack off my collapsed body. As she takes the arrow out of the bag, I feel the power fade and I can't wait to hold the arrow again. Psyche's eyes are ablaze as she gazes at it, and I lift my head and stare too. The way the colours seem to flicker, the way it refuses to be defined. It's beyond words. I clamber to sitting and reach out a hand.

'Better give it back to me,' I say. 'We don't want anyone seeing it.'

Psyche turns to me, smiling. But she makes no move to hand back the arrow. Instead, she stands up.

'Psyche?' I say. 'Can I have the arrow please?'

She doesn't answer, just looks at me with a frighteningly cold curiosity. Where have I seen that look before? Then I remember. Clive.

I try to get to my feet, but all the life has drained out of me. 'What are you doing?'

She rolls her eyes. 'Oh, the penny finally drops!'

I stare at her. I feel as though all the air has been sucked out of my lungs. 'You can't be working for him. You can't be! No! I had to persuade you!'

Psyche gives me a withering look. 'You had to think you were persuading me. Different thing.'

I struggle again to get up, but my limbs feel weak, all the strength that the arrow had lent me is gone, and then some. This is madness. How can she be helping Anteros, after everything he has done? I think back to the Eros and Psyche myth. Maybe Anteros shot her back then? 'Are you under the power of the arrow?' I ask. 'Is that it? Because, Psyche, what you feel for him, it isn't real. Search inside your heart. You must know this is wrong. You can fight it.'

She laughs. 'Oh Frida, you're such an innocent. You don't understand anything.' She crouches beside me. The arrow is just inches away. I try not to look at it. I have to wait for the right moment. 'You like to analyse people, don't you?' she says. 'See what makes them tick? Well, trust me, you're an amateur. Try living three thousand years and then see if human nature holds any mysteries.'

What I see in her eyes devastates me. She's angry and tired, but she's sane. She knows exactly what she's doing.

'Why?' I ask. 'You saw Troy. You know what he will do to us. How can you live with that?'

Psyche folds herself gracefully into a cross-legged position beside me.

'How can I live with it?' she asks. 'Let me tell you something about living, Frida. I've been down here for so long. At first I believed that Eros would come for us, that he would find a way. Then my daughter Pleasure died. Then my grandchildren died. And their children and their children's children. All of my lovers, and all of my friends. On and on, death and disease, pain and old age. Decades of it. Then centuries. Then a thousand years. Until there was only me, living with it.

'And all the time,' she says softly, 'there's Anteros, extending his influence over the mortals. I understand, Frida. I thought that what Anteros was doing was wrong at first. But time has a funny way of changing a person's perspective.' She shakes her head. 'You'd understand if you'd seen what I've seen. How they fall for his pretty corruptions again and again. The greed in the mortals. The violence. The way they have a chance for peace, but they choose pain every single time.' Her gaze is fathomless, unspeakable. 'Do you know what it's like to live for three thousand years, knowing it will never end? That I'll always be here, amongst this wretched species, in this unbearable world?'

'So, you're trading the arrow,' I say dully. 'For what?'

'A way out. A way back to Olympus.'

'There is no way back to Olympus! The gateway is closed!'

She laughs. 'That's what you were told. But Anteros closed it. If he wants to, he can open it again.'

I take in this information. 'It wasn't an accident,' I say. And of course, it all makes sense. 'Anteros wanted to be here.'

'Well, yes. Why would he want to stay on Olympus, where he was a nothing, a nobody, when he could be down here, ruling, as he has always wanted?'

The arrow is still just slightly out of reach. I shift position. 'You're not thinking straight, Psyche,' I say, desperately clutching for the argument that will change her mind. 'You think Eros is going to welcome you back, after you help his brother? He won't!'

Her face darkens. 'I have no interest in reuniting with Eros,' she says. 'Like I said, Frida, you understand nothing.'

I have to keep trying. If only I didn't feel so damn tired. 'Listen, Psyche, okay, this is a terrible world. But if you help me, we can change it. Make it better to live in.'

She raises an eyebrow. 'Wow. Have you heard the term "hubris", Frida?' she asks. 'It's the sort of excessive pride that offends the gods. Well, you're hubristic. You're so sold on your own ideas, your own magnificence; you don't stop to wonder whether you are seeing the world as you want it to be, not as it is.

'Like when you came to me to ask for help. You looked at me and saw what you wanted to see: a lonely woman grieving her lost love, just waiting for a righteous cause. You were so pleased with your own assessment of the situation, with how you managed to talk me round.

'And then, with your Oracle,' she goes on. 'How long did it take to convince you he was a liar? Three minutes? And why? Because you're so desperate to believe your own propaganda about relationships, about how people cheat and use and lie. That we women should stick together against the terrible men. As though anything is that simple. As though every human being, male and female, is not riddled with selfishness and greed and betrayal.'

Dan! The breath rushes out of me at the news that he knows nothing of all of this. What the hell have I done?

Psyche smiles at my stricken face. 'Don't worry about your beloved Dan, Frida. He's coming with me. Something to sweeten the deal. Anteros has always wanted his own Oracle.'

That's it. Enough. I won't allow that. I can't endanger Dan. It has to be now. In a sudden movement, I make a grab for Psyche's bag. But my arm doesn't move like it should and Psyche just stares down at me, smirking.

'Really, Frida, you are not the smartest of my bloodline. Although,' she says, considering, 'at least you did better than your father.'

My heart hammers. 'What are you talking about?'

'He came to me for help, too. Thought he could spare you if he elected himself as the chosen one. Back then maybe I even still believed the human race had a shot.' She snorts. 'He didn't even make it past the river spirit.'

My whole body is shaking now. It's too much. 'I swear, Psyche, I will not let you do this.' I struggle up, but my head feels fuzzy, my limbs are weak. And there's something wrong with my vision, everything seems to be fading.

'Feeling tired?' Psyche taps the flask. 'You've had Lethe water. Just give into it, Frida. You don't belong in the world of magic. You've been too human for too long. When you wake up, you won't remember any of this. Not me, not Anteros, not the arrow and not your precious Oracle.'

She bends down to me and whispers, 'You won't know anything until it happens.'

It's taking all the strength I have to keep my eyes open. 'Until ... what ... happens?'

Psyche smiles. 'Anteros is going to send you all a very special Valentine's message.'

My thoughts are fragmenting, and a mist has begun to rise in my mind. I hear Psyche's footsteps as she walks away and I focus on Dan's face in my mind. I can't forget him. I won't. But the Lethe water is too strong and when the mist comes up to meet me, there's no stopping it. I have just one moment to think about how stupid I have been, how utterly, utterly stupid, before the emptiness swallows me whole.

Chapter 31

I open my eyes and stare up at the ceiling. It's white. I glance at the walls, the bedsheets. White. My head aches and my mouth is cottony. I stare at the ceiling for a while, blinking and waiting to properly come to. Then I attempt to sit up.

'Frida? Oh, thank God you're all right!'

I turn to see Bryony's anxious face. 'Hey,' I say. My voice is weak and croaky. 'Where am I?'

'You're in hospital. Are you okay? Here, have some water.' She leans over me, holding a plastic cup and straw.

I take a sip. The cool water feels good in my clammy mouth.

I turn to her, my face creased with confusion. 'What happened? Was I in an accident?'

'You tell me!' Bryony says and she sounds half-scared and half-angry now. 'You were found in a street in town. Not the good side of town, either. You were unconscious. Frida, there were drugs in your system . . . '

I pause, the beaker of water halfway to my mouth. 'Drugs? What kind of drugs?'

Bryony stares at me. 'They don't know yet, Frida. What's going on?' She waves her arm at the machine that seems to be monitoring my vital signs, her voice breaking. 'You were unconscious!'

'Unconscious?' I rub at my head, and try to think of the last thing I remember. Oona. I had an appointment with Oona Simpson on Thursday. It must have happened after that.

'What day is it now?'

'Friday,' she says and when I still look at her blankly. 'The eighth.'

My appointment with Oona was over a week ago. My heart begins to beat uncomfortably fast.

'When did you last see me?'

Bryony frowns. 'I came over to yours last Thursday to drop off that box. Do you remember?'

I cast my mind back, but there's nothing after Oona but a blank space.

'No,' I say, 'I don't remember that.'

Bryony breathes in sharply and I see how scared she is, and that scares me. I feel myself starting to panic, so I just lie my head back on the pillow and try to breathe. Gather the facts. I'm sure this is just temporary amnesia. Maybe I have concussion. I feel my head and wince. Sure enough, there's a large bump, tender to the touch.

'What happened when you came over to mine?' I ask.

'I dropped off a box of your old stuff that we found in my mum and dad's garage,' she says. 'I invited you for Sunday lunch. You didn't answer my text on the Saturday, so I called you, and you didn't answer your phone.' She's close to tears as she says this, she feels guilty that she didn't try harder to contact me. I don't know how I know this, but it's coming off her in waves.

'I just presumed you were working, Freed, you know how you get. Then you sent us a card, saying that you were staying with a friend for a few days.'

I frown at her. 'Which friend?'

'I honestly have no idea.'

'Did I say anything about staying with a friend when you saw me?'

Bryony looks at me with concern that she's trying unsuccessfully to hide. 'No. Nothing.' She reaches out and pats my arm. 'Don't worry about it right now. Just get some rest,' she says soothingly. 'I'll speak to your doctor and find out what they know.'

I don't respond to this. This is all completely weird, but something else is nagging at me. Why can't I shake the feeling that there's something I'm supposed to do? I take a deep breath, lay my palms flat on the cool white sheets, and try to organise my thoughts. This is all like a bad dream.

'So, let me get this straight. I was found unconscious on the street?'

Bryony nods.

'Is my phone around?'

Bryony hands it to me. Slowly, I click back through my messages. There's nothing since last week. I struggle up onto my elbow and go through my emails and texts. Nothing after Thursday 31st.

No memory. No messages. Just a blank space where the last week should be. Jesus, was I abducted by aliens?

'I don't get this,' I say. 'The last thing I remember, I had a meeting with a client, and then—'

'Then what?'

I think about it, and I see something; a dark-haired man, I think, but it's like the wisp of a dream, the more I try to pin it down, the more it drifts away.

'Nothing,' I say, sighing. I push the covers back. 'I have to get out of here. I have to get back to work.' *And something else*, a voice whispers. *You have to stop him.*

Stop who?

Bryony is trying to push me back into the bed. 'Frida! You're kidding me! You've been missing for days and nobody, including you, knows where you have been. Then someone finds you with your head down a manhole in the worst part of town, with an unknown substance in your system. You can't just carry on like nothing has happened! Doctor's orders,' she adds firmly.

'Okay, okay,' I say. I tuck the covers back around myself. 'I'll stay. Listen, can you get me a cup of coffee?'

She looks at me doubtfully.

'Please, Bryony. You know how screwy I get when I don't have caffeine. Maybe stuff will start coming back to me in a bit.'

'Okay,' she relents. 'I'll ask the nurse if you're allowed to drink anything. And I'll see when the consultant is next calling round, I'm sure he'll want to ask you some questions.'

As soon as Bryony has gone, I push back the covers. Next to the bed I find a small wooden cupboard containing underwear, a black T-shirt, combat trousers and a hoodie and trainers. Apart from the bra, the clothes don't look like anything I would wear unless at gunpoint, but they're the only clothes there, and they're all in my size. As I pull the hoodie on, I stop for a second. It smells faintly of perfume: *Narcisse*. But I don't wear *Narcisse*. Before I pull on the trousers, I pat the pockets, looking for anything that will tell me where I've been. There's nothing save for a pretty, shiny black pebble in one of the side flaps.

I pocket my phone, then pick up my wallet and keys – something here, too, registers as odd, though I've no idea what – and then I place them in the hoodie pocket. Feeling bad about it, but obeying an inner urge I don't understand, I leave the hospital, sending Bryony a text as I walk.

Discharged myself. I'm sorry. I'll call you soon.

It's 10:30. I take a taxi to the office, and then walk around, checking every corner and cupboard. Everything is fine, except there's no Penny, which is odd. I call her. The phone gives a strange tone, and rings five times – three times more than it usually takes Penny to pick up.

'Frida,' she says when she does answer. She sounds flustered. Again: odd. 'Is everything okay?'

229

'Sort of,' I say. Best not to get into that right now. 'I'm just . . . wondering where you are, Penny?'

There's a silence. 'I'm in the Caribbean. On holiday. Remember?'

'Oh.' I regather my thoughts. 'Sorry. It's a bad line,' I give a little laugh. 'I didn't say where you are, I said how! How are you?'

Another confused silence. 'I'm fine, Frida. Great, actually. They're treating us really well here. It's a really great prize.'

'Prize?'

'Yes. I won the holiday in a competition. I told you that.' The concern is back in her voice. 'Is everything okay?'

'Of course,' I say. 'Yes. I just wanted to say, everything is fine and have a lovely time. I probably didn't get a chance to say that before you went, because I was rushing out to . . .'

I let this hang.

'You were going home,' Penny says. 'To prepare for your meeting with NeoStar the next morning.'

I absorb this information.

'Are you sure everything is okay?' she asks. 'Because if you need anything—'

'No, no. I'm absolutely sure I'm fine.'

'And the temp is working out okay?'

I stare around the empty office.

'She's almost unbelievably efficient,' I say. 'Now look, you enjoy yourself. When are you back? . . . Another week. Right then. Lovely. You take it easy.'

I hang up the phone. Interesting. Penny wins a holiday

230

the week I lose my memory. And I had a meeting with the biggest corporation in the world that I don't remember attending. But then, maybe I never got there.

My brain thuds dully in my skull. Does it mean anything? Or am I just chasing ghosts? There's something else, too. This should all feel odd, but it doesn't. This weirdness feels sort of . . . familiar. Which is kind of weird in itself.

I sit at my desk and try to work out what I know. When Penny left me in the office, I intended to go to a meeting at NeoStar. I open up my work laptop and check my electronic diary for the last week. There's no appointment for NeoStar anywhere, which is strange because Penny doesn't make mistakes. Having said that, I just phoned her in the Caribbean, where it is currently around seven in the morning, so I probably woke her up. Maybe she did get it wrong.

But then, if it wasn't to NeoStar, where was I going?

I pick the next appointment in my diary that day, and call Mrs Bartholomew's mobile number.

'Hello,' I say in a fake posh accent that vaguely emulates Penny's. 'This is a courtesy follow-up call to your appointment with Frida McKenzie last Friday.'

There's a pause, then Mrs Bartholomew says, with some consternation, 'There was no appointment! Ms McKenzie sent me a message informing me that the appointment would have to be rearranged due to a family emergency.'

There's a pause.

'Exactly,' I say. 'This is just a courtesy call to say that we will rearrange your appointment at the next available opportunity.'

'Actually, I've found another more reliable lawyer,' she says sniffily.

'Oh, well done you!' I say gaily, and terminate the call. A lost client. Great. But at least I know now that I didn't make that appointment. I stand and stare into the mirror. I'm shocked by what I see. I'm wearing barely any make-up and my face is pale. My hair is scraped back into a pony tail and it looks like it hasn't seen a decent product in weeks. And these clothes – I look like I've joined the army.

'What the hell happened to you?' I whisper to this mirror-woman. She stares back at me mutely.

I lock up the office and walk to my flat. Opening the door, I release a long sigh of relief. Everything is exactly as I left it. I walk into the kitchen, running my hands over the clean, tidy kitchen counters, picking up the cushions from my sofa and hugging them, like a demented actor from a home furnishings ad.

I put the kettle on, scoop coffee into the pot. As I make the coffee, my mind runs over and over the empty space in my head where the last seven days should be. I can see from the thin layer of dust, the dry soil of my plants and the letters piling up in the post-box that I definitely haven't been at home. I switch on the TV and sit down in front of the news. It's the tail end of the business news.

' ... we've all been waiting for. On Valentine's Day at 7 p.m. NeoStar will announce the winner of the only NeoONE phone in existence, in what has become the biggest competition of its kind in recent history. That's right, only ONE person in the world can win this incredible device, and the good news is, if you've bought any NeoTech in your life, you're automatically entered into the draw.' The news anchor smiles, flashing white, even teeth. 'So that's most of us, right? And if you haven't? You can enter online here.' He points to a URL scrolling along the bottom of the screen. 'Because trust me,' he continues, 'you do not want to miss a chance to bag THE ONE this February fourteenth! This gold-plated, phenomenally advanced device is being described as a "game changer" by the company and there's already fierce speculation about ...' As the news anchor enthuses on, I stare at the screen, hypnotised by the golden glimmer of the NeoONE phone. Then the story moves on to the Dow Jones index and I switch off the TV and pad into my bedroom.

This is better. Everything is here, everything is familiar, and I'm filled with an immense sense of relief. There's the beautiful bedspread I spent thousands importing from overseas; there's my lovely, comfortable bed with its ivory-painted frame and pocket-sprung mattress. I lie on the bed and crawl under the covers. This, after all, is what I've been looking for. Just peace and solitude and safety.

I fall asleep in minutes and, if I dream of anything or anyone, I don't remember it in the morning.

Chapter 32

I spend that weekend in my flat with the blinds drawn. Saturday turns into Sunday and Sunday turns into the next week, and I still don't go back to work. As the days roll into one another, it becomes clear that I'm hiding. The most frightening part about it is I don't know what I am hiding from.

On Wednesday I sit on my sofa, under the duvet I've dragged in from the bedroom, and watch a reality TV show in which would-be brides are pole dancing in a bid to woo a wealthy bachelor. I open another packet of biscuits. The programme finishes and then the news comes on and a woman has been arrested after stabbing her boss's fiancé with a hunting knife. She was in love with him, the report says, and became violent when he didn't return her affections. I watch for a minute. Sad times. Mad times. Then I grab the remote and click over to a 1970s police drama.

234

The phone rings. It's Bryony, again. I let it go to answer phone. Bryony thinks I'm suffering from depression or work burnout or that I'm addicted to drugs or something. All I know is that I want to sit under this duvet and eat custard creams. I feel bad for screening her, but I really don't want to listen to any more of her urgings that I should go to my doctor, take anti-depressants, try acupuncture, see a counsellor. She can't possibly understand how I'm feeling when even I don't understand what has happened to me, what it is I am seemingly grieving for. I haven't lost anyone, or anything. I still have my business, my home, my life, myself.

I lost a week of my life. That's all. *That's all.*

On the TV, a man in a crumpled mac is talking to another man. The latter's pointy-ended moustache clearly signposts his guilt.

Sometimes it's hard to tell the good guys from the bad guys, someone inside my head whispers.

I frown. Odd phrases keep popping into my mind, like echoes. But echoes of what?

I just need some rest, that's all. I decide to go for a walk, get some fresh air. It's a crisp February day and I like the thrum of the traffic and the busy, hurried, distracted people, the sense that everyone has a purpose. There are Valentine's Day displays in all the shop windows. The day for lovers is just one day away, and so it's time to get to work. Boost your stamina in the health food shop with 50 per cent off selected lines. Show her you're a real man when you wear this aftershave. Change your hair. Change your clothes.

Change yourself. Be someone else, and someone might just love you.

It's only when my hands go numb that I realise I've been standing staring at a cardboard cut-out of Cupid for a full five minutes. He's surrounded by red heart-shaped balloons. Drowning in them.

Do they know that red is also the colour of blood?

I shake my head. What is wrong with me? I keep walking. At one point, I catch sight of a newspaper stand that declares, *Will you find THE ONE? Valentine's Day fever builds as NeoStar competition deadline approaches!* It starts to drizzle and I pull on a hat. Eventually I realise I'm walking to the part of the city that Bryony told me I was found in. I'm a veritable Nancy Drew, looking for clues as to my disappearance. I walk up and down every street, waiting for something that looks familiar, something that might turn these dull sparks of memory in my head into a flame of understanding. But there's nothing at all but the litter-strewn pavements, the layers of graffiti over shuttered-up shops.

I start to feel lightheaded, and when I check my phone, I'm amazed to see I've been walking for two hours, and it has been hours since I ate. I pass a greasy café called Tony's and hesitate, backtrack and then peer doubtfully in the window. It looks terrible. I scan the streets, but there's nowhere else around here. I sigh. I'll just buy a coffee and anything that looks safe to eat.

Inside the café, I join the small queue. The woman behind the counter has six-inch dark roots and a very lived-in face. She smiles at me broadly.

'You all right, love? You look very nice, if a bit peaky.'

I stare back at her, nonplussed. 'I'm fine, thank you,' I say stiffly. 'I'll just take a cappuccino and a blueberry muffin.'

When my order is ready, I take the thin cardboard cup and the muffin and sit at one of the well-worn booths. I stare out of the window, stirring lumpy sugar into the coffee. I take a sip and then give a small sigh of pleasure. This place might be run-down, but at least the coffee is good. I peel off the muffin wrapper and am just breaking off a chunk to eat when the woman behind the counter appears at my side.

She says, 'I have something for you.'

'I'm sorry?' I say, frowning. 'I didn't order anything else.'

She squints at me. 'You don't recognise me, do you, love?'

'No, I'm afraid I . . .' I sit up straight. 'Hang on! Did I meet you last week?'

'Yes, pet. And he said that if you ever came back in here, and you didn't seem like yourself, that I was to give you this. And you don't seem like yourself, so here you are.' The woman hands me a small cardboard box, then turns around and heads back to the counter.

I stare at the box, then at the retreating woman, then back at the box. The package is just smaller than a shoebox, and sealed with masking tape. My name is written in black marker pen on the top. I think about taking it back to my flat to open it, but something tells me to stay, and since it must have been instinct that brought me back here, I decide to obey this inner wisdom. Steeling myself, I take a sip of coffee and then I ease away the masking tape.

Inside, there's a small bottle of water, a set of keys, three small plastic bags, one containing brown powder, one holding some small, grey, gritty-looking balls, and one filled with some dried green herbs. I remember Bryony's words. Shit. Drugs? Is that what I'm mixed up in? Underneath the bags I notice something else and I pull it out. It's a small plastic vial containing what looks like two blue contact lenses. Under this, there's a scribbled sticky note which on one side says 'Arrow=200: GODS' and on the other '122 Laerdroia' next to what looks like a hastily drawn sketch of a camel.

Right. Wonderful. Good to know. I look at the water and notice that the bottle also has a yellow note stuck to it. This one says, 'DRINK ME.' Ha ha. Funny joke. I stare around. Is someone fooling around with me now? But nobody is watching. Even the woman at the counter is just busy serving people. I unscrew the lid. It's deeply foolish to drink something just because a sticky note tells you to, but I'm sick of unanswered questions and the gaping hole in my head. I just want the truth. And that inner instinct is urging me on.

I lift the bottle to my lips and sniff. Screw it, I think, and take a sip.

Nothing. I set the bottle down. So. Just a silly practical joke.

Then I gasp in a huge, sucking breath, gripping the table, knuckles turning white as everything, all of it, comes flooding back.

Chapter 33

I have to force myself to unclench my fingers from the table. I'm trembling with the torrent of memories that have just rushed back into me.

I forgot everything. Psyche gave me Lethe water and made me forget it all.

Oh. My. God.

With trembling fingers I take the bags from the box. The grey balls are Ophiotaurus bombs. The green herb I recognise as a protection spell. The other bag of powder, I've never seen before. Then it strikes me. It's what Dan intended us to use to destroy the arrow. It must be. I take the contact lenses out of the box. What on earth are these for? I search for more, but there's no note, no explanation.

Shaky on my legs, I head to the counter.

'Cathy, when did Dan leave this box for me?'

She screws up her eyes. 'Would have been last Wednesday, late on, just after closing. Haven't seen him since; is he okay?'

'He's ... away,' I say. 'Visiting friends.' I know Dan trusts Cathy but I don't know how much she knows. No point dragging her into this. Okay, so, Dan left the box on Wednesday, after his vision, but before we started drinking. That must have been what he went to get – the Lethe water antidote, all this other stuff. Which means ... my brain scrambles to put the pieces together ... he must have seen at least some of what was going to happen.

I stand there, dumbstruck. Did he know I was going to betray him? Or just that he would be kidnapped? And why the hell didn't he say something?

I look again at the scribbled note: 'Arrow=200'. What does that mean? I try to think of anything that might link Anteros and the number 200. But there's nothing. Even his grand skyscraper only has 199 floors. Then something occurs to me.

What if it doesn't?

What if there is a secret 200th floor?

Suddenly, I'm sure that's it. That's where Anteros will be holding Dan and the arrow. I stare at the note. But how am I supposed to infiltrate somewhere that isn't even supposed to exist?

I pick up the box, then head upstairs. Dan must have planted something else. A plan. A way to get him out. But the flat is exactly how I left it, except for the bedroom. In here, the lamp is overturned and the duvet is thrown onto

240

the floor. My blood runs cold when I think of the men in black dragging Dan unconscious from his bed. Who knows what they've done to him. But no, he must be alive. Dan is an Oracle, and as such, he's useful to Anteros. Psyche said so. They won't kill him.

Though, of course, there are worse things than death.

In my room, I find the phone I left here, and I reread Psyche's message, enticing me to meet her outside. I'm sickened by her duplicity. She lured my father to his death. She has taken Dan away. She stole the arrow. And ... what was it Psyche said Anteros was planning to do with it? My head is still fuzzy, some of the memories remain unclear. I pick up the bottle and drink the rest of the water.

But it's too much. Psyche's words come back – *Anteros is going to send you all a very special Valentine's message* – but so, too, do the memories from before: my father reading me stories, handing me the necklace, and telling me that I'm important. Mum and Dad arguing, a bit at first and then all the time until I hide in my room with a pillow over my head, a knot of guilt in my stomach because what she hates about him, she hates about me, too. The day I came home from school to find him gone. The trip to the city, where I knew, somehow, that there was something wrong, something bad, and I fought then, kicking and biting, until they strapped me down and forced water down my throat with a tube.

And then I was good Frida. Well-behaved Frida. Sensible Frida.

I run to the bathroom, where I vomit long and hard, a

cold sweat breaking out on my brow. I kneel there, on the cold bathroom floor, shaking and crying at what I was, what I have forgotten and remembered. At what I have done. Because I remember what I saw on the news. NeoStar's 'game changer', all those people, dying to open that email at 7 p.m. And I can imagine only too well what Anteros is planning.

$$\longrightarrow$$

I don't know how long I sit there, my eyes glazed over, my breathing shallow, my pulse pounding hard. I just know that eventually my heart rate slows, a calm comes over me and, from somewhere deep inside me, something else wakes up. I stand shakily, and turn on the tap, splashing cold water on my face, then swallowing cold gulps of it. I have to visit my flat. Because another memory has come back, one hidden long ago.

I lock up Dan's flat, and head for home, carrying the protection spell in my pocket. I can't let Anteros know I've woken up – the only advantage I have right now is that they think I'm no threat. When I get back to the flat, I place my phone on the bedside table – let them think I'm still wallowing under my duvet. Then I head to the storeroom to find the box Bryony gave me. I move aside a slinky, a Barbie dressed in combat uniform, and a Polly Pocket doll. Nothing.

I go through the box, removing everything: dolls, comics, sticker albums, teddy bears. I know it is here. It must be here. Bryony brought me the box just after all this started, and that can't be just coincidence. I'm about to give up when I see something glinting in the flap of the base. I tease it out with my finger, then pick up it, dangling it from my hand. It's actually here. My gold necklace. The heart-shaped pendant, with an arrow shot through it.

I walk to the mirror in the hall and with shaking hands I fasten the necklace around my neck. It seems to glow on my skin, and, above it, the face that looks back at me in the mirror is pale, but determined. Anteros thinks the mortal race are puppets. He thinks he can twist us up until we're all like him, vengeful and hate-filled and black inside. I touch the golden heart.

I have to show him that he's wrong.

$$\longrightarrow$$

Back at Dan's, I stand in front of the sketch of Anteros. He looks confident, insouciant. He looks like he's enjoying himself. Then I turn to the other drawing Dan made. It's me, and yet it's not me. There's a light shining from those eyes that I don't recognise. A power that I don't have. I sigh. It's the Frida Dan was expecting to find, but it's not the person I am. He overestimated me. And it backfired on him, badly. I feel a stab of shame as I think about Dan, locked up somewhere in NeoStar, because of my weakness.

I shake my head. I'd better make a start. I sit at the table and re-examine the contents of the box Dan left me. If there's one thing all these books have taught me it's that being a hero involves props. If you're Heracles or Jason,

Perseus or Odysseus, you get a magic harp, a golden fleece or a celestially bequeathed sword. What have I got?

One by one, I empty out the contents of the box. I've got Ophiotaurus bombs, to use against Anteros and the guards. I've got the powder to destroy the arrow's power. What else? I take out the contact lenses and turn them around, mystified. Are these a disguise, or what? I turn the vial upside down and see the words 'Blocks 100% of harmful rays' printed on the base. 'But what harmful rays am I going to encounter inside a building?' I wonder aloud, and then stop short as something really, really terrible occurs to me.

No. It couldn't be. It's not possible. Except that, of course, according to my new reality, pretty much anything is. 'Oh shit,' I say, placing the lenses aside with a queasy stomach.

I pick up the only other clue I have, the scribbled note. I've already figured that Arrow=200 might mean the 200th floor. But GODS? That's a tad vague. And what does 'Laerdroia' even mean? I grab Dan's laptop and search for the word but it doesn't return anything meaningful at all. Puzzled, I close the lid. Something is nagging at my brain. I feel sure I've seen that word somewhere before. On a hunch, I check the book pile, and then every book on every shelf, running my fingers down the spines. Nothing.

I take a deep breath, close my eyes and try to picture where I have seen the word before. Something flashes into my mind and I realise why I can't find the book. It was the one Dan was reading the night he was kidnapped.

'Please be here, please be here, please be here,' I mutter to myself as I search the lounge. I move all the sofa cushions,

244

check the coffee table. Nothing. Then I see it, a tiny corner of its pale blue spine sticking out from under the armchair.

I fish the book out, and sit cross-legged with it on my lap. Not 'Laerdroia', but 'Caerdroia'. (I must remember to tell Dan he has terrible handwriting.) With shaking hands I open the book to the 122nd page. I think I actually hear my jaw fall open. Because there it is, the security system to beat all security systems.

The Cretan Labyrinth.

Chapter 34

I spend the next hour tracing a path through a scan I've made of the maze. That will be my map. Then, stretching my aching limbs, I finally head to the kitchen, where I find a bag of pasta and an unopened jar of pesto. I cook the pasta, staring into space, thinking about Dan. I miss him. I know I hardly knew him. I know what I felt for him wasn't based on anything real. How could it have been, amongst all the confusion, and fear, and certain-death scenarios? But I wish so badly that he was here, that I had listened to something else inside of me instead of my fear and paranoia. Instead of Psyche.

I eat pasta covered in the oily basil and parmesan, and, as the comfort food soothes me, I think about what I'm going to do. It's my destiny to destroy the arrow. Dan left me the ingredients I need to do that, which means he believed I could do it. I just wish I had his confidence in me. When I went into the Underworld, I was following an existing story and I had Psyche to guide me – and even then I very nearly didn't make it out. This is different. There is no precedent for what I am about to do.

But it's not just that. Even though I now have an idea of what I'm going to face when I'm up on the 200th floor, I still don't know how to access it. There's not a single scrap of information about the layout of the NeoStar building online. I've found the architects who built it, a huge global company called Armstrong, and if I could just get hold of their blueprints, I might find something I can use. But of course they don't put their building plans on their website for just anyone to see.

I fork up some pasta. I wonder what they're feeding Dan. Whether he's okay. I feel sick at the thought that he might not be. He could be in pain, scared. I have to get into that building. It's Wednesday evening. The email goes out at 7 p.m. tomorrow. I've only got twenty-four hours to do this. I push the bowl away, close my eyes and try to clear my mind of the mounting panic.

I think about my life. How Psyche stole my father away before he could prepare me properly for what I am meant to do. Her scornful words ring in my ears: *You don't belong in the world of magic.* And she's right, I don't. I belong in the world of law, the world of business, the world of money and justice and power and really, really good hair.

My eyes fly open as an idea hits me. Then why not use who I am? I have an address book bursting with grateful clients. There must be one of them who can get me some information about NeoStar that will help me infiltrate that building.

Once I have the idea, I'm convinced there's something in it. I immediately access my work contacts via Dan's laptop and start cross-referencing my clients and their ex and new spouses against NeoStar to see if there are any links. It takes several hours that I really don't have, but after going through my entire list, I've got three potential leads.

My recent client and happy customer Linda is best friends with the woman who runs the catering company that occasionally manage NeoStar corporate internal events. Roy, whose divorce was one of the first I handled after launching my practice, has a lovely new wife who works for a chain of florists that are an authorised supplier to NeoStar. But it's the third name that sends a flutter of excitement through me. This woman's husband works for a company that is a subsidiary of the architects who built NeoStar.

This one could be the key.

There's only one problem. She isn't actually a client any more. She's reconciling with her husband, and I'm going to need her to betray him.

I get up and grab my coat. I'll just have to hope that Oona is ready for the truth.

→

When I knock on her door, my heart is racing. And then, there she is, all pink and glowing, as though fresh from a spa.

'Frida!' says Oona. 'What are you doing here?' She glances down at her watch – Tiffany, if I'm not mistaken – and widens her eyes at the time. 'Did we have an appointment?'

'No,' I say. 'Listen, are you alone?'

'Well, no,' she says. 'Robert is working late,' a shadow crosses her face at this, 'but the children are upstairs. Why?'

'Can I come in? I have something I need to tell you.'

She bites her lip, politeness vying with discomfort, but being a well-bred sort politeness wins, as I was gambling it would. I follow Oona into a grand living room. A piano in the corner. Tasteful landscapes on the walls. The soft tinkling of classical music. Everything perfect, it occurs to me, just like a stage set.

'Would you like some tea, coffee?' Oona asks.

'Coffee would be great,' I say with enthusiasm.

Oona goes into the kitchen, speaks in a low voice to the help. When she returns her tone is civil, but guarded.

'So, Frida, how can I help you?'

I swallow. 'How are things between you and Robert?'

'Things are better. We're working through our differences.'

'Right.' I thought as much. She's giving me the same soundbite she'll be offering to her friends. I knew she wasn't ready. She's still deluding herself. Damn.

I don't have any time to mess around. I take a deep breath.

'Oona, I'm here because certain aspects of your husband's behaviour have come to light that you were not previously aware of. While I respect that you want to patch things up,

I wonder whether you might like to hear the full facts before you make that decision.'

Oona looks startled. 'Well, no,' she says. 'I mean, we have agreed that we will put it all behind us, so what good would it do, raking it all up again?' I hear Robert in those words and I frown. There's a long silence. I bite my tongue.

'Well, what sort of facts?' she asks after a minute of awkwardness.

'It's delicate,' I say. 'You might find this upsetting. I need to make sure you really want to know.'

She looks unsure, but I know she's hooked. Impossible not to ask the questions after I have dangled the bait. Her suffering is etched on her face, the sight of it appals me, but I have to do this. I have no choice.

'Just tell me what you've come to tell me,' she says flatly.

I take a deep breath. 'The young woman your husband was seeing at work. She wasn't the first. There have been at least two others before her.'

Oona turns from porcelain to pale. She blinks, wets her lips with her tongue, a nervous gesture that hurts my heart to watch. I remind myself again that the fate of the world is at stake.

'When did you say you had reconciled with Robert?'

'On the Saturday after I visited your office.'

I meet her eyes, my face serious. 'I'm afraid to tell you that Robert was with the young woman in question again on that Sunday evening, and on the Monday morning.'

Oona sucks in a breath. 'How do you know that?'

'It is my practice to track the spouses of my clients to

250

gain information that might be helpful in court. This occurred before our informal meeting in the gallery, where you changed your mind about going ahead with divorce proceedings.'

I'm only half lying. I do usually hire a PI but only once my clients have signed to it. But who needs an investigator trailing Oona's husband when you've got an indiscreet young woman's social media pages to browse through?

'Monday morning?' Oona says, her voice faint, and I know what's she's thinking, because I planted the thought there. Oona was having lunch with her husband hours after he'd fucked his younger woman.

'Are you sure?' she asks.

'I am. I'm sorry, Oona,' I say. 'I understand your hopes for a reconciliation, but I felt that you deserved to know the truth rather than continue under a false impression.' I hold my breath. It's a gamble. What I'm doing is entirely unethical, and if she directs her anger at me, and not her cheating scumbag of a husband, then all is lost.

'He told me it was over between them.' Her voice is small, little more than a whisper.

I nod.

'Why lie to me, why tell me that, when I already knew?'

'Because he thought that he could have his cake and eat it.' I look around. 'You look after this lovely house, you take care of the kids, you represent stability and comfort and the acceptable face of an affluent life. He doesn't want to give that up, but he also wants to have sex with other people. He knows you won't put up with that, so he lies.' I meet her eyes. 'Robert is thinking only about himself. It's time you did too, Oona.'

I'm pushing it now. I really need her to go for this, and I'm telling her the truth. But sometimes, often, the truth is too much and too soon.

'Why are you telling me this?' she asks, bristling. 'Is it because you want my business? Because it is extremely inappropriate. You must know that.' I hear in her voice the anger that I have been waiting for.

'I don't need your case, Oona.' I gaze at her frankly. 'I'll level with you. I'm telling you because I like you, and I don't want you to waste any more of your life on someone who doesn't care for you. And also because I need you to do something that will seem like a betrayal of trust, and I wanted you to understand that your husband is not a trust-worthy man.'

There's a pause. 'And what is it you want me to do, exactly?'

I take a breath. Here goes. 'I need Robert's password to his work's intranet.' Oona blinks at me. 'I know it sounds mad,' I say, 'but it's life and death that I have it, otherwise I would never have come here and said these things to you.'

Oona looks at me for a long time. Then she gets up.

'I think you should leave.'

'Oona,' I say hurriedly, 'you don't understand—'

Her stare is all ice. 'I understand that you have used my situation to take advantage of me,' she says, dignified in her anger. 'And I have quite enough of that going on, wouldn't you say?'

→

I walk from Oona's house, brooding over my words. I messed up royally. What kind of a hero am I anyway? What would Psyche have done in my place? Knocked Oona out and searched the house? Tied her to a chair and interrogated her? Probably. Perhaps I should have done the same. *You have used my situation to take advantage of me.* I shake my head. I should have been more careful, I shouldn't have told her the truth about her husband. I know better than to force things like that. What came over me? I pull my jacket closer around me and mull over what my next move could possibly be, when I feel a hand on my shoulder.

'Frida!'

I swing around, and stare at Oona in surprise.

'I'm glad I caught you,' she says, panting. She holds out her hand. In her palm lies a red flash drive.

'It's everything from Robert's hard drive. I copied it last week when ... well, you know. There's a list of passwords on there, maybe it'll be amongst them. The file itself is password protected but I cracked it.' She sighs. 'It's his own name with a zero for the o and a 3 for the e.'

'Of course it is.' I try to muffle a snort of laughter at this and fail. Oona gives a wan, resigned smile.

'Thank you,' I say, taking the memory stick. 'You don't know what you've done.'

She shrugs. 'I knew he was lying, you know. But I was willing to play along with it. And you took that opportunity away from me.'

'I'm sorry, Oona—'

'No.' She holds up her hands. 'I haven't been happy in this marriage for years. I love the house, the security, the prestige. But I don't love Robert, not really. I don't know if I even like him very much. I didn't want to accept that, but after what you just said,' she shakes her head, gives a gentle laugh, 'it's like I woke up.'

A chill runs through me. The power of the arrow, it's still inside me, faint, but there. It can change the way people feel. I shiver with the knowledge.

'Thank you.'

She nods, looking sad, but somehow more at ease in that sadness than I've seen her yet. 'I have to go.' She turns, and then stops, looks back at me. 'It's an odd question, but, does this have anything to do with the man I saw you with?'

'The man?'

'Yes, you were in the gallery with that dark-haired man. I saw you both together, as you walked in. You looked so very different, Frida. You looked ... happy. Real happiness. You don't realise that it exists until you see it for yourself.'

A lump forms in my throat. Do. Not. Cry. 'Yes,' I say, getting the words out with difficulty. 'It's connected to him, in a way.'

'Well, I hope you find what you're looking for, Frida.'

'I hope so, too.' I almost turn and then remember. 'Oona, please will you do me one more favour? On Valentine's Day, after 7 p.m., don't open any emails. Just stay offline and make sure your kids stay offline too. Please?'

254

She frowns at me, her expression searching. But eventually she shrugs and says softly, 'Okay.'

As I head back to Dan's flat I send Bryony a hurried text, warning her of a powerful virus that's doing the rounds and advising her not to open any emails for the next 24 hours. Back at Dan's I insert the drive into his laptop. I access the password list, and then I'm straight on to Robert's intranet. A few polite email requests from 'Robert Simpson', and, bingo, I'm granted temporary access to the parent company's archives. And here are the blueprints. The schematics. The plans. But it's a very specific area I want to know about and as I search, anxiety floods through me. Will I really find it here? Would they trust any mortal to know that there even is a 200th floor? Maybe they would, if they knew they could simply wipe their brain afterwards.

I have to believe the answer is here. I make countless cups of coffee and plough through hundreds of documents, but nothing seems to match what I am after. I'm about to give up when something catches my eye. Just one line of text. It could mean anything, but . . .

I read the words again, just to make sure, and then I think about the note Dan left. 'GODS'. That's it. It has to be. And I smile. Because now I know how to get up to the 200th floor.

Chapter 35

It's almost two weeks since I last approached the giant revolving door of NeoStar. As I head towards it now, preparing myself for what's to come, I'm reminded of that other Frida. So ambitious, so determined to make a good impression on the NeoStar bigwigs.

So utterly clueless.

Back then, I was in force-to-be-reckoned-with Frida mode. Or so I thought. This time, my own mother wouldn't recognise me. As I walk through the door, I see Mandy at reception and the horror comes rushing back. I swallow hard and paste on a smile. I need to keep my nerve.

'Hi,' I say in a high girlish voice completely unlike my own. 'I have a delivery.' The large tote bag I'm carrying over my shoulder holds four long, slim boxes. I take one out with a flourish. 'Roses,' I say conspiratorially. 'It's the day for it, after all!'

'Which floor?' asks Mandy, robotic as ever.

'There are a few, actually,' I say, smiling in the face of her frosty manner. 'Are you Mandy?'

She looks at me with more interest now. 'Yes, why?'

I give her my best full-wattage smile. 'I have a dozen pink roses for a Mandy Moran on the main reception.'

I hand the box to her, watching her icy façade melt fractionally as she opens it. 'They're very pretty,' she says cautiously, reaching out and touching one of the soft coral petals.

'Aren't they!' I practically squeal. 'The card will tell you who they're from.' I wait patiently as she finds the printed note that bears the name of Megan, her married lover, with a message reading: 'I'll call you later'. An expression of triumph crosses her face and I give silent thanks to Linda for this piece of gossip passed on by one of the catering staff.

'I also have deliveries for Irene Kowalski on 55, a Teddy Smith on 90 and a Clare O'Hara on 105.' Nothing on the higher floors. I don't want to alert any suspicion.

Distractedly, Mandy takes a security card and plugs it into the USB on her laptop. Her eyes keep travelling back to the flowers.

'Name please?'

'Sasha Jones,' I say. 'From Secret Garden Florists.' I point at the company logo on my shirt. God bless Roy for his speedy, no-questions-asked response to my random request. She quickly searches for the name online, confirms that I am who I say I am, taps a few keys and prints out

257

a pass. She's so keen to get back to her roses, she hasn't noticed that the real Sasha Jones is fuller in the face and a slightly lighter shade of blonde than the woman standing in front of her.

Mandy hands me a pass. 'You'll need this to access each of the floors using either the stairs or the lift. Please return it to me and sign out before you leave.'

As I queue to get through reception, I see to my dismay that it's the same security guard who was on duty the day they locked me in the meeting room. I hold my breath as the X-ray machine scans my bag, praying the protection spell will conceal what I need it to, then I flash the guard a broad smile as I walk through and collect the bag. Just another Valentine's Day at the office.

I get in the lift, making no eye contact with the two men waiting with me, and press 5, 5, star. The two men get out on 14 and, as I wait to arrive at my floor, I stare at my reflection. Blonde wig. Red lipstick. Blue contacts. Florist uniform. Perfect customer-is-always-right smile. And a NeoStar pass on a lanyard around my neck. So far, so good.

On the fifty-fifth floor, I get out of the lift, swipe in, and walk to acquisitions, where I hand a box to the first person I see, asking him to pass them on to a Ms Kowalski. I've sent them from her long-distance partner who lives in another continent and will remain uncontactable until seven this evening, by which time, either I'll have destroyed the arrow or none of this will matter anyway. I shake my head. No point thinking like that.

Aiming for an air that is efficient but unhurried, I head

back the way I came and take the lift to 90. There, I hand the third box of flowers (from 'a secret admirer!') to a nearby receptionist to deliver to the lucky Teddy, then head back to the lifts. I let a full lift go, then get in to the next one. With a pounding heart, I key in 199, and then hold down the star button. According to my research, this should give me an express ride up there. As the lift ascends at some speed, I watch the numbers tick upwards. My heart feels as though it is going to burst. When it stops with a jolt at 199 I reach for the door hold button but before I can touch it, the door begins to open.

I keep my eyes on the carpet. As the door slides across, I watch with horror out of the corner of my eye. I can't believe it. It's the worst kind of coincidence. Except, of course, there's no such thing.

It's Clive, deep in conversation with a woman with a grey chignon. The pair don't even glance at me. I try not to look at them but I can't help it, my gaze is pulled to their reflection in the mirror. My skin crawls as I watch Clive speaking. I see it now clearly, even in his mortal guise, the terrible thing underneath that smile. Something deeply corrupted. I look at the woman. She, too, does not look mortal, her eyes are shark-like, and when she speaks I see her teeth are rodent-sharp.

I fix my eyes down, and try to remember to breathe. Come on, Frida, I think to myself. Just don't give them any reason to notice you. The lift is almost back down at the 190th floor, when:

'I think you've made a mistake.'

I look up slowly. 'I'm sorry,' I say in my fake high voice. 'What do you mean?'

Clive gives that mirthless smile again. He nods at my bag, which still contains one box. 'Nobody wants those up here.'

I pout and reach into the bag. My fingertips brush the box, containing not roses but the Ophiotaurus bombs, as I pull out a piece of paper and pretend to check it. Then I put my hand to my forehead and give a girlish giggle. 'Oh my gosh! Yes, you're right,' I say. 'I read it wrong! They're actually for Lisa May on 99. Oh dear. Silly me, Valentine's Day gets me so giddy! It's such fun, isn't it?'

Clive and Grey Chignon exchange a look of malicious amusement. 'It will be this year,' Grey Chignon says. I see, then, how it really is just a game to them, and I can feel the anger rising inside me. Keep calm, Frida, I tell myself. I don't want to use the bombs unless I absolutely have to, although right now I would like nothing better than to knock Clive onto his oddly shaped arse.

Instead, I keep my sugar-frosted, inane smile intact until the lift arrives at 190 with a gentle bump. As the lift door slides open Grey Chignon steps out. Clive does not. I smile at him, and make a deliberate point of pressing 99, giving another silly giggle. Clive casts one more glance back at me, shakes his head, and leaves the lift. The door closes and I let out a long shaky breath.

I'm alone again.

I let the lift travel down thirty floors, then I type in 199 again and keep my finger on the star button. The lift zooms back up and, this time, when I hold the door closed it stays closed.

'Okay,' I say to myself. 'Quickly.' I take a deep breath and try to remember what I read. *Exclusive access is gained upon entry of a six-digit code.* A small scrap of information, I can only pray it means what I think it does. I stare at the panel. A six-digit code. How many different combinations does that give me? I bite my lip. No point thinking about that. Either what I suspect is right or . . . this is over.

I type in the numbers, surprised to find my hand isn't shaking: 7, 1, 5, 4, 1, 9.

7, 15, 4, 19.

G. O. D. S.

For a moment, nothing happens. I'm sure my heart really does stop then. If this code is wrong, then this whole thing is over before it has begun. Then I realise: I haven't pressed the star key. I reach out – this time my hand *is* shaking – and I touch the button carefully, almost reverently. Immediately, the lift hums and ascends rapidly, leaving my stomach back down on 199. I swallow hard. This is it, then. No going back now.

When the lift door opens, it's onto a white corridor. At the end of the corridor is a white door. I can't believe it. It worked. I did it! Somewhere through this door is Dan. The arrow. And Anteros.

I screw up my courage and step out of the lift.

Chapter 36

The room beyond the door is completely empty, except for an enormously grand stone statue looming above the only exit. I approach it, gazing up in awe. It's a tremendous piece of ancient art, with the head of a woman, the wings of a large bird, and the haunches of a lion, one planted each side of the door. I reach for the handle and—

'I am the Sphinx,' the statue roars. 'No man shall pass.'

Jerking and scrambling backwards, I stare up at the creature, open mouthed. Oh dear. Not a statue at all, then, but a real living Sphinx. Jesus! How come Dan didn't think to warn me about that?

Then I get a flashback of the camel. Oh.

The beast regards me.

'You shall not pass,' it says in a voice that's dry and crumbly as old stone. I feel myself trembling and quickly scold myself. Snap out of it, Frida. You've faced a three-headed hell beast. Don't let this thing rattle you.

'Well, I sort of need to be somewhere,' I say, aiming for a breezy tone. 'I've got a meeting with Anteros.' I gesture past the beast. 'If you could just let me—'

'YOU MAY NOT PASS,' it booms. 'Unless . . .'

'Unless?'

'Unlesssss . . . you answer a riddle.'

'I'll be honest, nobody told me anything about a riddle.'

'Do you accept?' the creature asks, implacable.

I look around. There's no way out of this room but through this door.

'What happens,' I ask, 'if I get it wrong?'

As I watch, the beast opens its mouth, displaying two rows of pointed teeth, then snaps its jaws shut. There's my answer.

What the hell. 'Okay,' I say. 'I accept the challenge.'

The Sphinx smiles, like it's just seen dinner arriving. There's a long, dramatic pause before it speaks.

'Here is the riddle,' it begins. 'What has four rooms, but no roof? Two entrances, but many ways to exit? Can be broken, open or closed? Can be full, but if ever found empty, will become a mere tomb?'

There's another long silence. I realise the riddle is finished.

I bite my lip. 'How long do we have?' Probably I should have asked that before I started. The Sphinx just stares at me. It's enjoying this, I can tell.

'Okay,' I say, 'forget it.' I start to run over the information. 'Four rooms, but no ceiling. Okay, what has rooms?

263

A tepee? A tepee doesn't have a ceiling, does it? And um . . . a tent can be closed or open?'

The Sphinx is licking its lips. Its teeth are sharp little daggers and its eyes are dead pebbles in its dusty face. I wonder when it last had a meal.

'No, not a tent,' I say hurriedly. 'That's not my answer. I dunno, a bungalow? No, that has a roof.'

I try to calm my hammering heart and review the information. 'Four rooms. One way in, but many ways to exit. An exit – a way out like, what?' I can't think of anything, my mind is blank. I remember something I read, about the riddle told to Oedipus. The thing about these riddles is they don't mean what you think they mean. So maybe a room is not really a room, in this instance. What else can a room be? What else has entrances and exits?

I have no idea.

I move onto the next part. 'What can be broken? What can be open? What can be closed?' I shake my head. 'A bottle of wine? A set of venetian blinds? A . . . ' I'm running out of time. My heart is skittering so loudly I fear the beast will hear it. I sense from the expression on its face that it knows I'm not going to get the riddle. I realise dimly that I am rubbing the heart pendant between my thumb and forefinger, an anxious, unconscious gesture.

And then it comes to me.

I run through the question again. *Four rooms but no roof?* The heart has four chambers. *Two entrances, but many ways out.* That could be the two atrium, many ways out, many ways to die. *Can be broken, open or closed.*

264

Broken hearted, open hearted, closed hearted, yes, that works. *Can be full, but if ever found empty, will become a mere tomb.* An empty heart has no blood pumping through it, which means it has stopped. And also, an empty heart is a loveless heart, like a tomb. Practical *and* poetic. Nice.

I face the Sphinx.

'Do you have an answer?'

I can tell by the slavering look it gives my thighs that it's pretty sure I don't.

'Yes,' I say.

The beast blinks its dusty eyes. Then it grins, a merciless smile of greed and cruelty and hunger. 'What is your answer?'

'A heart,' I say. And then, a little louder: 'The answer to the riddle is a heart.'

The Sphinx rears towards me, hissing, and I stumble back. Oh God, I was too hasty. I've got it wrong. This is where it ends.

Chapter 37

When I open my eyes, the beast has settled back down, and the exit door is open. Breathing out a huge sigh of relief, I run through the doorway before the creature can change its mind and eat me anyway.

As I enter the next room, I have to stop and wait for my eyes to become accustomed to the gloom. A couple of lamps shed a feeble glow onto the deep red walls. Some lazy, woozy jazz is coming from somewhere. As my eyes adjust, I see a bar running along one wall, a line of optics and glasses hanging above it. There's a woman, on a stool, her back to me. And on the back wall, lit by a corona of white, there's another door. The door I need to get to.

'Hello?'

The woman swivels around on her stool and surveys me with amusement. I recognise her immediately. Why wouldn't I? They have a picture of her decapitated head on the wall of the boardroom downstairs. I had suspected she was here, but I'd been praying I was wrong. No such luck.

I approach slowly, making sure I don't look her in the eye. Medusa holds a cherry on a stick in one hand and a cocktail in the other. Out of my peripheral vision, I see the snakes undulating around her head, rhythmic and menacing. When she sees me, she laughs, and stirs her drink with her cherry, and then slowly, deliberately, inserts the cherry into her mouth and bites it.

'Company!' she says. 'Wonderful. Come, have a drink.'

I let out a sigh. What is it with these mythological types, always wanting you to hang out with them?

'I'm in a bit of a hurry, actually.'

Medusa smiles. It's hard to judge without seeing her eyes, but I don't think it's a friendly smile. The snakes start to hiss in unison and the gorgon puts a hand to her head, the quick, coquettish pat of a debutante, causing the snakes to calm and fall back in waves.

'Have a drink with me,' she says. 'I insist. And, please, dear, there's no need to keep staring at the floor like that.' I watch out of the corner of my eye as she touches a finger to the spectacles she's wearing and tap, taps her nail on the clear glass. 'Protective lenses. Completely safe. You won't come to any harm while I'm wearing these.'

Giving in – there's no way I'll be getting past her if I don't do as she wishes – I walk over to the bar and take a seat facing her, keeping a tight grip on my bag. As she fixes me a cocktail, I look at her properly. She takes my breath away. Firstly, of course, there are the snakes. About two dozen of them, of varying thickness, every pair of beady eyes trained on me. She wasn't born this way. I read about her. She was beautiful once. The snakes were a punishment from a goddess for impurity, and I see that Medusa has been cursed, not only with the mother of all bad hair days, but with skin covered with scales. Her eyes are the yellow marbles of a python, one black slit for a pupil. She's wearing a tight snake-print satin cat suit, zipped down to reveal a Grand Canyon of cleavage, and is sporting wickedly high snakeskin stiletto boots. Yeah, I think, why not make a feature of it?

'I thought you were supposed to be dead?' I say.

'And I thought you were supposed to have lost your memory?' she returns, a snake snapping in time with her words. Then she shrugs, smiles and deftly mixes and hands me a cocktail. 'You read that I was beheaded by Perseus?' she asks. 'Pah! The mortals always like to believe they will triumph in the end. It's a story they tell themselves. That they can banish the monsters. That good defeats evil.' She reaches for a packet of cigarettes and lights one with a shiny silver lighter, then sucks in a lungful of smoke. 'They're just stories.'

'You were a mortal once, Medusa,' I say. 'Didn't you used to want good to win over evil?'

She narrows her eyes and blows smoke into my face. 'That was a long time ago now.'

'I need to go through that door,' I say, nodding my head to that beckoning rim of light. 'I need to stop Anteros.'

Medusa raises an eyebrow. 'You know I'm not going to

allow that.' She pours straight gin into her glass, tips more into mine.

'Why are you protecting him? Wasn't it the gods who did this to you?'

She laughs, and the jagged sound sends the snakes into a frenzy. 'My dear, that's exactly why I'm protecting him. Anteros is not on the side of the gods. He has formed his own tribe. And once he's destroyed the human race with that arrow,' she smiles bitterly, 'the gods are next.' I stare at her. Her eyes are green, yellow, orange, black. Her gaze is a fire.

'You can't trust him.'

'You don't understand,' she says. 'You are brave, but also foolish. You should leave now, while you can.'

'I can't leave.'

She shrugs and reaches a hand to her glasses and says, sadly, 'Then you must die.'

'No!' I grab her hand. As I make contact with her skin – the arrow, it's close, it's lending me its power – I feel her emotions full strength. I get it all. The true horror of what happened to her that day so long ago.

She was serving as a priestess of Athena and had sworn to remain a virgin. But Poseidon found Medusa in Athena's temple and, overcome with lust, raped her. Athena then punished Medusa for being defiled, cursing her so that anyone who looked directly upon her would be instantly turned to stone, dooming Medusa to be alone for ever. She was so scared, she felt so wretched, she thought she deserved it. Now she just wants revenge. She burns for it. Would let millions die for it . . .

I jerk backwards and let go of Medusa's arm. She stares at me, shocked. I stare back at her, equally appalled.

'What did they do to you?' I whisper.

Medusa's face is impassive. She shrugs. 'This is their nature. We are nothing but animals to them.'

'Medusa,' I say, 'who do you think incited Poseidon to attack you?'

She frowns.

'Remember how Anteros made Apollo fall in love with Daphne, just because Apollo criticised his archery prowess?'

'Poor Daphne,' Medusa murmurs. 'She did make such a lovely tree, though.'

'And how he fired an arrow at Actaeon's heart, so that he gazed on Artemis when she was bathing, and she turned him into a stag and he was eaten by his own hounds?'

'Yes, so what?'

'It's always Anteros. Whenever anything horrific is done in the name of passion, he's to blame!'

'No,' she says.

'Yes.' I feel the power of the arrow and I push the thought, feeling her emotions, and an ability, faint but definitely there, to make her see the truth. 'Have you forgotten that he's a god? That violence is his nature, too? He manipulates people. We are all just his puppets.'

Her emotions are tumultuous. She might sense that I am telling the truth, but she clings to her lust for revenge like a lifeline.

'Medusa, listen to me. I know that I'm just a stupid mortal. And I don't know how this world works. But I can only tell you what I just felt. Athena cursed you, but it is your hatred, your fear, your rage and lust for vengeance that keeps you trapped like this. And Anteros is using that for his own means, just like he uses everyone's unhappiness.'

She shakes her head, the snakes whirl, their eyes bore into my skull.

'I'll never rest until Athena is suffering as much as I have suffered!'

I touch her hand and give it everything I've got. 'You're poisoning yourself, Medusa. Every day that you relive it, you attack yourself again. Please, let it go.' I feel it, a shift, like a change in energy. Medusa stares at me and, to my amazement, the colour of her eyes begins to change, from black yellow to warm hazel. It's working! I'm curing her!

Then her snakes rear up, and they dart into her face, jabbing her with tiny vicious bites. Medusa blinks and, just as quickly, her eyes are blazing fire again, and her face is stiff with anger. She throws off my hand. 'You think your little parlour games will work on me?' she snarls. 'You don't know who you're dealing with.'

She lifts her glasses and hits me with the full glare of her petrifying gaze.

Chapter 38

And . . . nothing.

Medusa stares at me, blazing with anger. The snakes droop dolefully around her head. 'Why aren't you stone?' she booms.

I tap my temples, blessing Dan for his forethought. 'UV blocking contacts. Apparently they work on whatever it is you've got going on, too.'

The gorgon sinks back down onto her bar stool and picks up her drink. 'I should rip your eyes out,' she says, but it's lacklustre.

'I'm sorry,' I say. 'It's nothing personal. I just don't want to be turned into a statue. I mean, not in this outfit, anyway. How embarrassing.'

This doesn't raise a smile. 'He's through there,' she says dully, inclining her head to the doorway. 'Your lover boy. He's chained up in the Labyrinth. That's what you've come for, really, isn't it? Not the arrow. Stupid humans, following their hearts to the death for what they think is love.'

I'm already heading for the door. When I get there, I turn back. Medusa is pouring herself another drink, her posture defeated.

'Thank you,' I say.

She turns to me then and her eyes are hard. 'Don't thank me,' she says. 'When you find out what he's got planned for you, you'll wish I had turned you to stone.'

As Medusa turns away, I open the door and step through from the darkness to the light.

$$\longrightarrow$$

My first impression – and one that will endure throughout – is that the Labyrinth is torture. A thousand fluorescent bulbs cast a forensic light over hundreds of corridors of stark white stone. I knew what to expect, but even so, I'm daunted. There is something repulsive about this place, its absolute lack of colour, its unrelenting passages. I open the last box in my bag and, buried under the protection spell, I find a ball of red string. I take hold of one frayed end and tie it to the door handle. I need to trace my route, for when Dan and I leave.

IF you leave, a little voice nags but I push it away. Returning to the box, I take out the map and pen, then quickly mark my location with an X. I can't afford to get lost. There are no landmarks here. No identifying signs. Just wall after wall, each one blurring into the next.

Then I begin to walk, the red thread unspooling behind

me. 'Forwards, and then turn right,' I mutter to myself. 'Left again, forwards then next right.' All I can think about is making the next turn, ticking it off, checking I am exactly where I think I am. It crosses my mind that if I'd tried to come here without the map, I'd have gone insane long before I starved to death.

Each time I turn, I am met with exactly the same view. It's starting to mess with my head. Blank wall after blank wall stretching out into infinity. I feel myself starting to panic. Don't think, Frida, I say to myself, just walk. One foot in front of the other. Easy does it.

Eventually, as I track the turns, I get into a kind of hypnotic rhythm, like riding a wave. It's the arrow, I realise. The arrow is reaching out to me. I close my eyes and try to feel for it. To gain strength from it. I just want to touch it again.

As I get closer to the middle, I get a feeling. A not very good feeling. I don't think I'm the only person – thing – in the Labyrinth. Sometimes, distantly, I hear snorting, a sort of snuffling that I can't identify. I was so busy working out the route through this maze, I forgot to reread the myth. What is it that lies in wait in the Labyrinth again?

I shake my head. Nope. Not going there. I press on.

The maze is so huge and so complex that, in between navigating myself through its corridors, I have plenty of time to rehearse what I am going to say to Dan when I find him. How sorry I am. How stupid I've been. It also allows me to focus on my plan. Find the arrow. Destroy the arrow. And if Anteros or anyone else discovers us I'll use the Ophiotaurus bombs. That should buy us enough time.

Time. Time seems to be leaking away in here. I check my phone. I arrived at the NeoStar building at two and it is now almost four. How is that possible? It gives me just three hours before Anteros sends his message.

Almost there. Whatever I think I heard before, there's nothing here now but me, muttering to myself, going slightly mad. *Turn right, now left, left again straight on, now right.* I've been working my way through the maze so long that, when I turn a corner and emerge into a wide, square space, I'm taken aback.

Because he's there. It's Dan, fastened to some sort of elevated pillar.

'Dan!' I shout. My voice echoes in the emptiness. I hurry over. As I get closer I can see that there are dark circles under his eyes, a few days of stubble. He looks awful. But my heart soars. He's alive!

'Dan!'

He jerks up at the sound of my voice and his eyes are wide. He smiles and it's a wonderful thing to see. Worth everything I've gone through so far. But as I run to him, he glances over my shoulder and I see something else in his face.

Fear.

'Frida,' he says as I approach, 'you have to hide. It's coming.'

'What's coming?' I dart a look over my shoulder. 'What is it?'

The sound is getting closer now.

'The Minotaur!'

I stare at him. 'Right. Shit. That was it. Minotaur.'

Dan is laughing, I think he might be slightly hysterical. I

have to act fast. Stuffing the map into my bag with shaking hands, I step up onto the plinth. Behind me, I can hear the frothing, snorting, pounding of the beast as it approaches and realise with horror that, in tracing my route, I may have led it right to us. I grasp the ball of string and hurl it as far away from us as I can.

'For God's sake, Frida!' says Dan. 'What are you doing? Just run!'

'No,' I say shortly, in a tone that brooks no argument. I assess the situation. Dan is shackled to a metal pole with metal chains. Luckily, I've come prepared. I pull a pair of bolt cutters from the bag, and snip through the chains on his arms and his legs. Dan throws off the shackles and climbs down as I pull the map from the bag and stare at it. 'This way!' I shout and we pelt down corridor after corridor. But no matter how fast we go, that snorting, frothing threat seems only moments behind.

'Here!' I shout and we head down another corridor of blank walls. I trace us on the map, preparing to turn right, but when we do, there's nothing but a solid wall.

A dead end.

I stand there, staring around, eyes wild. 'Shit!'

Dan raises his eyebrows. 'So nice of you to rescue me, Frida,' he says drily. 'I was beginning to worry that I wasn't going to have the opportunity to be gored alive by a man-bull after all.'

'Hang on, hang on, I'm thinking,' I snap. I've only been in his company for two minutes and already he's back with the sarcasm.

'Do the bombs work on this thing?'

Dan shakes his head.

'No.' I sigh. 'Of course not. That would be too easy.' I close my eyes. There must be a way out, it cannot end like this.

We both hear it at the same time and look at each other. The slavering, steaming, terrible sound as the Minotaur rounds the corner. We've got thirty seconds, tops.

'Frida,' Dan says, grabbing my hand and pulling me to him, 'listen, I—'

I feel what he's going to say before he even starts and I make a beak with my hand and then close it. 'Stop with the pre-dying speech, please? I have a brilliant idea. The only thing is, it involves going back there and facing that thing. Okay?'

Dan nods. 'Okay.'

I smile. 'Then, let's do it.'

And so, against all instinct and common sense, we walk together, hand in hand, towards the Minotaur.

I gasp when I see it. I can't help it. It's magnificent. Covered in tawny brown fur, risen on his hind legs like a man, but with hoofs, a shaggy chest and the snorting, steaming head of a furious bull. It's about one and a half times the size of a man, and as it sees us, its black eyes seem to shine a little brighter.

I point to a gap in the wall. 'We need to be covering that,' I say in a low voice.

'Just inch over, very slowly,' says Dan. 'It gets excited by sudden movements but it can't see as well when you're still.'

We take tiny steps sideways until we are covering the opening.

'Okay,' I say. 'Now, make some noise.'

He glances at me. 'Seriously?'

'Yes.'

He shrugs. 'Come on,' bellows Dan, shooting me another glance that is equal parts terror and trust. 'Come and get it! Wooo!'

As he does so, I reach into my bag and my fingers close around something smooth and round. The Minotaur paws the ground with its hoof. I think I see steam rising from its nostrils. As it charges, I turn to the space in the wall directly behind me – what I pray passes for a door in a Labyrinth – and I cast the black pebble to the ground.

'Okay, now we stand firm,' I say, turning back around. Dan and I grip each other's hands as the slavering, crazed man-bull-beast thunders towards us. In a few seconds, we'll almost definitely be impaled on its terrible horns. Dan squeezes my hand even harder and I feel what he's feeling. Every atom in him is screaming to get out of here.

'Don't move,' I say to him, through gritted teeth. 'Just wait.'

The Minotaur bears down on us now, it wants to tear us apart, wants to feel the flesh rip under its power. I feel this coming off it, intense, sickening, its desire to destroy is so strong. I have to drag my focus away from its mesmeric hatred. I have to hold my nerve. I wait until we can almost feel the bull's manic breath on our faces and then . . .

'Now!'

We spring apart as the Minotaur, propelled under his own terrible momentum, thunders into the gap in the wall that has been transformed into the opening to the Underworld. The descent is steep and we hear the beast struggle, legs going from under him, furious and confused at this unexpected territory. It scrambles to recover itself, turns to make another attack, and we can only watch and hope and, yes, the atoms are changing again, the air excites as, before our eyes, the doorway closes and becomes the Labyrinth once more.

Dan stares at it, at me, and at the gap again, as though the bull's head might come back through, tearing a hole in reality.

'Wow,' he says.

He turns to me, a strange look on his face.

'What?' I ask, laughing out of sheer relief that the idea worked.

He meets my eyes for a long moment. 'Nice disguise,' he says eventually, tugging at the wig.

I smile. I can hardly speak, there's so much to apologise for, my words are bottlenecking. 'Dan, listen, I'm so sorry, I—'

He makes a beak with his hand and closes it. 'Frida, you are hereby forgiven,' he says. Then he wraps his arms around me in a huge hug and I feel his emotions and I almost cry then, because they're exactly the same as mine. We stay there like that for two whole precious minutes, until I force myself to pull away.

'We don't have much time,' I say. 'I have to get to the arrow. Do you . . . ? I mean, you can leave . . . if you want? Take my pass; it'll get you out of the building.'

'What and miss all the fun?' Dan shakes his head. 'We're a team, Frida. I'm not going anywhere. Just tell me what you want me to do.'

I nod. 'I have the powder for the arrow. I'll take care of that.' I take the Ophiotaurus bombs from the bag and hand them to him. 'If anyone turns up, use these. We don't have much time. The email goes out at seven.'

'Email?' Dan asks.

'Anteros's game changer,' I say. 'You know, the one-of-a-kind gold phone that's been all over the news? I don't think it exists. The message everyone will open, hoping to find The ONE . . . Well, let's just say I think they're going to get more than they signed up for.'

Dan turns even paler. 'You think he's going to infect them with the power of the arrow?'

'I'd bet my life on it,' I say grimly.

As we trace our way through to the other side of the Labyrinth, I tell Dan everything that happened after Psyche turned up at the flat, and he tells me what he knows: he awoke tied up in the Labyrinth, only too aware that I was out there, my memories gone. Every day, he was mentally willing me to go to the café, to be given the box and remember. But he had no way of knowing whether I would.

'What, so you didn't see that bit happening?' I ask, horrified. What if I hadn't gone for a walk that day? What if Cathy had been on her break when I got there?

Dan shrugs. 'Everything that is meant to happen happens,' he says.

280

'For someone who's been tied up and thrown to a Minotaur, you're pretty philosophical.'

He just smiles at me. 'Well, you're here, aren't you?'

I feel a glow inside, then, which has nothing to do with the proximity of the arrow. 'When we get out of here,' I say, 'we are going to the café, to have a cup of coffee, and talk about normal stuff.'

'Sure,' Dan says. 'Normal stuff like . . . ?'

'The weather!' I say. 'Or TV. Or sheds!'

'Sheds?' He grins.

'Sheds!' I say.

He stops and looks at me intently. 'Frida, there is nothing I would like more in the world than to talk about sheds with you.'

For some reason this strikes me as the most romantic thing anyone has ever said to me.

'Then it's a deal,' I say. And we walk on.

Dan is weak from his time spent tied up and terrified. It takes us a long time to reach the Labyrinth's end. When eventually we find the final door, it is past six o'clock. Less than an hour until the message goes out.

I can feel the arrow. It's there, on the other side. It calls to me.

'Are you ready?' I ask.

Dan holds up the bombs in answer.

'Then let's go,' I say.

And we step through the door together.

Chapter 39

The final room is even more amazing than the last. Above us, a glass ceiling. Ahead of us, a curved glass wall. And in the centre of the room, a magnificent black marble statue, at least ten feet tall. There's no mistaking the subject. The long hair, the butterfly wings, the bright eyes that somehow seem to shine with energy. It's Anteros, poised in the act of firing an arrow. His very own altar to himself. I shake my head. It tells me everything I need to know about him. Well, everything except where he's keeping the arrow.

Dan scans the room. 'If you are right about the email, we need to look for a computer. He must have the arrow hooked up to something to harness its power.'

I nod but don't move. 'Wait,' I say. I close my eyes and tune into the arrow, quieting my heart and just letting it call to me. Its magic reaches out, like a magnetic pull.

I open my eyes. 'Over there.'

We hurry over to the other side of the room and yes, oh thank God, it's the arrow. Not connected to a computer but embedded into a huge golden throne that looks out over the city. Below, the normal bustle of metropolitan life goes on, oblivious. I can just imagine Anteros sitting here, playing with our lives, like this is his very own Olympus.

Dan approaches the throne and stares up at the arrow, eyes wide. 'Wow. It's . . . '

'Yeah,' I say vaguely, because as I turn to look at it, I only have eyes for the arrow, too, and I hardly know Dan is there. It sings to me, beguiling my senses, declaring our affinity. I reach up and caress the flight, and I feel again the power of it. I stand on my tiptoes and lift it down, slowly, reverentially, and cradle it in my arms.

'We need to be quick, Frida,' Dan says. 'You need to sprinkle the powder from flight to tip to remove its power.'

I can hear him, but he's far away, his words so small, and my body can't or won't respond. Instead, I continue to stroke the arrow, feelings its power pulsing through me.

Dan grabs my sleeve. 'Frida!' he says. 'The powder!'

I snap out of it. 'Ri . . . right, yes. The powder,' I mutter, flushing, unsure of what just happened. Focus, Frida, I tell myself. Focus!

'Maybe it would be better if you don't touch it?' Dan suggests.

'Good idea.' Placing the arrow onto the marble floor, I take out the powder. I pierce a hole in the plastic bag, and hold it over the weapon. The arrow's colour seems to change, then, as though it can sense what I am about to do, as though it is offended, appalled. My hand stops.

'Can you do this?' Dan asks.

I stare down at the arrow, wanting nothing more than to clutch it to my breast, to feel the bliss of its magic again.

'Frida!'

I blink. 'I can do it,' I say.

I kneel and shake the powder over the arrow. The first few grains trickle over the shaft of gold. That's when I hear an amused voice say: 'You know, I thought you'd be taller.'

I jerk at the sound, diverting the powder from its course so that it falls uselessly onto the marble floor. Dan and I have time to exchange a single, stricken glance, then we turn, as one, to face the mighty god of anti-love.

I've seen hundreds of images of the more famous god of love over the years, and only one of his brother. But still, when I see Anteros, I recognise him immediately, as though somehow he is intimately familiar to me. Dark, where his brother is golden haired. Strong and muscled, where his brother is slender. Brooding, where his brother is glowing. His eyes are black-brown, his hair the same colour, long and artfully unkempt. He's wearing a very sharp, very expensive suit. He is, I would be remiss not to point out, extraordinarily handsome.

I swallow hard and shake my head, trying to clear it. Where Clive's aura was repellent, Anteros's is as magnetic as the arrow's. Dangerous. I hadn't prepared myself for that.

'Frida,' Anteros says, as though we are old friends catching up, 'you made it!' His tone is as smooth and warm as hot syrup. It's only then that I notice Psyche standing a short distance behind him. By the door are four security guards, each one larger than the last. We're trapped. But it's okay. We have a plan.

I flick my eyes right.

'Now, Dan!'

Dan hurls the bombs at them and, as a cloud of dust fills the room, I bend and start scooping the powder from the floor onto the arrow, desperate to finish the job. What happens next is a jumble of confusion. Through the haze I'm dimly aware that the guards are still conscious and moving towards us. I can't see anything, just smoke and the outline of bodies. I scrabble on the floor, hearing shouts and the sound of fists hitting flesh and bone.

Hand clenched, I'm ready to throw what powder I have gathered onto the arrow, when I'm grabbed around the waist. I lash out with my foot, cracking the guard a good one on the jaw, but my limbs are instantly gripped by another guard, then another, then another. My hand is forced open, the powder falls from my right fist. I fight. I try. But it's no use. There are too many of them.

When the smoke clears, Dan and I are being held by each arm by the men in black, and Anteros is holding the arrow. I look at Dan, eyes wide.

Anteros clicks his fingers and the guards shove us roughly

onto our knees, in front of him. 'Sorry to disappoint you,' he says pleasantly. 'When I heard you had got hold of some of the old magic, I made sure that we had some counter-medicine, just in case.'

I look at Dan. He shakes his head, a tiny movement: *Don't try anything.*

Anteros takes a step towards me, leans down and lifts my chin with a finger. His touch burns me. 'I'm glad you came, Frida. You mortals are usually so flimsy. You break so easily. But not you. You're different.'

Deliberately, I turn my gaze from Anteros to Psyche. 'You believe that you can trust him?' I ask, my voice trembling. 'That he'll give you what you want? That he'll risk opening up the portal to Olympus, when Eros and Zeus are waiting on the other side? You're just as gullible now as you were back in that myth.'

Psyche's face is cold and closed and she doesn't even look at me. 'Anteros,' she says, 'we don't have time to play with the mortals. Just lock them up.'

But Anteros doesn't shift his gaze from my face. '*I* say what happens to her.' His voice is low, and dangerous.

Psyche doesn't seem alert to the threat. 'She's a liability! They both are. Just get rid of them! After the email goes out, you can—'

Languidly, Anteros flicks his hand and a guard grabs Psyche.

'What are you doing? Get your hands off me! Anteros, tell him to get his filthy hands off me!' Psyche elbows the guard in the stomach and breaks free, a second guard grabs her,

286

and she bends, twists and throws him easily to the floor. But there are a dozen more where he came from and, impressive fighting skills or not, she can't take them all.

Still Anteros doesn't look at her. He only has eyes for me. 'First things first, Frida. You've left my Labyrinth empty. When I free my Minotaur from the Underworld, he's going to need something new to hunt. Who should it be? Your Oracle or Psyche?'

I glance at Psyche. Her face is filled with anger but I see something else there now. An expression I've never seen her wear. She's frightened.

'You can't do this, Anteros. We had a deal!'

'Psyche is immortal,' Anteros says to me musingly. 'So the Minotaur could gore her again and again, and she'd still live. Don't you think that's fun? Or perhaps you'd rather see your Oracle back there? Though of course, once he is dead, he's properly dead. That's the sad thing about being mortal.'

I look at Dan.

'Frida,' he says. 'You—'

Anteros clicks his fingers and the guard gags Dan.

'No conferring,' the god says cheerfully. 'So, what will it be, Frida?'

'I won't choose.'

Anteros shrugs. 'Then I'll send both,' he says, nodding. The guards start to drag Dan and Psyche out of the room.

'No! Wait!' I say. I see the look in Dan's eye, but I can't do it, I can't sacrifice him. I won't choose her over him, not again. I think about my father – how he trusted her, how she let him die down there – and I harden my heart.

'Take Psyche,' I say.

'No,' cries Psyche, terror in her voice, all trace of bravado gone. 'No! No! Anteros, don't do this. I got you the arrow. Frida, please, you heard what this means for me, pain that will never end. Please, please don't do this!'

I meet her eyes. After everything she has been through, all the things she's seen, this terrifies her. And I feel it – the sorrow at her thwarted escape, the realisation that there are worse things than a lonely life on earth. Much, much worse. I pity her, I do, she's my family, I can't do this to her. She sees it in my face and grabs her chance.

'Frida,' she says, 'this isn't you. You're one of the good guys.'

Bad choice of words.

'Sometimes it's hard to tell the good guys from the bad guys,' I say. Dan can't look at me as Psyche is dragged away, howling loud enough to wake the dead.

'Well done, Frida,' says Anteros admiringly. He makes a gesture to the remaining guards. 'Chain him up and tie her to the throne.'

Three guards haul Dan violently over to the wall and, when he struggles to escape them, one deals him a blow that knocks him half-unconscious.

'Dan, are you okay?' I shout, but I'm being pulled away from him, forced onto the golden throne, my wrists and ankles tied, as Dan slumps, bleary-eyed, against the wall.

Anteros surveys both me and Dan with a look of great satisfaction. 'Leave us,' he says and the men in black make their exit.

A silence descends, then. In front of me, the city stretches out, lights twinkling in the darkness. Anteros comes close, the arrow in his hand sending out a hum that I can feel in my bones.

He gazes down at the weapon, and then holds it in front of me. 'Beautiful, isn't it? Do you feel its power? Do you understand, now, what it is capable of?'

I struggle against the restraints, desperate to get my hands free.

Anteros smiles. 'Soon,' he says. He reaches above me, his body brushing mine, as he places the arrow back in the throne. Then he reaches out and strokes my hair.

I squeeze my eyes shut.

'Interesting choice: the blonde, blue-eyed look. Trying to emulate someone?' He pulls the wig from my head. 'Open your eyes,' he says gently. I shake my head. 'Frida,' he says, his voice a poisonous caress, 'I don't want to have to get rough with you.'

I open my eyes. With terrible care, he removes first one blue contact, then the other.

'There,' he says. 'That's so much better. No point pretending to be something you're not, is there?' He stares at the necklace. 'What's this?' He picks up the heart and I shiver as I feel his hands against my bare skin. A frown crosses his face, and I realise he doesn't know what it is. He's never seen it before. For some reason, this gives me a spark of hope. Maybe he doesn't know everything. Maybe there is still a way.

Then he pulls the heart with a harsh jerk and the necklace

snaps and falls to the floor at the foot of the throne. 'Did you think that would protect you? A cheap chain?' He laughs. 'I'm not a vampire, that is not a cross, and, trust me, there will be no happy ending. Everything is already in place. Even if you had destroyed the arrow, you wouldn't have been able to stop it. Surely you realise that now?'

'What happens when they open the email?' I ask dully.

Anteros stares out over the city, his eyes unfocused, as though he's seeing not what is, but what will be. 'They'll go insane with love for the first thing they see,' he says. 'Possessed by the arrow's power, they'll turn on one another, consumed by their wanting. They'll attack and torture and destroy each other, in a carnival of blood and pain and horror to dwarf the Trojan War. They'll do it all for love.' He turns to me, his eyes shining. 'And it will be . . . magnificent.'

Horror fills my chest so I can hardly breathe. I knew it. I knew what he had planned, but to hear him explain it oh-so-casually, as we look out at the human world below, it's too much devastation for my heart to contain.

'You're sick,' I say.

'I'm not the one who's sick, Frida. Surely you understand that. Do you know much about your legendary grandfather, Eros? No, I don't suppose you do, only what you've seen on all those moronic displays down there. Well, let me tell you a few things. Eros was a fool. A fantasist, especially when it came to the mortals.'

I look down at my dark city, lit up with pockets of activity, people together and alone on Valentine's night. All those innocents, their phones and tablets just inches away from their fingertips. In ten minutes, Anteros's gift will change everything. I should have warned them. I should never have imagined I could stop this. *Have you heard the term 'hubris', Frida?* I think about Bryony and pray she read the text message I sent her. What will become of her, of the kids?

What will become of us all?

'Think of everything I've done as a three-thousand-year experiment,' Anteros is saying. 'If humans were meant to love purely, as Eros imagined, then nobody would be buying what I'm selling. And, yet, I'm the most successful business-man in mortal history.'

Anteros's beautiful face is filled with passion and my heart sinks. He believes everything he's saying. He's a zealot to his own cause.

'You may rail against me now, Frida, but I was fair. I gave mortals a chance. Everything I made for them – every piece of filth and debauchery I dreamed up, every paranoid thought, every affair, every betrayal, every iota of self-hatred – they had the free will to walk away from it. I was testing them. And they proved to me, to everyone, who they really are. They'll scrabble to open that email, so desperate to be the special one, the chosen one.' His eyes shine madly. 'I'll make them special.'

'No,' I say. 'Please. You can't!'

'Save your breath, Frida. The experiment is over. Love loses. It's finally time to make my presence known. In the end,' he says, 'you get the love god you deserve.'

As I stare at Anteros something snaps in me. I recognise it, dimly, as the same kind of cold fury I felt after Billy left me, not immediately after, but months down the line when all of my careful supplications and polite yet heartfelt pleas had done no good and I realised, finally, that he wasn't going to change his mind, that I had nothing left to be careful *for*. Nothing left to lose.

'That's a lovely little story,' I say. 'But you're lying to yourself if you think this is some noble truth-seeking mission. This is revenge, pure and simple.'

This hits the target. Anteros narrows his eyes.

'We didn't know you,' I press on. 'We refused to worship you. And after three millennia, there are still only a handful of people who are aware you exist. You want to be seen, to be acknowledged.' I laugh. 'You'll punish us, and then you'll – what? – reopen the portal and avenge yourself on your brother, on Zeus, all because nobody ever gave you the credit you think you deserve? It's pathetic.'

Anteros leans down to me and strokes a finger down my cheek.

'I'm glad to see such spirit, Frida. I've been following your progress for a long time. Seeing how you operate. You believe you know best. You delve into the hearts of your clients, and make them give you their secrets. I must admit, I always assumed this so-called champion would be a man, but hey,' he winks, 'I'm all for progress.'

I glare at him, hatred in my eyes. 'Bite me.'

He smiles, delighted at this. 'I should have seen it long ago. Frida McKenzie, divorce lawyer, punisher of the weak, avenger of those who are spurned in love. Look how you manipulated that poor heartbroken woman into giving away her husband's secrets. Look how well you play the game.' He leans in again, too close. His beautiful black eyes lock with mine as he whispers, 'And you enjoy it, don't you? You're just like me.'

'I'm nothing like you,' I say through gritted teeth.

'Don't resist it, Frida,' Anteros says softly, his voice a deadly caress. 'Did your pet Oracle neglect to mention the alternate meaning to the prophecy?'

A bolt of fear shoots through me.

I tell you what you need to know.

I dart a glance at Dan. There's an expression in his eyes that I can't quite read.

'I know what the prophecy says, the same as you do,' I tell Anteros, but there's a bird fluttering in my chest.

Anteros smiles. 'I don't think you do. Let me educate you. In the ancient Greek, the exact wording of the prophecy delivered by the original Oracle was, *Through the coming of a descendant of love, he who hidden reigns over the mortal world shall meet his match.*'

'In other words, I'm going to beat you,' I say, but my voice cracks. I feel uncertain. And there's that feeling again, of the ground shifting beneath my feet. Anteros leans in, so close now that I can feel his breath on my cheek, and can feel, too, the power that's coming off him, dark and terrible and, yes, seductive.

'Or,' he says, 'you're going to join me.'

I look at Dan again, and what I see in his eyes now slays

me. Because it's true. It's what he always knew. This is the secret he was keeping. That I am destined to rule with Anteros. My body begins to shake with fear.

'No!' I say. 'You're wrong. That person you described, that's not me any more. I've changed. I'm not your match.'

Anteros looks at me lovingly. 'Wrong, Frida. Look how easily you condemned your own flesh and blood to an eternity of pain. Did you show mercy? No. You are exactly like me. You just need to be reminded of your true nature.' I see, now, that he is wearing a bow, crafted from dark gold. He must have been waiting for us. This whole thing, just a trap.

He holds out his hand and the arrow flies into it from its place in the throne. This is his magic, only too eager to do his bidding. He grins. 'Finally,' he says, 'I can show your puny little world who I really am.'

I watch, frozen, as he loads the arrow into his bow and its colour changes, from honeyed gold to something much darker.

'Are you a little angry that your Oracle didn't tell you the whole truth?' he says. 'Of course you are. Well, don't worry. I'm going to make your pet the first one you kill.' He sees my horrified expression. 'Oh, didn't I mention that? Zeus and Eros's rules mean I can't kill a mortal. But you can. And once you've felt the power of the arrow, that kind of act will come very easily.'

Anteros faces me and draws the arrow back. I close my eyes. He's wrong, I don't blame Dan. I understand what he was doing. He gambled on me. He believed in the good in me. Dan. Wonderful, gorgeous Dan. Funny, exasperating

Dan. The man I could possibly have grown to love over time; the man I will soon very probably kill.

'Frida,' Anteros says, 'look at me.'

I look at him. His eyes are deep, black and ardent, filled with the madness of the lost. Then he transforms, and it's breathtaking. His huge wings unfurl in purples and blacks and greys, darkening at the edges like dye-fed flowers. I see him, clearly now, in all his godly glory: a black angel, a demon, a winged warrior of bad love.

How easy it will be for me to worship him.

Will I know who I am, when it happens? Or will I be trapped inside myself, killing for Anteros, all the while banging my fists against the inside of my mind, pleading to be released? Anteros holds the arrow taut, and I stare down the shaft, frozen in fear. I realise now that, all this time, I have been holding out for someone to rescue me. Dan or Eros. My poor dead dad or even Psyche. Surely someone will save me? Surely it can't end like this?

But as I look up, Anteros gazes into my eyes and an inner darkness blooms within me. Nobody is coming. Love does not save the day.

'Frida,' Anteros begins, his face a picture of self-satisfaction, 'you will—'

'Another speech?' I say. 'Do me a favour and just shoot me already.'

His dark eyes gleam. 'I thought you'd never ask,' he says.

And then he fires the arrow straight into my heart.

Chapter 40

I suck in a huge gasp of air as the arrow hits, squeezing my eyes shut as the pain explodes in my chest and then spreads in shockwaves across my body. Because this is not a magical or a metaphorical injury. This is visceral, excruciating; metal slicing through fat and bone and muscle, piercing my heart. At first there is searing, agonising pain that blots out everything else and turns my world black. Then the throbbing torture travels from my heart all over my body, until I become it, or it becomes me, and there is pain, only pain.

I moan softly, my mouth slack, as gradually, out of that inky blackness of agony, something else emerges.

Pictures. Pictures of me. As a two-year-old I fall over, scrape my knee and wail and my mother doesn't come; as a three-year-old my dad sings to me; at five, a boy at school I like pulls my hair and steals my ruler; at twelve, I kiss

Richard Douglas, who I ardently believe is my one true love. Aged sixteen, I have sex for the first time and don't feel much of anything until five days later, when he still hasn't called me, and I go to his house and key his car.

At university, I fall for a guy on my course and when he goes back to his ex-girlfriend, I tell his professor that he cheated on his exams, then get drunk and sleep with him, too. I have frequent, drunken sex with near-strangers after that, and I believe I am strong when really I am scared, and I believe that I am free when really I am trapped in the game, and I'm pinned by the arrow, helpless to do anything but watch this documentary of the heart, as the arrow's power fires me up from the inside.

Then it's Billy and he's different, he won't leave me, he sees me like nobody else has ever seen me, he looks right into my soul, and I need him and I'm addicted to him and I hide my fears and I dull down my edges, and I tiptoe around him because when it is good it is the best, and when it is bad, it is because of something I have done, and I start to hide myself inside a better version of myself, but I can't hide my need, it seeps out like poison, and he starts to grow colder, and we argue and he lets me down, and I sends text messages that go unanswered, leave voicemails that explode into violent arguments, and then, blissfully, we are together again, we will never let anything come between us until the next time, and I lose weight and I bite my nails and I lie awake at night wondering where he is, and what I did wrong, and what I can do to put it right, and I do everything I can to make myself loveable, and then he leaves me anyway, and when my heart breaks, it breaks with a kind of terrible happiness, because I always knew it would happen and now at least it has.

The vision expands and I'm not Frida McKenzie any more, I'm changing, dissolving, soon I'll be mixed with the air. There's Dan's wife, watching him, knowing that there's another woman in his head, stealing her way into his heart. There are the nights she spends listening to him calling my name in his sleep. There's the ring she takes off and places on the kitchen table. There's the note she leaves, because she can't bear the relief she knows she will see on his face.

The images come fast now, rapid-fire pictures of strangers: the woman who cheats on her sick husband with his brother and a girl who keeps returning to the man who beats her and the one who marries for money and the one who marries for security and the one who never marries and hates the ones who do, and it hurts, and they're lost, and they're the children of the lost, and they hand on misery just like that poet said and it's hateful and poisonous and why can't they see that it just doesn't work? That love is something terrible and cruel. That love is a con. Why don't they just give it up?

I open my eyes. The visions have faded and Anteros is all I see now. His wings are outstretched and he is magnificent. He is the answer. He is what I have been looking for, though I didn't know it. It is so, so obvious! And I won't hold on any more, I won't try to keep faith in something that has never once proven itself worthy of that faith.

298

A sweet sickness blossoms within me. The arrow contaminates my blood, and it offers me everything I've ever wanted: certainty, security, truth; one position fixed forever to which I can always come home. There's such delicious pleasure in allowing the power of the arrow to burn through me, asking me to consent to the darkness, to stop striving, to give myself over to him.

It feels *good*.

There's something else, something nagging, like a tiny fly buzzing just out of sight. I am dimly aware that it is the heart necklace, I can see it glinting there on the floor. But so what? It isn't magic. It can't help me. It's just a worthless trinket. The dark magic in my blood is softly lulling me. *Forget about the necklace. Let me have your heart. Everything is easy. No one will ever hurt you again. Give in to me*, the darkness whispers, *just seal me inside your heart and we can be done with all of this for ever . . .*

The light is almost gone now; it's just a pin prick in the darkness. The light is the gap in the doorway of my heart as it closes. In a few moments the transformation will be complete and I will be his. And things will be better. Anteros is right. I am no hero. There is nothing I can do now to stop what is going to happen. He's too strong. He's made of the same stuff as the arrow energy; a relentless, unstoppable force.

The heart glimmers. The light gets smaller. And it's almost done. You can't help them. They're weak and lustful and depraved. So give up. Give in to it.

Except . . .

Except what?

Except . . . something. Something, but what is it?

It washes towards me like something carried by the ocean, near, then far, then near again. And then, it's in front of me. The knowledge, complete and undeniable. Anteros has filled me with power.

The power I need to stop him.

I am suddenly all attention, but calm, too, like everything is happening in slow motion. I let the knowledge inform me. And it tells me this: the power that runs through me has no agenda, it simply wants to be.

What it becomes is up to me.

You always have a choice, Frida.

Now I don't try to fight the darkness. That's not the way. Instead, with every ounce of my being, I open my heart as I focus on the small dot of light from my childhood necklace, light that has all but vanished. As I watch, it seems to grow fractionally. Yes. Yes. And as the light grows, slowly, slowly, I can feel a different kind of energy beginning to tingle in my limbs. Gradually the feeling turns into a golden lightness, then a joyousness, flooding through my body, reversing what went before.

It crashes through the doors of my heart in wave after wave of golden light.

I open my eyes and see my reflection in the black window, and I'm not myself any more. The reflection is that of a golden, glowing goddess, but I recognise her. It's the Frida that Dan drew in his sketch.

I stare out at the city below. One minute until the arrow's magic is released on the mortal world.

I pull my arms and the shackles pop like paper chains. My gaze rests on Anteros, calm, remote.

Anteros frowns. 'What is this?' he asks.

'This?' I reply and smile. '*This* is who I really am.'

Thirty seconds.

I stare down dispassionately at the golden arrow sticking out of my chest, then I pull it out, looking at it with cool fascination.

Anteros stares at me. 'Frida, stop. I command you.'

I laugh as I reach out a hand and Anteros's bow flies from his arm and into my hand. I am powerful, more powerful even than him. And I think: this is what Eros saw. This is what Anteros fears. This immense power. There's a seed of it in every mortal.

Twenty seconds.

I load the arrow. I look at Anteros and I see through him. His awesome power and his terrible isolation, and the black hole inside him. The untold capacity in the mortals that he sees, and fears, and despises, and will never, ever be able to own.

Ten seconds.

'You can't stop it,' he says, nonchalant. 'Even if you shoot me, there's nothing you can do. Your people will end up mad, crazed, killing each other in horror and bloodshed, and it is exactly what they deserve.'

I stare at Anteros, *seeing* him, a gift of the arrow magic. I see fury. I see madness. I see cruelty. But there's something else. Something at the heart of everything he has ever done.

Five.

Vanity. Control. Power.

Four.

This is his Olympus. And everything comes from here. And then, I understand.

I switch my gaze to the statue he has erected to himself, an altar to his greatness because the mortals never built one. Those eyes, yes, they gleam, but not with life. With power.

Everything comes from there.

Three.

The goddess energy surges in me, and I narrow it down to a point, and send it into the arrow.

Two.

I switch my aim to the statue.

One.

Anteros's expression turns from triumph to rage.

Fire.

The arrow flies true, and pierces the eye of Anteros's statue. There's a single moment of absolute silence, and then a pulse of incredible power rips through the building, as the statue explodes in a shower of sparks and fire.

Then silence.

I send my goddess consciousness out to the people below, a kind of inner listening that the old Frida, the mortal Frida, doesn't even understand.

Is it done?

And the answer comes back: *It is done.*

I see Anteros, by the window, as still as his ruined statue, beautiful in his fury. He holds his hand out to the broken effigy, calling his arrow, and without thought my arm

302

extends too. We watch the arrow quiver in the burning socket of the eye, wanting to be free, to be reunited with a love deity.

Then it shoots out and lands in my palm and in one smooth movement, I close my fingers around it, load it into the bow and aim. We stare at each other, then, two immense and ageless beings, locked in an endless moment. *You could finish this*, whispers goddess Frida. *Shoot him now. Enslave him to you.*

But human Frida hesitates, and that is all it takes for Anteros to push open that huge window, letting in the frigid night air. He gives me one last look – a look that will haunt my dreams for a long time to come – and then he's gone.

'Frida!'

I turn slowly to see Dan tugging at the bolt that holds his chains. Oh, this mortal. His dreams, his fears, his fathomless love for poor, flawed Frida. I train the arrow on him, his eyes widen in love and awe and terror, and then I fire the arrow into the bolt, setting him free.

Then the world starts to dim, darkness creeping in from the edges.

'Frida,' Dan shouts. 'Frida!' But his voice is faint, and so very far away, as the goddess power rushes from my body and I sink to the floor.

Chapter 41

Three months later

I stand in front of my office, the keys in my hand.

The thing about having had a goddess of love emerge from your innermost being is it's not really an experience that lends itself to divorce law. For one thing, I've been left with some sort of residue, an ability, faint but definitely there, to pick up on the emotions of people, like a radio tuned to a new, unexpected wavelength. I don't know how long it's going to last, but while the power is still inside me, surrounding myself with emotionally fraught couples is probably not the wisest idea.

Best to close up my practice for a while until I work out what's next. Besides, I've got other kinds of work to do. Dan used the powder on the arrow while I was still unconscious, destroying Anteros's magic for good. (Would I have destroyed the arrow, if it had come to it? Better not to ask that question.) But now, there are other duties: tidying up the magical elements left behind after Anteros's disappearance, for one thing, with the help of Dan's well-connected family. Making sure Anteros's allies pose no threat. Though, with their leader gone, Clive and his buddies have been only too eager to broker peace.

Cut off the head to kill the beast – isn't that what they say?

I take a last look at my office, then I lock the door and start the walk into town. Summer is coming, you can smell it in the freshly mown grass and the sun-warmed pavements and nowhere does summer like this city of mine, with its energy and its enthusiasm, always hoping for a better day. And is it my imagination or is there a growing sense of peace here, since the events of February 14th?

I pass the library and see the lions guarding the entrance. The Cathedral. The cinema. The courts, where I once thought I knew so much about everything. The streets are busy with people making the most of the sunshine, sitting by the fountain, gathered at pavement cafés with their friends and lovers.

I take a seat outside the Town Hall, and something casts a huge shadow against the fledgling sun. I look up. NeoStar. Except it isn't NeoStar any more. Anteros's message reached the mortals all right, just not in the way he'd hoped. When millions opened that email – 'WILL YOU FIND THE ONE?' – it infected their devices with a virus that wiped their hard drives and filled their screens – a nice touch, this – with rows of tiny arrow-pierced hearts. And, of course, there was the small matter of the non-existent golden phone. Share prices plummeted after that. A crisis of confidence, the business reports said. Ineffective leadership in the aftermath. And then, the inevitable liquidation.

I feel bad for everyone who lost their jobs. Goddess Frida didn't care about such petty trivial things as security and money. Mortal Frida does, though. Mortal Frida cares a lot. But if this is what the goddess left me with, if this guilt and this lingering connection to the mortals' emotions is the price I have to pay for stopping Anteros, then I guess I'll have to bear it.

I feel a presence beside me and I turn.

'Hey you,' Dan says. He hands me a coffee and we sit in silence for a while, staring up at the building. I take the postcard out of my pocket and hand it to him. Dan glances at the picture, a beach in Sicily. He turns it over. No words, just my address.

'It might not be from her.'

'It's from her,' I say. 'She wants to let me know she hasn't forgotten. I get the feeling Psyche is not someone I wanted to make an enemy out of.'

Dan shrugs. 'She made an enemy of herself. She made her choices.'

I nod and sip my coffee and stare up at the building, anxious for movement.

'Is it time?' I ask.

'It's time.'

And it is. We watch in silence as the NeoStar logo is dismantled, letter by letter. Soon, there is only the arrow, shooting upwards, a symbol, now, of a promise unfulfilled. And then that, too, is gone.

'Do you think he'll come back?' I ask.

Dan puts an arm around my shoulder. 'I don't know, Freed. But, three months and no visions. Maybe we've seen the last of him. And if we haven't? Then the gods know where we are.' He smiles at me and I smile back. We're not a proper couple. Not yet, anyway. I need time to work everything out, to work myself out. There is, after all, the little fact that Dan didn't tell me Anteros was going to try to convert me to his cause. Secrets, even ones kept for a good reason, are still secrets, after all.

But still, I feel happy when I'm around Dan, a different, easier kind of happiness than anything I've been used to. I've learned enough to know to pay attention to that feeling.

'But in the meantime,' he's saying, 'let's not go looking for trouble, okay? Let's just be two perfectly ordinary people having lunch together.'

'Ordinary people,' I say. 'Lunch. Talking about sheds. That kind of thing.'

'Exactly,' says Dan.

I touch the pendant around my neck.

We walk down the sunlight-dappled street. As we get near Tony's Café, there's a moment where I see a figure, dark, bright-eyed, holding a golden bow, and I have a terrible idea that it's Anteros, come to take his revenge.

But it's just a busker setting up a harp, and he begins to play such beautiful music, and as we pass him he gives us a hopeful smile so I stop and throw some money into his hat, and then I follow Dan into our favourite run-down café, to enjoy a little ordinary happiness.

Author note

I can remember exactly when I first had the idea for *The Gods of Love*. I'd just finished reading C. S. Lewis' *The Screwtape Letters*, in which a senior demon writes letters to his rookie nephew instructing him on how to tempt a human away from 'the Enemy' (aka God) and towards 'Our Father Below' (you know who). I loved this metaphor. What impressed me most were the banal, everyday activities the demons used to steer the unsuspecting 'patient' off path. As Screwtape himself counsels; 'the safest road to Hell is the gradual one'.

I closed the book and had the very clear thought: I want to do this, but about love. I only needed to look at my own past romantic entanglements to see how easily we humans are led away from our best interests and into territory distinctly more hellish.

In *my* novel, I decided, the unseen force for good would be the Greek god Eros. But who would head up the Bad Romance department? After all, Eros doesn't have such an obvious opposite as God.

So I did a bit of digging and I found out something interesting: Eros had a brother I'd never heard of, called Anteros. According to myth he was benevolent, the god of love returned. But, then, also according to myth, he was the son of Aphrodite (love) and Ares (war).

Love and war. Interesting. So here I had a younger brother to Eros, a love god of equal power but one whom hardly anyone had ever heard of. I wondered what being ignored all these millennia might do to an immortal whose very purpose was to be worshipped. And a god who understood the inner workings of love but who despised humans? What might he be capable of?

What if, I thought (really getting into my idea now) this god had been living amongst us all this time, corrupting love in various invisible ways (the safest road to Hell, after all, being the gradual one). And what if that wasn't enough? What if Anteros's end game was something so bloody and epic that the mortals would never forget his name again?

And there, I had my antagonist.

All I had to do was create a mortal capable of defeating him.

Confession time: Frida's role originally went to a guy. Why? Had I, too, been brainwashed by all those adventure stories that cast the male as the hero? I don't think it was that, or not only. I think I created a male protagonist because I was writing about love and relationships, and having been utterly heart-broken myself not so long before, it was all still quite raw. I wanted to write about this stuff, yes, but from a nice safe distance.

But no. One of my favourite writers, Stephen King, says in *On Writing*, 'For me, writing has always been best when it's intimate'. I get that. This first attempt wasn't intimate enough, it didn't work, and eventually I put the idea away.

But there was a character in that early draft who kept on speaking to me. Frida had guts, a nice line in sarcasm and I liked her a lot. While I went about my daily business, (which included, perhaps not coincidentally, vanquishing my own romantic demons and meeting my now partner), Frida was elbowing her way from her position as love interest into the role of hero.

As she did, something magical happened: the novel, having everything it needed, knew exactly where it wanted to go.

All I had to do was let it.

Interview with Nicola Mostyn

What genre is The Gods of Love?
Absolutely brilliant question. When you find out, please do let me know.

Okay, serious answer. I used to write a lot of features and it would drive me mad when a musician or artist would say wankily about their work: 'Oh it really can't be pigeon-holed.' As a journalist, that did not help me AT ALL. Also, I've been a bookseller, so I understand more than anyone the need to be able to – literally – put a book in its correct category.

So trust me when I say I was not willfully aiming to write something that couldn't be pinned down. But I have to write what I love and it turns out what I love is humour, strong female protagonists, magic and mythology as metaphor and analyzing the hell out of romantic relationships.

Put all that together and you get *The Gods of Love*. I'll leave it to those poor booksellers to decide where it belongs.

How much of your own experience is in *The Gods of Love*?
Oh lots! Not directly – I mean I've never had to grapple with a three-headed hell beast (insert own internet dating joke here) – but the book has definitely been influenced by my own romantic experiences and how I now think about love. Through my twenties and much of my thirties I was chasing what I thought was love, but my relationships were not working out and

seemed to be taking me further away from myself.

And it wasn't just me. I saw the same in the relationships of many of my friends, in society, and also reflected in books and films, as though it was all perfectly normal. It made me wonder – how are we still getting it so wrong? There's a great quote by social psychologist Erich Fromm in his book *The Art of Loving*: 'There is hardly any activity, any enterprise, which is started with such tremendous hopes and expectations, and yet, which fails so regularly as love.' He wrote that in 1956. They didn't even have Tinder in 1956. But then, in another of his books, Fromm said: 'Love is the only sane and satisfactory answer to the problem of human existence.' So, you can see why we're in a bit of a pickle.

Describe your writing schedule.

When I'm working on a project, the first thing I do when I get up is write Morning Pages, as recommended by Julia Cameron in *The Artist's Way*. Three sides of A4 longhand, a stream of consciousness splurge onto the page, which clears away some of the unhelpful brain chatter I generally have floating around in there. Then I sit at my desk and I write fiction until lunchtime. I usually aim for one chapter a day. I am somewhere between a seat-of-the-pantser and a planner. A strict plan robs all the magic for me, since I get my best ideas as I'm writing. But then, if I have absolutely no idea where a book is going, I'm liable to write about seventeen novels in one. So, much as I try to do in life, I have a vague idea of where things are heading and follow that path until my instinct tells me there's somewhere more important I need to be.

Why do you write?

I'll paraphrase a great quote I saw on Twitter: 'I write because it's as close to magic as I'll ever get.'

What are your influences?

I've always been a huge Stephen King fan. I love weird tales and, of course, he's an incredible storyteller but more than that he's interested in the darkness and light in human hearts and I think his books explore that beautifully. Other writers I count among my favourites are Margaret Atwood, Donna Tartt and Ira Levin for fiction and David Sedaris, Cynthia Heimel, and the late Joseph Campbell for non-fiction.

What is your advice for aspiring writers?

The best way to learn is by doing. I learned to be a journalist by doing it, and I learned to be a novelist the same way. Don't wait for anyone's permission. Be tenacious. Wear your rejections like badges of honour; in fact, celebrate them. Also – and this goes for anyone, not just writers – don't listen to anyone who tells you it can't be done. People who've buried their own dreams have a vested interest in you not achieving yours, because it'll hurt them too much if you do.

What are you working on now?

I'm working on the sequel to *The Gods of Love*, which is called *The Love Delusion* and follows the story of Frida and Dan after the fallout of Valentine's Day. I'd love this pair to find the happiness they deserve, but I've a feeling Anteros isn't quite finished with them yet . . .

Acknowledgements

Much like the gods, published novels only exist because people believe in them. As such, I'm eternally grateful to the following people:

To my agent Susan Armstrong for her faith in this book from the very beginning, and to my brilliant editor Anna Boatman, designer Hannah Wood, and the wonderful Piatkus team, whose love for this story brought out the very best in it.

To my companions along the writing path; Maria Roberts, Sarah Tierney and Emma Unsworth – without our annual writing pilgrimage my life would be much the poorer (though my liver may be grateful).

To Adrian Hemstalk, David Lloyd, Rhian McKay and Rachel Galbraith-Marten for their invaluable feedback and encouragement.

For keeping me sane, Kellie Barratt, Paul Connery, Teresa Wilson, Steffy Cooke and Elaine Swords.

To my parents, Jennifer and Alfred, and my sister Amanda, whose constant, unwavering belief in me is its own kind of magic.

And to Nick Brown: the gods were truly smiling on me the day I met you.